PRAISE FOR *NETHERWORLD*

"The Chronicles of Koa is a wonderful story full of likeable characters, a clear world, and a fun mission."

—KIRSTIN L. PULIOFF, AUTHOR OF *THE ESCAPE OF PRINCESS MADELINE*

"It has a fantastic story, twists and turns throughout, and some mysteries you won't see coming. I'm looking forward to reading more of her books as she writes them. The Chronicles of Koa #2 will certainly be a day one purchase for me!"

—THOMAS RAY MANNING, AUTHOR OF *ENERGIZE (FROM THE LOGS OF DANIEL QUINN)*

"The ending had me on edge. I have to say I have not read a vampire novel like this one before."

—GLENNA MAYNARD, AUTHOR OF *BEAUTIFUL STRANGERS*

"The author has created an engrossing world with vampires, angels and other mythical creatures. And not just any mythical creatures, her creations were... awesome!"

—MORGAN JANE, AUTHOR OF THE *SANGUIS CITY* SERIES

NETHERWORLD

THE CHRONICLES OF KOA
BOOK ONE

K.N. LEE

Captive Quill Press
Fort Mill, SC 29707

This is a work of fiction. Names, characters, places, brands, media, and incidents are either the product of the author's imagination or are used fictitiously. Any resemblance to similarly named places or to persons living or deceased is unintentional.

Library of Congress Control Number: 2015905974

ACKNOWLEDGMENTS

Writing this book has been a rewarding experience. I would like to thank those who provided support and believed in me during this journey. I must first thank my editors, Ann Wicker of East Oak Media and John Davis, as well as my proofreader, Maggie Dallen. I would also like to give thanks to my beta readers, Jacqueline Pfahl, Melinda Metz, and Angelica Grier.

Also, thank you to J.M. Rising Horse Creations for my fantastic cover art. You are a magician! Thank you to Colleen M. Albert, The Grammar Babe, for being the best fairy-godmother ever.

My friends, Facebook page fans, and Twitter followers have also given me so much support and helped me push through all of the doubts and fears that come with writing a book. Thank you all!

Lastly, I must thank my lovely mother, Brenda Williams. She has always been there to motivate me and believed in my talents even when I was a little girl creating books out of cardboard wrapped in wallpaper!

Table of Contents

To my grandmother
Brenda Lee Cooper

CHAPTER 1

THE CLOCK STRUCK MIDNIGHT, and for once Koa didn't have anyone to track…or kill.

A buttery aroma wafted into the air as Koa opened a bag of freshly popped popcorn. There came a low purr from behind and she glanced over her shoulder at the stoic black cat that sat on the countertop.

"Smells good, Raven. Doesn't it?"

Raven stared back with her ethereal green eyes. The cat blinked, and licked her paw.

Koa shrugged and blew her dark blue bangs out of her eyes. "Fine. More for me."

Through the archway and into the grand hall, Koa walked through the large empty manor. There was a chill in the air, but Koa didn't mind as she wore nothing but a black lace panty and bra set. The sound of her soft footsteps echoed, and she found herself humming as she always did.

She didn't pay any mind to the gothic statues that glared down at her on either side of the wide corridor. There was a time when Koa had been frightened by her father's relics. As a girl she would avoid walking down the hallways at night for fear that they would awaken and grab her with their cold stone hands.

Now, Koa was used to the statues of angels and demons. She barely glanced at them anymore. Such things were a part of her daily life and she no longer feared their artistic replicas.

It took her a few moments to cross the cold marble floors to the large den she had converted into an entertainment room. Koa used a remote to turn off all of the lights. She lit a scented candle just as Raven brushed past her leg. She rubbed her soft fur onto Koa's bare flesh.

The scent of vanilla made her smile.

Koa flopped onto the plush sofa and put her feet up on the ottoman. She sank into the cushions and closed her eyes in bliss. "Halston has given me a few nights off." She turned on her television. "Finally, I get to catch up on some reality TV!"

Raven seemed to roll her eyes and Koa grinned. "I know," she said as she relaxed her back on the orange pillows and popped a handful of popcorn into her mouth. "I can be such a girl sometimes." She laughed to herself. She was happy. Life had been so busy lately with the rise of supernatural crime that a single moment of solitude was rare.

Koa glanced at Raven and held her arms out. "Come sit with me."

Raven snuggled next to her and rested her head on Koa's lap. Koa smiled and stroked her black fur. Sometimes it seemed as if Raven was all she had left in the world, besides Halston.

Koa just started to crunch on a kernel when she heard the faintest creak in her hallway. It was so faint that she almost didn't catch it. She didn't want to catch it. She wanted the night to go smoothly, but it was the way Raven's ears perked up that confirmed that Koa had indeed heard something.

Scrunching her small nose, Koa grumbled and put her bowl of popcorn down on her glass coffee table. All of her senses were heightened. There was a definite warning deep in the pit of her stomach. She sniffed the air. There was the faint stench of coal and something rancid.

Odd, she thought, frowning. She had smelled that distinct odor before. It was not from this world. *Very odd*.

Raven looked down the dark hallway and made a low sound of warning deep in her throat. Her black fur stood on end. Koa shushed her with a hand.

She came to her feet and headed toward the sound. She could feel that someone was there. Like the telling smell of oncoming rain, Koa had an uncanny sense of knowing when something bad was about to happen. She hoped that this time she was wrong.

Her heart thumped wildly in her chest. Her one day off, and someone decided to bother her. Raven lowered her head and waited back on the sofa.

"Scaredy-cat," Koa mumbled.

Koa softly tiptoed into the darkness. She now wished that she was properly dressed. She didn't want someone catching her in her underwear. She sighed. She was probably overthinking things. Two-hundred-year-old French manors tended to creak in the night. Koa should have been used to the sounds after all these years of living there.

The truth was that Koa was still afraid of the dark, and with good reason. She froze when something crashed to the floor. She quickly pressed her back against the wall and waited. One of the statues had broken.

Voices.

Koa cursed in her head. Someone was definitely in her house. Her breath quickened. Koa could hear Halston's voice in her head, telling her that it wasn't worth it—that she should run. She didn't run.

Instead, she peeked around the corner of the wall and saw flashlights. The harsh, fluorescent light pointed in her direction. Two men. Bald and big. They were dressed in black with tattoos all over their pale white faces and scalps. They clutched silver-barreled crossbows.

Koa's face paled. Their black eyes searched her hallway.

No, Koa thought with cold realization. Her skin crawled with dread. *It's not possible.* "Syths," she whispered in a hiss. They heard her. Four black eyes looked up and met hers.

Koa pulled back. Her pulse raced. These were creatures of folklore and mythology, but Koa knew the truth. Such creatures did exist. It was just that they shouldn't be in the human world. She gulped. Something was definitely wrong.

"Shit!" *No time to run now.* Boots stomped down the marble floor. Dread washed over her, making her skin feel prickly.

Two Syths, equipped with crossbows. Koa knew what those arrows were laced with. Her stomach pumped with anxiety. Why were they in her house?

Raven came around the corner and leisurely sat in the middle of the hall. Koa's anxiety was replaced with fury. No one had ever invaded her home.

Koa glared over at Raven.

"Fine. Just sit there and let me do all of the work," she said to the black cat. Koa yelped as a large hand reached for her long black and blue hair. She grabbed the hand and with a push off the ground, she leapt.

Her feet climbed up the air as if by invisible stairs. With a surge of energy, she took flight. She grunted as she lifted the large man's weight off the ground and flew upward. He used his other arm to direct the point of his crossbow at her.

Koa's eyes widened and she pursed her lips. She saw the red poisonous bolt ready to be released. The second Syth waited below as Koa went higher and higher up the tall, vaulted ceiling. It was cold up there, and pitch black, but Koa could still see the Syth's illuminated face.

An arrow zipped past her and she gasped. "Come quietly, Koa, and we won't have to hurt you," the Syth below shouted. "Our master doesn't want you dead. He just wants us to bring you in."

She snorted. "No thanks. I like my world just fine." Koa looked down at the Syth whose hand she held. It was rare to see one of his kind.

His lips curled into a malicious grin. "Yes, come quietly, my pretty," he whispered. His voice was like nails on gravel. "You know you don't belong here with the humans…"

Koa gazed into those soulless black eyes and felt her stomach churn with dread. They were like small, black beads. The tattoos around his eyes were inscriptions of a dialect that didn't exist in this world. Someone was letting rogue nephilim out of the Netherworld.

"And neither do you," she said and with an evil grin, she let go of his hand.

He cried out and fell nearly fifty feet. Koa heard a satisfying crunch of bones. She smirked. Still, it wasn't enough to kill a Syth. Those bones were probably regenerating already. Koa hadn't encountered many since she'd become a Netherworld agent, but Netherworld beings were extremely hard to kill.

Koa darted away from another arrow and into the darkness of her empty manor. She stood on the ceiling, upside down, yet defying gravity as she looked down at the two shadows below. She considered all of her options. She could fly out of that window ahead or she could go back and kill them.

Syths were dangerous. She couldn't let them get away. But her weapons were in her vault. In order to reach her vault, she would need to go past the Syths. How silly of her to think that she was safe. Not even her home was sacred anymore.

Nearly five years as an agent in Halston's Netherworld Division, and Koa was still caught off guard.

Koa frowned. Halston was right. She should have moved a long time ago. She could already see Halston's self-satisfied smile. She hoped she'd make it out alive to see that smile again.

Something caught her attention: a glittering light below. Raven's green eyes glowed.

Like a bolt of lightning, Koa shot through the darkness to Raven. Determination filled her veins. She could make it. She had to.

Bolts bounced off the walls and sparked along the floor. Her heart pumped, but her face was set with purpose. She smiled when she saw her Lyrinian sword lying on the floor, like a beacon of hope in the darkness.

The second Raven stepped away from it, Koa grabbed the silver hilt. A jolt of power slammed into her palm and flooded her body. She gritted her teeth and embraced the euphoric pain the sword caused her. The blade shot out, lengthening from the size of a small dagger to that of a full-sized sword. The jagged blade was a dark metal, rippled with black engravings.

Netherworld dialect.

Koa grinned. Once the initial pain subsided, the power made her feel invincible. The Lyrinian sword had been her father's. He had trained her to use it when she was only a little girl. This weapon was not of this world—and would not be put away until all evil was vanquished.

"Thanks, Raven."

The cat seemed to nod.

Koa cried out as a bolt nipped her right cheek. The pain was surprising. It sizzled. Blood dripped from her face as her hand shot to cover the wound.

Her green eyes went dark. She balled up her fist and tightened her grasp around the sword. She narrowed her eyes and turned around. They pulled the triggers on their bows and heard empty snips.

Koa gave them a cold grin and yet there was no amusement in her voice. "You picked the wrong girl to mess with."

They were out of bolts. Both Syths skidded to a stop. Almost frantically, they reached behind them and into their quivers to reload.

As Koa took a step forward, their eyes went wild with fear of the small girl before them.

Koa held her sword's black blade at her side. It pulsed with craving for blood—the blood of the evil ones that would increase its power.

Charging at them, Koa was lifted to her toes and. She spun and slashed one of the Syths across his side, a sizzling sound filling the air around them. Her white teeth flashed as the blade burned an iridescent red at the first taste of blood.

The blade craved blood and she would sate it.

It didn't stop at the bone. It didn't even pause. The glowing blade sliced through his spine with ease until the man was cut in half. It sped up only when it came through his other side and into the cold air of the manor.

The Lyrinian sword's red light encased the black blade and heat radiated along her flesh.

She clenched her jaw as the blade went cleanly though the other man, separating him at his waist. Their cries filled the entire manor as she sliced them to bits.

Both Syths lay on the floor in pieces. Koa kicked their crossbows away, not that they had hands connected to their arms anymore. Her chest heaved as she stood over them. Smoke rose from the blade of her Lyrinian sword. Koa watched their pale white faces, waiting. Blood pooled onto her floor. She watched it gather around her bare feet.

Raven sauntered over. She sat down and licked her front paw. Her green eyes looked up innocently into Koa's matching green eyes. "Shall we leave now?" she asked, in her mother's voice.

Koa's shoulders slumped. She looked over at the cat. "Yes." She nodded and looked down at the blood pooling between her white toes. "But first, I must clean up this mess."

CHAPTER 2

KOA SAT BACK in her wooden chair and watched as Halston entered the little bistro. She hid her smile as his eyes scanned the room. He was like a golden light, come to spread joy throughout the room. She wasn't the only woman to notice him. Koa was very aware of the looks he got whenever he stepped into a room.

She sipped her coffee and sighed. She wasn't ready to tell him about the night before, but Halston was more than her best friend.

He was her boss.

Halston didn't have to look long for her. Koa tended to stand out, especially in the countryside of Paris. Her pale face, green eyes, and long blue hair were a stark contrast to everyone in the room. The fact that she was Korean didn't help her blend in either.

Their eyes met and his the corners of his lips lifted into a smile.

How could anyone have a more perfect smile? Koa set her cup down and rested her elbows on the table top. She twirled her hair with her finger as she watched Halston check his watch.

Always late, she thought with an impish grin. For someone who loved rules and decorum, Halston never seemed to think twice about punctuality.

Halston shrugged as if he just realized that he was thirty minutes late and it wasn't a big deal.

Bright blond hair was revealed once he took off his navy fedora and crossed the small room with tables set close to one another.

Perfect white teeth smiled at Koa as Halston stood before her.

Koa secretly enjoyed the dirty looks the other women were giving her when they realized that this masterpiece of a man had come to see her.

"Good morning, Koa," Halston said, sitting across from her. He reached over to take a piece of her bacon. Koa slapped his hand.

"Hands off," Koa scolded as she hid a mischievous smile. "You didn't even ask."

Halston's eyebrows drew in as he sat back. "Someone's moody today," he grumbled and motioned for the waitress.

Koa folded her arms across her chest. "And someone's late…"

That perfect smile returned. It should have made her grimace. Instead, it did exactly what he wanted it to do. It softened the lines in her face, making her smile in return.

"I apologize. Why couldn't we meet somewhere familiar? I've never heard of this place"

"I like it here. Don't question a Parisian about her bistros."

"But you don't know how hard it is to get out here with all of the sheep in the streets and whatnot. And you're not really Parisian — you're Korean."

Folding her arms across her chest, she leaned back in her chair. "I'm offended, Halston. I've lived in Paris since I was six years old. That's long enough to be considered a true Parisian."

Halston swiped one of her macaroons and popped it into his mouth. "Pardon me, Mademoiselle. You will forgive me, right?"

Koa rolled her eyes, but her smile widened without her permission. She could listen to him just talk for hours. "Sure. This time." She flicked her bangs out of her eyes. "How could anyone resist that British accent?"

Halston shrugged with a grin. "I suppose it has its perks."

Koa didn't think Halston knew just how much it affected her. He could ask for anything.

The tiny waitress took his order. She made eyes at him as if Koa wasn't sitting right there. Koa shook her head. Good thing Halston wasn't her boyfriend or husband; she might have felt inclined toward jealousy. She put her elbows onto the table and drank from her small café au lait.

Koa rolled her eyes as Halston spoke in French. He told the waitress how she looked like Audrey Tatou in *Amelie* and the girl swooned — her cheeks reddening as she giggled.

Koa almost wished she could show her fangs to the waitress and wipe that smile off her cute little face, but she resisted. She would be good today. Leave it to Koa to contemplate outing the entire vampire race to the poor, blissfully ignorant humans.

The waitress sauntered off with a beaming smile. Halston turned his attention back to Koa. She wondered if he knew that he'd just made that woman's day.

"Why, sir," Koa said as she mocked a British accent. She put the back of her hand across her forehead and pretended to be one of the girls from her favorite Jane Austen movies. She batted her eyelashes. "Aren't you just the most charming, handsome gentleman I've ever laid eyes on? I could just hand you my sweet innocence right here on this table." She burst out laughing and Halston made a face.

"Your British accent is dubious at best," Halston said with a chuckle.

"It's not that bad. I've worked with you in London long enough to have picked up a little of the accent."

"Not nearly enough," he muttered.

"Funny," she said.

His smile faded. "You look tired."

Leave it to Halston to figure something was wrong within the first five minutes of arriving. She was surprised he didn't notice sooner.

Too busy flirting with doe-eyed waitresses, she thought, taking a sip from her coffee cup.

His gaze roamed over the surroundings.

"Thanks. That's *exactly* what I needed to hear this early in the morning. You look as if you just fell from Mount Olympus. Congratulations for making me feel like a spotted monkey."

Halston sighed. His face turned serious. This was the face of her boss.

"Out with it. What happened?"

She carefully sat her cup down before her and leaned in. "Syths. Two of them. Ugly bastards, bathed in the stench of burnt coal." She grimaced at the memory. "I'd say they'd only been in our world a few hours."

"What?" he whispered, his eyes widening with the levity of what she'd just told him.

"They attacked me, Halston. In my *house*."

"Are you *sure* they were Syths?"

Koa tilted her head, giving him a blank look. "Want to go check the graves I dug for them? You know, just to be sure?"

Halston let out a long breath.

"Give me some credit. I may still be the *new kid* in the division, but I think I know my Nephilim."

Halston shook his head. "There have been more unusual deaths of children lately, particularly little girls. Bloodless corpses are scattered about in the streets." Halston looked at her. "I told you, Koa. I told you a long time ago. You cannot stay there anymore."

Koa grinned then. She knew he would say that.

"What are you smiling at? This is serious."

Koa laughed lightly and shook her head. "Nothing, Halston. Nothing at all." She drank some of her coffee. She looked at it with a perplexed expression as something dawned on her. "I thought you told me that the nephilim were locked in the Netherworld. I thought they could not get free."

The Netherworld, the world of the nephilim, creatures of supernatural origin, had been her main study since the death of her father. From all that she learned, they were not supposed to be able to come and go freely. There were supposed to be rules and boundaries keeping the human world safe from those creatures. Someone was deliberately breaking those rules.

"I never said that. They can come and go as they please, if they have permission. And I am the only one that can do such a thing."

Koa sat up straight. "So, there is no one else that can give them permission? How could they have escaped?"

Halston waved her to settle down. "I'll handle it," he said. After a moment of silence, he lifted his brows as their eyes met. "I want you to move."

Koa examined his face. It was apparent that he feared for her safety. Unfortunately, she feared for her own as well.

"Whatever you say."

"Really?"

"Let's say we go shopping for houses today, shall we?"

"That was almost too easy," Halston said.

Koa put money on the table. "Don't press your luck."

*   *   *

Koa wasn't sure if it was the professional thing to do, but whenever she and Halston weren't on missions or working, he always reached for her hand when they were walking together. Koa never protested, it was instinctual and her hand would slide into his naturally.

They walked down the gray pavement and stopped before a newly developed high-rise. Koa looked up into the sky. It was tall. She would be able to fly out whenever she wanted, as long as no one was looking.

She frowned. *This is not going to work.*

Her father's mansion was her home. How could she leave it? She still remembered when he had come back for her and Raven. For years, Koa and her mother had lived in a one-room cottage in Daegu, South Korea.

Each day Koa would look out their window and wait for this elusive father of hers to return to the woman he had impregnated and the child he had held only once. Raven had been confident that he loved them both, and that he would come back for them, when the time was right. So, she would sit on the floor and spend the entire morning cooking for the field workers while Koa struggled to learn how to hide her fangs and resist slaughtering the people of that village.

Being a half-blood was hard. It was hard not having a vampire father around to teach her how to curb her cravings. She could eat food, but each week, the blood lust would hit her and she would be bedridden until Raven brought her blood from an animal. Koa would never forget just how good a mother Raven had been when she was still human.

Koa sighed, pushing the memory of her mother's beautiful face away. It always stung her heart to remember such things. The curse had almost ruined them. Halston had been the one to help them cope with the curse that had been put on her mother. She gave Halston a sidelong glance and squeezed his hand.

"So, what about this one?"

Koa didn't hesitate. She shook her head. "I don't like it." She motioned around them. "There are too many people around. It's not safe. People can be nosy, and you know how I get when I'm hungry."

"I suppose you're right," Halston said with a sigh. He checked his watch. "But Koa, I'm not going to be able to find you another secluded manor in the countryside. Homes like your father's manor just aren't practical. Sooner or later you're going to have to get used to being around people. You can blend better than any vampire because you can walk in the sun. You must get used to life with humans."

Koa frowned. "Come on Halston, I've watched *Pride and Prejudice*, *Emma*, *Sense and Sensibility*, I know. Europe is made up of such things. Go to London and make one of the lords move out."

"Just being a Jane Austen fan doesn't make you an expert on England, Koa." He chuckled louder. "I don't think that's exactly how we want to relocate you, by moving a lord out and eliciting a bunch of unwanted attention."

"Who cares about unwanted attention?"

Halston's smile faded. "I do."

Koa folded her arms across her chest.

Gently unfolding her crossed arms, Halston stepped closer. He brushed her bangs from her eyes. "You're being bratty right now," he told her softly.

Just having him so close made her heart beat a little faster.

Her tongue went dry.

The smell of blood everywhere filled her nostrils and made her dizzy. She nearly stumbled and held onto Halston's arm.

He held her up. His voice was concerned. "The hunger?"

She nodded and took a deep breath. "I need to get to Wryn Castle."

"Are you sure?"

"Yes, I haven't had human blood in weeks."

Her fight with the Syths the night before had drained her a lot sooner than usual. She and Halston had developed a schedule for her feedings. The battle last night had thrown it off.

He held her hand and patted the back of it. "I'll take you. I want to keep an eye on you."

Koa shook her head. "No. You cannot come. They don't take kindly to *your* kind."

"And I don't take kindly to theirs either."

Koa looked up and gave him a coy smile. "But you like me, don't you?"

Halston let out a breath and looked away. "Of course I do, Koa. You're not a typical vampire though."

"Good. But you know that I must go alone." Koa looked around to make sure no one was close enough to hear her. She lowered her voice.

"The Wryn are not bad vampires. They are the best kind that we could ever hope for. At least they don't kill people. I swear, they are all registered and they follow the rules the Netherworld Division has set."

"Fine. Be careful, Koa."

She nodded and looked away from his concerned eyes. She knew how much he hated that she was about to go to the castle of one of the oldest vampire clans in Europe.

CHAPTER 3

BLOOD WAS LIKE liquid chocolate to Koa.

She savored the flavor and the euphoric rush the moment its warmth touched her tongue. Eye closed in bliss, colors flashed behind her eyelids.

Koa licked Ian's neck clean with three long strokes, leaving two small puncture holes. As she wiped her mouth, her canines returned to normal.

"Are you done, Mistress?" Ian spoke to her in an almost timid voice, as if he didn't want her to be finished. He craved more. Koa rolled her eyes and crawled from on top of him. He reached for her and she pushed his arms down by his head.

Koa lowered her tone. "Did I tell you to speak?"

Ian shook his head and she smiled. She enjoyed such dominance. It excited her that such an attractive young man thought of her as a goddess.

"Good boy." She played with his soft hair and sighed. "I'm sorry, Ian, for being so rude. I didn't mean it."

Ian had such an innocent face. She wondered how many hearts he had broken with that face. It was odd to think that they were the same age. Sometimes Koa contemplated what a normal life would have been like. College, boyfriends, parties… it seemed like such a foreign idea to her.

She traced his lips. There were many times when she'd almost kissed him, just to remember what a kiss felt like. She trusted Ian, and felt safe, therefore she didn't want to ruin the arrangement they shared. It was far too valuable, for both of them.

She had just drunk a full blood meal, and she still felt like sleeping for a week.

Still, Ian was beautiful, smelled nice, and looked at her with pure adoration. She almost leaned down for a kiss. His lips were soft under her fingertips. She craved physical satisfaction beyond a meal. Her skin crawled with desire.

Koa snatched her hand back and hopped off of him. She darted to the door and held it open for him. "Run along."

Ian gathered his backpack and did as he was told. He was enamored. She could see it in his eyes. She wondered if he knew just how strong she was. Even though he respected her, chances were, Ian only saw a small girl with a pretty face. He smiled at her as he left the room. He was attractive, but Koa was saving herself for someone else.

Koa didn't make eye contact with Ian. She didn't want to look her meal in the eye at that moment.

Koa sighed. She supposed Ian wasn't just a meal, he was her pet, and he had been so for nearly three years.

Lexi, the keeper of the castle and one of the four leaders of the Wryn clan, came around the corner and stopped before her door. Koa smiled at her. They were both friends and business associates. She was just as small as Koa, but far more advanced in her vampire skills.

At over two hundred years old, Lexi still looked like a woman in her early twenties. She had bouncy brown hair cut just above her shoulders and large dark brown eyes. She wore the tallest heels Koa had ever seen and skimpy dresses.

Lexi watched Ian walk down the hallway and gave Koa a sidelong glance. "When are you going to use that *lovely* young man for more than his blood?" She smirked.

Koa rolled her eyes but laughed. "He is more like a brother than a lover." She raised an eyebrow. "If he's so 'lovely,' why don't you take him to your bed? You have my permission, but you cannot glamour him. I don't want him confused about who his mistress is." Koa grinned. "I doubt you have a chance with a sweet human like my Ian."

Lexi flicked her hand. "I don't want that little boy. You are more my type." Lexi winked and reached for Koa's long dark hair. She sniffed it. "Just as soon as you get over your Goth phase. What's with the blue hair and thick black liner?"

Koa flashed an amused smile and leaned against the door. She folded her arms across her chest. "Great, everyone is insulting me today. Let's all pick on the poor little Asian girl."

Lexi leaned in close to Koa's ear. "Oh, sweet pea. One night with me will have you forgetting your name, let alone your race." She frowned. "And you're a mutt anyway. You're not a full Asian, just as much as you aren't a full vampire!"

Koa burst out laughing. "Don't make me tell Greta that you're flirting with me. I know it's blondes that you really like. And sorry, I'll never go blond."

Lexi folded her arms. "Greta is one of many. You think she has any say in what I do?"

"One of many, huh? Sounds exhausting," Koa said as she imagined having one boyfriend, let alone many.

Lexi glanced behind Koa into the room. "Staying the full night this time? You waste so much money paying for a night when you only stay an hour or two."

Koa grinned. "Are you complaining?"

Lexi shook her head. "Of course not. I'll accept as much money as you're willing to waste. But come on, have a drink with me. We can have a girls' night out." She thought a moment. "That is what you kids are calling it these days?"

Koa cringed at being called a kid. Just because she was twenty-one, didn't mean she hadn't seen enough of the world and been through enough to make her just as seasoned as Lexi. Koa's watch buzzed over on the side table.

"I have to go now, Lexi." She began shuffling Lexi away from her door. "If I don't see you on my way out, book me for the same time next week." She remembered something and turned serious.

"I almost forgot. Please transfer a thousand pounds out of my account and into Ian's. Tell him that I don't want him staying at shabby hostels anymore. I can smell it on him."

Lexi nodded. "Sure. Good night then."

"Night." Koa closed the door and darted over to her side table. Halston's face appeared on the bright face of the watch. The fluorescent light only illuminated his pale skin, making him look more angelic.

She smiled and pushed the side button.

"Good evening, Halston," she purred rolling onto her back and holding the watch over her. He stared down at her for a moment.

"How was your supper?" Halston asked.

"Young. Fresh. Eager. The same as always."

"Well, it's better than the alternative. I know you. You'd never forgive yourself if you killed someone for a meal."

Koa sat up. "Unless they deserved it," she noted. "I'd forgive myself just fine."

"Well, don't get too eager with those college kids. We don't want any accidents."

Koa scoffed. "It was an honor," she said. "For him." Her grin widened.

Halston shook his head in disapproval.

Koa's smile faded in mild annoyance. *Why does he have to be so good all of the time*? It was practically in his DNA to be the good guy.

"Besides, Ian is not just some college kid. He is special, and I don't feed from anyone but him. We have a good arrangement. You don't give the Wryn clan enough credit for what they've done for the registered vampire population."

Halston gave her an odd look. He cleared his throat. "You don't… sleep with him? Do you?" He seemed embarrassed to even ask the question.

Koa laughed lightly. "Of course not, Halston. What do I look like? Ian is hot, sure, but I could never."

"He's hot you say?"

"Oh yes, Halston. He's like totally drool-worthy. I mean, I can't keep my panties dry whenever he looks at me," she joked, mocking an American accent. She gave him a look under her long thick lashes. "Jealous?"

He remained serious. "Then, tell me. What do you do with him?"

Koa peered at him, curiously. *Why does he care now?* She looked up at the ceiling and blew her bangs out of her eyes.

"I don't know, Halston. It starts with a seductive smile. Then, there comes the glamour. Just like any person I've ever fed on, I press on his thoughts a little here and there. He dreams while I drink. He dreams of all of his deepest desires coming to true. And then, when he looks at me, it's instant infatuation. They see me for the first time after I drink, and to them, I look like an angel. No offense," she said to him, cringing at the word angel. It sometimes made him withdraw when she mentioned it.

Halston looked at her for a moment, and then nodded. "It all sounds pretty intricate."

"It is. I'm not sloppy. Even a full-blood can make a mess of things. I may be young when compared to other vampires, but I've developed my own little ritual. And it works."

"And no one dies."

She nodded, with a small smile on her lips. "That's right. No one dies." Koa rolled over onto her belly and set the watch in front of her. "See, I'm a good girl. I promise."

He seemed to perk up again. "Good. Meet me at the safe house. We have a mission."

Koa shot to her feet. "Really? I get to work with 'the boss' tonight?"

Halston smiled. "Indeed. And you'd better follow orders."

"Don't I always?"

"That's up for debate."

Koa smiled. She slipped her skirt on, and then her black leather boots. She pulled her blazer over her tank top and slipped her watch back on.

Halston waited patiently on her screen. Koa ran toward the balcony and with a leap, she jumped over the edge. The wind blew at her face furiously. It was late fall. She didn't care. The chill didn't affect her. She closed her eyes as she descended from the dark tower of Wryn Castle.

Wryn Castle was an exclusive venue. It had once been a gothic castle, and now, the vampires had transformed it into a modern hotel of sorts, where fresh college kids were delivered by room service. It was one of the few places that didn't tolerate reckless killings of their charges.

Koa, and everyone else who were members of the Wryn Castle were unique, for they had mutual arrangements with their charges.

"Mission? Will this be fun, or will I have to get dirty?"

"Depends on how you play it. Oh, and I found you a new home."

Koa breathed in the cool fresh air. "New home?"

"Right. In London. Now you can be close to your beloved Wryn Castle."

Koa raised an eyebrow, letting her body pick up speed. "London?"

She glanced at the watch with a grin. "Bringing me home to mother, Halston. So soon?"

Halston returned the grin. "Giving you what you asked for. You really are spoiled, did you know that? And five years isn't so soon, Koa Ryeo-won."

"For me it is." Koa swept to the side. She avoided a tree branch from slapping her in the face and ascended.

"Nonetheless, no, Koa. I don't have a mother, remember."

Koa nodded. "Of course not." She thought of her own mother then and felt a brief stab of guilt. The pain of remembering her mother before the transformation was too much. She pushed the memories of her mother's beautiful face and her smile out of her mind.

"London it is," Koa said with a nod, and she flew into the darkness.

*   *   *

The next morning, Koa could tell that Halston was pleased with his work. They had been out all night, tracking rogue vampires and making them either register or leave the country. Halston did not tolerate any human deaths due to vampires, not in his territory. There had been no jokes or smiles last night. When he was the boss, there was no denying his authority.

Now, Halston was her friend again, and full of cheer. He presented the quaint little cottage to her like a gift. She cared too much for his feelings to show her disappointment. The cottage was small and bleak in comparison to her father's manor in Paris. Sure, it was cute, and made of stone like something in a Jane Austen movie. That should have made her happy, but she hated to admit that she wanted something a little *more grand*.

Koa would miss the vineyard and gardens of her manor. She and Raven would read classic literature and enjoy the grounds for hours. Those days in the garden had been her first glimpse into the romantic British lifestyle she had read about and longed for.

Koa thought about the grand piano in her father's music hall. She would close her eyes and play with Raven curled on top, listening in painful bliss. The music always reminded them of when her father used to play before they sat down to formal dinners.

Koa remembered how much she enjoyed those nights. Formal dinners had been unheard of in Korea, when one or two small meals a day had been a privilege.

She sighed and hid her true feelings for this little cottage that reminded her too much of her days of poverty. Halston had no idea what this meant.

"It's nice. A bit small don't you think?" She asked offhandedly to not reveal just how deep her hatred for it was.

Halston shrugged. "I don't think so. It's quite a gem. It's lovely on the inside. Three bedrooms, a nice little kitchen... not that you cook," he joked under his breath. "It's well-kept and secluded."

Koa looked around. She could see cottages a couple of yards away on each side. "It's hardly secluded." She pointed with a skeptical look. "I can see into the neighbor's yard. That means the humans inside will see me when I come and go. That's dangerous. What if I want to fly? You do recall Rome, don't you?"

Koa could still remember the faces of the couple who had seen her take off from one of the buildings. It was a good thing that no one believed their fantastical stories of a flying girl.

Halston winced at the memory but didn't address it.

Koa could tell that he was a little annoyed. The Rome incident was one of those times when Halston had told Koa not to do something, and she had done it anyway.

"We'll build a privacy fence, a stone one, just like the sturdy stone your house is made of." He held his hand out for her hand. "Come on, let's take a look inside and you'll see what I mean. Raven is waiting."

Koa sighed and put her hand into Halston's. They went inside and she was surprised by how much natural light it got. That was a good thing. No sneaky vampires would dare hide out and wait for her in this house.

She smiled at her mother when she came running down the stairs and leapt into her arms.

"This house is lovely, Koa," Raven said as Koa snuggled her under her chin. "I've always wanted a nice cottage like this."

Koa sighed in defeat. She flicked her bangs out of her eyes. Her mother loved it. It was official. This was their new home.

"Yes, Mother," she grumbled. Koa pursed her lips. Raven gave her a look.

"Koa," Raven whispered. "You cannot call me that, not even in private. You never know who is listening or spying on us."

"She's right," Halston added. He opened the shutters on all of the windows and let even more light into the cottage. "Never let your guard down. Even at home."

"Yes. I forgot. It's hard to call you by a pet name."

Raven purred. "It's all right, darling. We just cannot take any chances. Our enemies think I am dead. We must keep it that way."

The thought of someone finding her mother and harming her made her throat tighten with fear. "I understand." She shoved horrible thoughts of her mother being killed out of her head and tried to distract herself. She looked around, trying to figure out where she would put all of her things. If Koa would be forced to live there, she could at least try to make it feel like home.

Halston hooked both thumbs in his belt loops and looked proud. "Right. I'm going to head back to the safe house. You get settled and meet me there at sunset. You're with me again."

Koa nodded as he left the house. She met Raven's eyes. "Another mission tonight, Raven. Sure you will be all right here by yourself?"

Raven's eyes glittered. "You underestimate me, Koa. You forget it was I who saved you the other night when those Syths had you running around like a chicken with its head cut off."

"I know," Koa said. "What would I do without you?"

Raven rubbed against her leg. "That's something I hope we never have to worry about."

CHAPTER 4

HALSTON DIDN'T MIND helping Koa find a new home. He enjoyed being needed. He sat in his car for a few moments contemplating her facial expression when he presented the cottage to her. It was obvious that she didn't like it.

Now, he frowned and as he waited for her in the safe house. He leaned back in his desk chair. That young half-blood was hard to please. It was their joke that if something was too easy, then Koa lost interest pretty quickly. Finding a new home wasn't easy. She didn't like being around too many people. She loved her father's manor, but things had changed. The Netherworld was catching up with her faster than he expected.

Halston had hoped that they would have more time to prepare. Now it seemed that Koa would have to face her demons a lot sooner than anticipated. He rubbed his temples. He did not think that she was ready.

A loud scream broke Halston from his thoughts. The sound seemed to come from far away, like an echo. There was desperation in that scream as it grew louder and closer. He felt the blond hairs on his skin stand on end.

Micka and Rohan both looked up from their work stations. They came to their feet in unison and reached for guns that were strapped underneath their desks.

Halston sat up and watched as Galena fell through the inkwell portal. There was a loud shriek as the black liquid spit her out onto his clean, white floor. Galena collapsed and Halston ran to her.

Halston left his seat and slid to Galena. He held her head up from the floor. Galena looked like a frail, crumpled rag doll. She was covered in blood. Her eyes were wet from crying and her blond hair was sticky with something foul.

"Don't let him in!" Galena called out weakly. She squeezed her eyes closed and started to weep. Her entire body shook with her racking sobs.

Halston's heart pumped with worry. He looked over his shoulder at the two agents that looked at him with fearful eyes. They lowered their guns. This was not normal… even for Netherworld agents.

"Get me a clean, wet cloth and some water!"

Rohan nodded and rushed to complete the task. Micka stood ready, with her gun pointed to the portal, in case someone followed Galena.

Halston pulled Galena's hair from her face and she screamed. He withdrew and noted the bruises on her face and the cuts in the corners of her mouth. He drew a breath and looked at the inkwell portal. The portal stood in the center of the safe house. It was a large circular device held stationary by shiny black brackets. The portal was only supposed to be used in dire situations. There had to be a major emergency, for once a portal was revealed, the person escaping could easily be followed. The last thing Halston needed was a nephilim coming through that portal and causing havoc… or worse, damaging equipment in his laboratory. He wasn't done with his latest invention.

He looked down to see Galena looking up at him. He held his breath. He'd rarely seen such terror in a person's eyes. The way she looked at him spoke volumes. She had been frightened nearly to death.

"Galena," he said. "What happened?"

Her face contorted and she started to cry again. Her sobs came from her soul. They were sorrowful, deeply hurt, cries of pain. Halston felt his skin grow cold. This woman was one of his best agents. She was human, but she was one of his best. From the poor streets of Russia, Galena had been orphaned early after vampires killed her parents.

Halston had found her just the way he found most of his Netherworld agents: angry, ready for revenge, and trying to seek that revenge in foolish ways. He had found her, trained her, and put her out there to be a spy. Halston had given her the tools to find her parents' killers, and bring them to justice.

Halston didn't seek out to simply kill all vampires and other nephilim, he tried to protect the humans. Sometimes that meant finding vampires that were willing to try a new life. Those vampires, like the Wryn clan, were open to finding 'pets,' people who sold their blood for money or care. They registered with his Netherworld Division, and lived their lives clean and free of murder and chaos. It wasn't a perfect arrangement. There were still vampires that loved to kill, and resisted the Netherworld Divisions of the world that tried to bring order.

Rohan knelt down and handed Halston a wet towel. Halston wiped Galena's face clean. She winced and jerked away. Like a frightened animal, she crawled far from both of them. Her eyes darted around the safe house.

"Did they follow me?" Galena's voice came out ragged and almost too soft to hear.

Micka ran up with a bottle of water and paused when she saw Galena with her back pressed against the wall. Galena grabbed her by the leg. Micka's almond-shaped brown eyes looked to Halston.

"Don't let them hurt me anymore," Galena begged.

Halston sighed and came to his feet. He didn't move closer to Galena. She was too afraid, and he didn't want to make the situation worse. He stood there and thought about what to do. She had been missing for about a week now. There was no telling what she had been through. He put his hands in the pockets of his trousers and looked down at Galena.

"Galena," he said. "We won't hurt you. You are safe. We are the only ones here. Rohan, Micka, you, and me." He knelt down and looked at her with a small, friendly smile. "I'm Halston. You do remember me, don't you?"

Galena tilted her head and stared at him. Her eyes were as big as saucers, and for a moment, Halston doubted that she recognized him. Her shoulders slumped and she slowly nodded. "Yes. I remember you, Halston."

Halston nodded. "Good. Good girl. You remember that I am your friend, and that I care about you, right?"

Galena let go of Micka's leg. She ripped the black stockings the woman wore with her ragged nails. Halston noticed that her fingernails had blood caked into her cuticles. Micka adjusted her glasses but ignored her ruined stockings.

"I remember," Galena said. She folded her legs and rested her head on the wall. She looked exhausted.

"What happened?"

She shook her head and her bottom lip trembled. "I've been through a lot in my life, Halston," she said in a wavering voice. "But nothing like this."

Galena looked from Rohan to Micka. "I will tell you," she said. She met Halston's eyes. "And only you."

Micka and Rohan got the point. They both collected the files that they had been working on, and took them to a back room of the safe house.

Halston stood and walked over to Galena. He sat down beside her and looked toward the secret hatch door at the far end of the safe house. He didn't want to sit right in front of her. Whenever someone did that, it just made the conversation feel like an interrogation. He wanted Galena to feel comfortable.

He reached for her hand and she flinched but didn't run. Halston had a soothing effect. He took her hand and cradled it in his own. Somehow, that relaxed her.

Galena took a deep breath. "It was last Monday." A tear fell from her eye. Halston gently brushed it away. He pulled her hair from her face and tucked it behind her ear. "I found the man you had me look for. Bund. I was surprised that he was a young guy, but that also made me feel a little more comfortable around him," she said and looked to Halston. "You know what I mean?"

He nodded. He knew Bund's game.

"But once he got me inside, he changed on me." She hugged her arms and shifted her weight. Her brows furrowed. "There were so many of them, Halston. I told them, I would only sell my blood to the one you sent me for." She closed her eyes. "But they didn't listen." Her voice lowered. "They locked me in there. Somehow, Bund knew I was coming. He knew you had sent me. He punished me."

Halston clenched his jaw. He should have never sent her alone. He couldn't understand how Bund could have known that Halston had sent Galena. Halston had to remember, Bund was smarter than he seemed. Like Halston, Bund was a great deal more than he appeared to be.

He didn't say anything. He waited for Galena to go on. He knew it was hard for her, but he needed to know what they were dealing with.

She took a while to continue. She kept looking at the portal to make sure no one was going to step through.

"I might as well spit it out, right?" Galena asked the question, but Halston could tell that she was speaking to herself.

He nodded anyway. "Go on. It's just the two of us. Whatever you tell me will stay between us. I won't tell a soul."

Galena gave him a look. Her gray eyes narrowed. She pursed her lips and examined his face. "Not even Koa?"

Halston's eye twitched, not because he was lying, but because Galena seemed to have suspicions about his relationship with the young vampire. He knew that would be a problem if people suspected that he and Koa were more than professional associates. He would have to find a way to eliminate such suspicions.

He swallowed and shook his head. "Not even Koa."

Galena looked unsure. She watched him for a while longer and sighed. She looked down at her feet. "You know… it's all right if you like her. We all like Koa."

Halston pulled away from Galena.

She watched him. "You don't have to go all pale on me. We all see it."

He didn't know what to say, so he said nothing.

Galena slumped against the wall and stared at the portal again. "Well, there were so many of them that I lost count, but they raped me, fed from me, and kept me locked in a cage."

There was a long stretch of silence. Halston held her head to his shoulder and she started to weep again. It was unnerving to hear that woman cry. She was always so strong, even cold. She had been broken.

She looked up and rubbed her face. She threw her hands up. "Bund didn't even feed from me! You know what he said to me? He said that I was too *old*. What the hell?"

Halston shook his head. He knew Bund's preferences. Children gave him more energy than adults.

"Bund just watched the others with a stupid grin on his face!" She slammed her fist into her thigh so hard that Halston feared she'd bruise herself. "I hate that man more than anything in this world," she said through clenched teeth. "Please, tell me how to kill him."

Halston took her fist and gently opened it. He took her hand into both of his. "You don't worry about it. I'm terribly sorry that I put you in that situation, but even I can't kill him."

Galena's shoulders slumped. "Great."

He tilted her chin up. She was still shaking a little. "But, I know someone who can get rid of him. *Forever.*"

"Well, I want to be there when you do it, so that I can spit in his face."

"I'll try to arrange that." He smiled for her, hoping it would soften her angry face. Tonight… his smile wasn't working.

"If it wasn't for one of the dumber vampires, in his drunken stupor, forgetting to lock the cage, I would still be there. I might be dead now."

Halston patted the back of her hand. "It's all in the past now. I don't want you to worry. I can erase this event from your memory, if you'd like." He came to his feet and held a hand out to her.

Galena took his hand and pulled herself up, but she held tight to his hand. Her eyes were serious. "No, Halston."

He tensed. The tone of her voice was unexpected. She sounded like herself again, cold and serious. She looked… ready to hurt someone.

"I don't want to forget. I need to remember this. You're not getting out of letting me spit in his face when you kill him."

Halston nodded and tried to take his hand back. She held steady.

"Listen," she said. "There's more."

Halston sighed. "What else?"

She leaned in close to him. Her eyes were hardened, her grip unyielding. "He knows about Koa."

There was little in this world that would make him react recklessly. He would have to restrain himself while he listened to what the Russian woman had to say.

CHAPTER 5

THE SAFE HOUSE was an unassuming abandoned warehouse that Halston had purchased decades ago. The entire strip of land was abandoned. Once a power plant, no one dared come near it for fear of radiation exposure.

Koa had the suspicion that Halston probably had a dozen or so safe houses. Whenever one was compromised, he always had a backup, and he didn't always tell her his plan. He was clever. People tended to assume that such an attractive man couldn't possibly be such a genius. They didn't know that he was always at least ten steps ahead of them, and that his brain functioned at a superhuman level. They could never guess that he was not, in fact, human.

She walked into one of the secret entrances in the back and covered her head with her hand. The exposed pipes still tended to drip cold water onto her head. It was dark and silent, except for the incessant drips. She rolled her eyes and lifted herself a few feet off the ground to avoid stepping into the black puddles that covered the flooring.

Halston was good. This was all a diversion, in case anyone dared come inside. They would see the oil spills and the oozing green gases that seeped into the air from cracked pipes along the wall. Anyone would be discouraged from going any further, but Koa knew better.

She ignored the mutilated rats and followed the labyrinth-like tunnels to a small door that one might never have noticed because it seemed to blend into the darkness. The door was rusted and covered in a slimy film of green goo. She pulled the hidden lever and pushed. With a creak it opened, and her eyes were affronted by bright lights.

Koa groaned and hurried inside. She pushed the door closed and set the lock on the digital keypad attached to its back.

"Glad you finally decided to join us," Halston called.

Koa sighed and turned to face him. With clean, white walls, the sterile space reminded her of a lab or a hospital. The constant buzz of electronics hummed in the background. The sleek white desks and long bare tables were spaced apart like a study hall.

Halston's love for technology was apparent at first glance into that room. He had flat screens everywhere and prototypes for weapons and various gadgets and devices. Everything was neat and tucked away into its proper place. Then then she saw it, locked away in its glass case.

Halston's infinity gun.

Koa shivered as she looked at it. She loved that weapon. She almost wanted to trade in her Lyrinian sword, just to wield that shotgun one time. She'd only ever seen Halston use it a handful of times, and each time she had been appalled by its power. He refused to let her touch it.

She shifted her gaze to Halston and Galena, a female assassin from their Russian office. She gave Koa a forced smile and returned her attention to Halston. Koa felt the tension in the room. Galena looked as if she had been crying. Her dull blond hair looked dirtier than normal, and she had suspicious cuts on her arms that were barely hidden by a bunch of bangles.

Galena had first been seen by Al, their recruiter, and later brought into the Netherworld Division by Halston. She was a charge, or 'pet' for hire, similar to Ian in that she sold her blood to paying customers, but Galena worked with the most notorious of them all. Now, she went undercover for the Netherworld Division and sought to expose the most evil of the vampires and kill them. She was ruthless, cold, and calculating.

Koa swallowed and silently took a seat a few feet from them. She glanced at Galena and saw that her eyes were red and swollen. She had bruises on her cheeks and neck.

Koa didn't like to see that. Koa looked at Halston with questions in her eyes. He gave her a look that begged her not to ask any questions.

"Right. Here's the plan. Galena, I want you to go home, clean up, and rest. Let me know if you need anything. I want you to consider this a vacation." He looked to Koa and then held up a holograph device that showed her a small, shabby, building. "Koa, you and I will visit the Oracle."

Galena stretched her long legs and took a deep breath. "What if he finds me?"

Halston clenched his jaw. "It's not you he wants. I will take care of it."

Galena's voice cracked. "I don't know, Halston. He seemed different from the others."

Koa tensed. Galena was frightened, which made her feel worried.

Halston sat before Galena and his face softened. Galena looked at him with fresh tears in her eyes and Koa felt a tug at her heart. Halston took her hands inside of his. Halston could be the most serious man she'd ever met, and he could also be surprisingly tender.

He spoke to Galena and Koa leaned forward to hear him. She couldn't wait to find out what had happened to their most trusted informant.

"Listen, Galena," Halston said. "I will not let anything happen to you. Wear the earrings I gave you and I will track your location. I have two of my best Shadows following you. They will be like bodyguards and defend you if anyone tries to hurt you again. I don't care if they're human, vampire or whatever, the Shadows will provide a defense for you if you need it. And if someone tries to hurt you again." He handed her a vial.

Koa's brows lifted. This must be serious. Vials could only be bought in the Netherworld, from the Alchemist.

"You throw this, and you run like hell." He gave her a pointed look. "Got it?"

Galena nodded and looked down at the black vial that Halston placed in her hand. She curled her fingers around it and attached it to the holster underneath her skirt. She wiped her eyes but smiled. "Thank you, Halston."

Halston nodded and wiped the tear from her cheek. "Don't mention it."

Galena gave a confident nod. She obviously felt better about what she now had to do and came to her feet with her head held a little higher than before. Koa watched Halston sweep his hands behind Galena and two Shadows emerged from the floor. They were translucent beings that walked in unison behind the woman.

Koa never liked Shadows. She sat back in her cold metal chair and watched them vanish. They might have vanished from their sight, but they still lingered unseen, and would follow and protect Galena.

Koa shivered. She remembered when Halston had attached Shadows to her one time. She could always feel their cold, unearthly presence. Sometimes Koa would look behind her and frown, wondering if they were still there.

Galena didn't seem to mind. She was comforted by the knowledge that they would always be with her.

Galena nodded. "I'll be at my cottage in Greece." Halston nodded and came to his feet. He folded his hands behind him as she gathered her bag and headed for the exit.

Galena gave Koa a look. Her gray eyes made Koa hold her breath. There was something hidden in them that made Koa afraid.

"Good luck out there, Koa." Galena's voice lowered. "Watch your back," she said and left the room.

Once the door was secured, Koa shot a glance at Halston. "What happened? Tell me?"

Halston sighed and leaned back against one of his computer stations. He shrugged and looked off toward the door that Galena just went through. "We have a problem, Koa."

Koa frowned. "Obviously."

He gazed at her. He looked paler than usual. Koa sat on the edge of her seat. Something was definitely wrong.

"I think something is brewing. A war, perhaps. Someone is letting nephilim out of the Netherworld at an alarming rate. They are gathering and mobilizing."

Koa felt her face flush. "More Syths," she whispered.

Halston shook his head. "Not just Syths, but Netherworld vamps and even demons."

Koa fell back in her chair. "Why do you think that, Halston? Why would they mobilize?"

Silence.

Koa saw that Halston was holding back. She sat up. "What is it?"

Halston ran his hands through his hair, making it messy. "You remember who killed your father?"

She could feel herself shaking. She ground her teeth. "How could I forget? It took us a long time to find out who did it."

Halston sucked in a breath. "Well, Bund has returned."

Koa put both hands over her lips, as if in prayer. One of her deepest fears was being realized. "He is free? From the Netherworld?"

Halston's silence answered her question. Koa whimpered and felt acid from her stomach enter her throat. Fear washed over her like hot water. She covered her mouth. "No, Halston."

Halston held his hands out to calm her down. "Did I tell you to start worrying? I have this under control."

"Halston, he killed my father."

Halston sighed in exasperation and turned away from her. He slumped into his chair at his computer station and began typing away. "I have a plan, Koa. Don't I always have a plan?"

Koa nodded. Her throat felt dry. When Halston found Koa and recruited her, it had been only weeks after her father had been killed in a Parisian alley. Koa had only been seventeen, and just returned from a nightmare that she couldn't remember, to find her father killed and her mother cursed to live as a cat.

It would be an understatement to say that Koa had turned to the dark side for a while. She didn't like what she had become, but Halston had given her direction. Halston helped her find out who had killed her father. Someone named Bund. For five years, Koa thought about what she would do once she found that person, and yet, she was fearful of him. Her father had been the strongest vampire she'd ever known.

Her father had trained her, loved her, and protected her. She felt her adrenaline start to simmer. She might get her revenge sooner than she thought.

"Now, I need you to trust me. Can you do that?"

Koa nodded again, but her entire body felt as if it had been stuck with pins and needles, like a foot that had fallen asleep. Was she ready to face her father's murderer?

She grabbed her arms and massaged them. She tried to shake off that horrible feeling of fear. She didn't like it. She didn't like being reminded of the horrific events of her past.

"Halston." Her voice sounded almost childlike. Koa couldn't explain why she almost felt like a child again. A terribly frightened child.

He stopped typing and turned his attention to her. "Koa. Don't. Just don't."

She pursed her lips. "But, you don't even know what I was going to say!"

"You were going to ask me if you could go to the Netherworld."

Koa lowered her head and pulled a loose string from the hole in her jeans. "Perhaps, I could go there and find out what is happening. Maybe I can find out the truth about my past. I mean, look at my sword…" She held the hilt out toward him.

He didn't look at it. He knew already.

"There are *Netherworld* symbols on it. How could my father have such a weapon? Why did he take me there as a child?" More questions crowded Koa's mind, but she was afraid to ask them. "If I knew the answers to these questions, I could have my memories back. I mean, an *entire* chunk of my adolescent life is missing!"

Halston didn't speak for a moment. Koa's eyes brightened. There was hope. Maybe he would finally let her go. Maybe she could finally recover the missing memories of her past. He didn't know what it was like to lose years of memories and have no clue as to why.

All she knew was that her father had taken her to the Netherworld when she was twelve. Then there was nothing… a white void. When Koa woke, she was in a strange place with no recollection of what had happened, or how much time had passed.

Halston finally broke his silence. He shook his head. "No. It is out of the question. You are not ready."

Koa's eyes narrowed. "How the hell can you say that? How do *you* know? You may be the 'boss' in this Netherworld Division, but you don't control me!"

Halston shook his head. "You don't get it, Koa. I don't want to control you. I am trying to protect you."

Koa sneered. "Yes," she said sarcastically. "I suppose it's for the best. I suppose I'm not meant to have my memories back. I mean, they are *my* memories and all."

Halston gave her an odd look. "Perhaps you don't know just how lucky you are to not have those memories back. Have you ever thought of that?"

Koa glanced at him. "What do you mean?" Her face was hot with rising rage. She hated being told what she could and couldn't do. She was an adult, not a child. "What do you know, Halston?"

Halston's watch began to ring. He answered it and Koa sighed. He hung up and came to his feet. "The Oracle is ready to meet with us. Let's go."

Koa nodded and watched Halston arm himself. For the first time, she felt as if Halston was hiding something important from her. He wouldn't tell her what happened with Galena, but she had an idea.

She frowned down at her hands. She couldn't shake the feeling, but she felt a small spark of doubt that she could fully trust someone who kept so much from her.

Halston glanced at her, and it was as if he could read the concern on her face. She thought that he would say something, dismiss her doubts. She wanted him to. Instead, he simply nodded for her to follow and left the room.

CHAPTER 6

KOA WAS a little taken aback by their means of transportation. Out of every car that Halston had, they drove an old sedan to the Oracle. She was confused. There were so many better ways to get there — that is, until she saw where the Oracle lived.

They arrived at a tiny flat in a lower-class complex. A seedy hole in the wall that most people of means would try to avoid. Koa knew better than to judge, though. Her childhood home wasn't much better. She knew what it was like to be dirt poor.

She overlooked the dilapidated buildings and pot holes in the street and looked into the faces of the children. They played in the street with nothing more than their imaginations. She knew what it was like to not even have a toy. Most people would have felt uncomfortable in this neighborhood.

Koa felt the exact opposite, and she was glad that Halston had chosen the old sedan instead of a shiny Maserati or Mercedes. She would have felt ashamed in the midst of these unfortunate people.

Halston stopped the car and they stepped out into the sunset. Halston closed the door and looked over the car at her. "Are you ready?"

Koa nodded quickly. "I am. I've been waiting to finally meet her." She smiled and Halston did the same.

"Good. She has been looking forward to meeting you too. Don't forget that she can be dangerous though."

"Please, she's a sweet old lady," Koa replied as she followed behind Halston to the woman's flat.

"And she can be more dangerous than a man with a gun," Halston said over his shoulder.

Koa just nodded when they stopped before a door. Halston knocked.

Koa smiled at a little boy who nearly ran into her. The little boy returned the smile, and she giggled at his missing two front teeth. He hid and peeked around the corner as if playing with her. He made a silly face and hid again.

Koa covered her eyes and pretended that she was scaring him when he peeked around the corner again. He burst out laughing. Koa beamed. She loved children more than anything. Sometimes she wondered if she'd be able to have a child someday.

Koa should have never been born. Vampire children weren't born to human mothers. As far as Koa knew, she was the only one.

The door opened and Koa turned her attention from the child. She waved to the boy before she stepped into the flat. The Oracle was a small Chinese woman. She wore a warm smile on her thin lips. Her wire-rimmed bifocals made her dark eyes look abnormally large. She wore a red nightgown that seemed like it needed a wash. There were food stains all over it.

"Koa, right?" the Oracle said with a heavy Chinese accent.

Koa nodded. "Nice to meet you."

The Oracle looked her up and down and nodded. "Come in."

Koa had to hide her disgust as she entered the flat. It was a small home, and unlike Halston's safe house that was an illusion on the outside, this place was just as rundown on the inside.

Koa covered her nose. The smell of cat urine made her want to gag. The smell was as intense as ammonia and with Koa's heightened sense of smell, she felt like she might faint if she breathed it in too deeply, so she took small, quick, breaths behind her hand.

The house was a cluttered, revolting mess. The Oracle seemed to be a mixture of a hoarder and a victim of a chronic obsessive-compulsive disorder. Koa watched her step away from the door and flick the light switch four times after she closed the door. She spoke Mandarin under her breath in what sounded like a chant.

Koa and Halston stepped to the side and waited for her to complete her rituals. She touched the doorknob a few times to make sure that it was locked, before turning her attention to them. She waved for them to follow and walked down the narrow hallway to the back of the flat.

A cat jumped onto the Oracle's shoulder and seemed to cradle her head as she walked. Koa grimaced at the stains in the old, disgusting carpet. There were open cans of cat food scattered about and small piles of cat feces. Koa wanted to vomit. She averted her eyes and swallowed the acid in her throat.

"No time to clean up today," the Oracle said. She pushed a pile of newspapers off her tattered sofa and motioned for them to have a seat.

Koa wanted to stand, but she didn't want to offend the older woman. She sat on the very edge of the sofa and kept her hands and legs close, so that she wouldn't have to touch anything. A cat ran under the coffee table and looked up at her with its yellow eyes. Koa smiled at it, almost expecting it to say hello. No, only her mother could do such a thing.

"You come much sooner than I expected," the Oracle said. She sat in a rocking chair and folded her hands in her lap. "I am surprised."

"Your messenger came by this morning. I saw no reason to wait," Halston said.

Koa listened. She was so anxious that her knees bounced with nerves. The Oracle knew so much about both worlds, and Koa felt like such an eager novice on the subject.

"Well, I suppose that is just as well." She leaned back and her eyes settled on Koa. "It is nice to finally meet you."

Koa nodded. "Yes. Nice to meet you too, Oracle. I've been waiting for Halston to bring me here for quite a while."

The Oracle's smile spread across her small, sagging face. "Well then, now that we've met, you can visit me anytime. I teach you a thing or two about life." She glanced at Koa's hand. "You married?"

Koa was aghast. She shook her head and pursed her lips.

The Oracle grinned. "How old are you?"

Koa glanced at Halston. She was uncomfortable already. "Twenty-one."

The Oracle waved her hand. "Oh, just a baby. Still... not too early."

Koa looked away. She pretended that she didn't hear.

"What are you waiting for?" she asked.

Koa giggled nervously. *Change the subject lady*, Koa thought.

The Oracle sat back in her chair. "I married one man. At nineteen. He was good man." She nodded her head at the memory. "He never judge me for what I am. When he die, I lost more than love. I no longer care what happen to me. I give up."

Koa looked at her. She felt bad. She looked around. It made sense. She wondered if the Oracle's home had been this messy when her husband was alive. Something told her that it hadn't.

"Because I treat him good, he good to me." The Oracle pointed at her. "But you see? All men the same. Rich man, poor man, white man, Asian man, black man… all the same. Just pick one." She laughed. "You cook for them, you clean, you take care of them, they all yours. They have no reason to act up." She laughed harder. "Understand?"

Koa glanced at Halston who just looked ahead at the Oracle with an expressionless face. Koa couldn't help but narrow her eyes. "Yes," she said, but she had no idea what the older woman meant. Koa didn't think all men were the same. She'd seen too many evil men out there to have her ideas changed by a strange woman with bifocals as big as saucers.

The Oracle scoffed and slapped her knee. "Nonsense. I know you don't get it, child."

Koa's face turned red. She hoped to God that the Oracle couldn't read minds.

"But one day, you will get it." The Oracle stared at her.

Koa nodded. She tried not to think too much… just in case the Oracle could read minds. She tried not to think about how disgusted she was to sit in that smelly house and have cat fur all over her clothes. She tried but she couldn't help but to think those things. Koa and the Oracle were in a stare-off with Koa trying to figure out if the Oracle was fiddling in her head, and the Oracle simply giving her an intense look with her magnified eyes.

Halston cleared his throat. He was all business on this night. "The message said that you linked with someone. Someone from the Netherworld."

The Oracle ignored him. Her eyes narrowed as she continued to look at Koa. "You want something, child, don't you? You want to know the truth of your past."

Koa nodded. She leaned forward in her seat so much that she nearly fell off.

"I sent the message because I wanted Halston to bring you here. I wanted to finally meet the girl of prophecy."

Halston looked at Koa. He looked perplexed. "But…"

Koa smiled and looked to the Oracle who winked at her. The Oracle had tricked him.

"Do not worry, Halston. I did not lie to you. I did link with someone from the Netherworld last night, and that link wanted one thing. They want Koa. Koa the key… and she must be used to set the world right again."

Halston turned to the Oracle. His brows were furrowed in annoyance. "Is it true then? Is he behind everything that's been happening lately?"

The Oracle nodded. "He is."

Koa looked from one to the other. "Who are you talking about?"

Halston sat back and Koa nearly yelled at him not to. He would get cat fur all over his clothes. She restrained herself.

What is wrong with you? Koa thought to herself. *That is not important right now. Focus.*

"Then we have lost already." Halston ran both hands through his hair. Koa knew that meant he was worried. His brain was already trying to calculate a solution. He was lost to them for now. He would not speak until he thought of a solution.

Koa put her hands on her hips and leaned forward. "Who is *he*?"

The Oracle shrugged. "The Bringer of Death."

Koa raised an eyebrow. "Sounds a bit dramatic…" Koa hid her rising apprehension. Such a title, said by the Oracle, must be serious.

"Well, he the creator of the 'new world' vampires. Before him, nephilim were only in the Netherworld. He the reason we have vampires in the human world. He also the one who ordered your father killed."

Koa frowned. "Bund killed my father, who are you talking about?" Koa felt her skin tighten.

"Bund is general. He not the commander in chief. He not a king. The king… he is free. You should be afraid of *him*. Humans all over should hide their children from Bund, and lock their doors to keep Greggan out. They are a terrible pair. I'm thirsty." The Oracle smacked her lips together. "Want some tea?"

Koa sat frozen. She couldn't speak. She shook her head to the Oracle's question. The Oracle shrugged and came to her feet. She walked back to her kitchen. Koa heard cabinets opening and being slammed shut. She heard dishes clanking together.

Koa nudged Halston. "Is she talking about who I think she is? Is it really the king of the Netherworld?"

Halston groaned. He rubbed his temples. "No, Koa, there isn't just one king of all the Netherworld, just like there isn't one king for all of the human world. Greggan is but one, though he is one of the worst that we could dare to face."

Koa grabbed his arm. "He's the reason my father was killed? He's the one who sent Bund to murder him?"

Halston shrugged his shoulder to his ear and made a face. "Well, yes. Well, not necessarily. Sure he sent the order, but there's a little more to the story."

Koa shook him. "Tell me, then!"

The Oracle returned with a platter of tea cups and a tea pot. She set the tray on the table that was covered in dust and poured Koa a cup.

She simply sat there, staring off as the Oracle handed her the cup of tea. Koa didn't have the energy to protest. There were too many thoughts in her head. She absentmindedly drank a sip and frowned.

It's cold, she thought, but didn't dare say it.

"The only way to solve this problem is to send the girl back." The Oracle spoke directly to Halston.

Halston shook his head. "I cannot let her go there. You know that." He stood and reached for Koa. "Let's go."

Koa took his hand.

The lights in the room turned blue and everything in the room seemed to glow. "Sit down."

Both Koa and Halston froze. The Oracle's voice took on a dangerous tone. Halston gave Koa's hand a reassuring squeeze and sat back down. Koa looked around and felt a cold chill sweep through the room. She held her breath and looked at the Oracle.

The Oracle's face seemed to be shrouded in darkness and shadows. It was eerie. Her bifocals turned black and hid her eyes.

"I want peace in my world. My link knows the only way is to return the girl to her proper place."

"Your link has his motives."

"Do not speak," she hissed. She was on her feet and towering over them. The Oracle was a small woman, but somehow Koa felt intimidated and looked away from the dark glasses.

She gripped Halston's hand as fear crept into her. She wished she knew more about what was happening.

"They will keep coming after her, until you return her." She waved a hand in the dark and Koa gasped. Mists swirled around before them. White swirls of air that danced in the dark revealed a tall gate of some sort. Koa felt her heart pound. She had seen this gate before. It was the Gate to the Netherworld, the portal that some of the nephilim had escaped from.

"You are smart, Halston. Smarter than the men of this world. Clever and resourceful. Use your skill to find a way around this bargain. Give them what they want, and get what you want." She leaned forward. "Find an ally… outthink your enemies."

Koa watched Halston's face. He was on the same track as the Oracle. "An ally? Do you think he will help us, after everything?"

The Oracle shrugged and sat back down. "One way to find out."

The lights returned to normal and they were surprised to see that the Oracle was sleeping. Her little snores filled the room. Halston pulled Koa up and put a finger to his lips.

She nodded. They quickly and quietly walked out of the den. They left the tiny flat, and Halston didn't stop when they were outside. He hurried with Koa in tow until they were at the car.

He held her door open. "Get in."

They drove off much quicker than when they arrived. Koa looked out the window. She was already formulating a plan of her own. She couldn't trust Halston to give her the freedom to search for answers, so she would have to do it without him.

If he wanted to keep secrets from her, then she would do the same. She knew of a nephilim clan that would definitely have answers. She just didn't know if they'd give them to her without a fight.

Koa sighed and gave Halston a sidelong glance. She was tempted to tell him her plan, but that spark of doubt nagged at her once more. She shook her head and looked out the window at the dark streets. Soft rain began to fall.

I guess I'll just have to find out on my own.

CHAPTER 7

HALSTON DROPPED KOA OFF at the safe house. She would be occupied with paperwork that would last her for at least a couple of hours. He hoped that was enough time for him to execute his plan. Now, he stood before Koa's new cottage with the passenger door open… for Raven. She ran from the house, jumped over the gate and scurried into the front seat.

Halston closed the door and looked around. No one was around. The night was dark and quiet. He walked around to his side and got in.

"Where is Koa?" Raven asked.

Halston knew that would be her first question. She was a good mother to the girl. He wished she didn't have to get cursed.

"At the safe house. I gave her enough paperwork to keep her busy for a while."

Raven curled into the leather seat and looked at him with big green eyes. "Well, you know Koa…"

Halston shrugged a shoulder. "Yes, I do. I thought the same thing, but she has no idea what I have planned."

"You better hope she doesn't. My daughter can be more than a bit headstrong at times. I still worry about her as much as I did when she was a toddler."

Halston smirked. "Who are you telling? I learned that the day I met her."

"So, it's true then, Bund is looking for Koa?"

Halston's face turned serious. He nodded. "Yes." He tightened his grip on the leather steering wheel.

"Do you think he means to kill her?"

"No," Halston said. "If there is one thing we can depend on, it's the fact that Bund will do anything for payment." He gave Raven a look. "And Greggan pays very well."

Raven shivered. "Too bad it's not money Bund wants."

Halston thought of all the children's bodies he'd seen sprawled around London. They had been mutilated, gutted, bled, and left in artistic poses, as if to taunt Halston. Bund had a particular taste for little girls. Halston's stomach turned at the thought of what that foul creature had done to the poor children before he killed them.

Raven sighed. "I can't help but think we need to do what we've been trying to avoid these past few years. Maybe we should go ahead and send Koa back now, before it's too late. Jax is the only one who can free me from the curse, and I need to be free so that I can help protect her. I am the only one that can get rid of Bund... for good."

Halston thought a moment. He watched the dark road ahead as they cut through the countryside. Rolling hills passed by and he glanced at the full moon. Too many bad things happened on nights with full moons. He was glad that, for once, the full moon was on their side. They would need the power that it held for what they were about to attempt.

"You need me, Halston. I can only do so much in this ridiculous, body."

"I know. But the cost is much greater than the reward. Koa is not ready yet."

Raven sat up. Her black fur mocked eyebrows and she bunched them in dismay. "How do we know if she'll ever truly be ready? We cannot shield her from the truth forever."

Halston knew she was right. He just cared too much for Koa to watch her suffer. He wished he could keep her past from her forever. Once she knew the truth, he feared she would never look at him the same.

"Halston?"

Raven broke him from his thoughts. He looked at her. "Yes?"

"If you refuse to speak about the Netherworld, at least tell me what happened with the Oracle?"

Halston sighed. "Jax."

Raven inched closer, eager to hear more. "Yes... I knew it! Another sign that we need to act now! Go on... what else?"

"He's been linking with the Oracle lately."

Raven seemed to smile. It looked odd on her feline face. He tried to picture her smile from before the curse. It was difficult.

"But that's good!" Raven exclaimed.

Halston shook his head. "Why is that good? He's the enemy as far as I'm concerned."

"But he can free me! We need him."

"The price we pay for the things we need," Halston said under his breath.

"Exactly. But it's not your need, Halston, it's mine. And I deserve to be changed back. If not for me, it needs to be done for Koa."

Halston didn't reply. His head was full of too many thoughts, doubts, and scenarios. There was truth to what Raven said. He knew that soon he'd be making the journey back to the Netherworld. The Netherworld held too many of his secrets. He couldn't admit that he wasn't ready to face the past.

CHAPTER 8

KOA CREPT THROUGH the narrow alleyway as soft rain trickled down onto her head. She welcomed the cool shower. She needed something to calm the nervous anxiety that began to fill her belly. She knew it would take more than a sword and a straight face for these vamps to take her seriously.

The evening was late and Koa had grown tired of paperwork. She had more important things to attend to. When Halston dropped her off, she had almost blurted out what she was planning. Instead, she pursed her lips and left without a word. She couldn't let him even suspect what she was doing.

Koa approached the lair of a secretive nephilim clan that had escaped into the human world centuries ago. They were quiet and kept to themselves, because they were smart. Not only that, but they were afraid. They were hiding… and now Koa knew who they were hiding from. A common enemy. That was all the leverage she had against them.

Koa had never encountered a Netherworld vamp. They were a completely different breed from the vampires walking around in the human world. The vampires of the human world were considered new world vampires, the children that were created by the Netherworld vampires in ancient times.

New world vampires could not reproduce because they had once been human, and so their only way of increasing their numbers was to bite and turn other humans. They were not as powerful as the Netherworld vamps, because Netherworld vamps were born from pure-blood mothers and fathers.

Koa knew that what she was doing was dangerous, but as Halston liked to always say, Koa preferred to learn the hard way. If it was too easy, then she just wasn't interested. This time, however, Koa could feel deep down that this was not a good idea. She almost turned back—that is, until she smelled blood.

Human blood. Her eyes nearly rolled back into her head at the overwhelming scent. It wasn't just a hint of blood. It was a feast of it.

Spilled blood. She pushed her anxiety aside and checked to make sure her sword was intact. It was attached to her belt and in its closed state it wasn't much bigger than a dagger in the guise of a simple baton.

Her face was set in newfound determination as she walked up to the metal door. She cracked her knuckles and drew a breath of the cool night air.

Koa needed answers. She refused to wait any longer. All she wanted in the world was to avenge her father's death and break her mother's curse.

Koa knocked twice and waited.

Koa expected to be immediately dismissed once they took a look at her, but when the young looking vampire opened the door, she was beheld with bewilderment. The tall, gangly lad stuttered when he laid eyes on her. His eyes looked her up and down.

Koa felt her stomach flip. He knew who she was. *This is not good,* she thought, but stood her ground.

"Wat you want, ey?"

Koa had practiced so many answers to this very question. Now as she stood before a real Netherworld vamp, her throat went dry.

He stared at her with the same wide-eyed expression. He blinked. His eyes were a dark blue, like the sea at night, and were set under the thickest eyebrows she had ever seen. His face was thin and hollow as if he was malnourished. She could see the bones in his face.

"Your leader," her voice cracked. She swallowed and tried again. "I wish to speak to him, or her."

He nodded and rubbed his fist in his hand. "Right. Right. Come in then."

Koa watched him step out of the way and hold the door open for her. She looked into a large open studio and gulped. The Netherworld vamps were everywhere. The place was set up like a lounge. The lights were dim and cast a soft orange glow on everything. Koa hated how loud her heels sounded on the gray concrete floor.

There were women walking around in nothing but their panties. They walked around as if in a trance. *Glamour*, Koa thought as she watched some of the rough looking vamps feast on the women who did nothing but sit in their laps with blank expressions on their paling faces.

There was a cloud of smoke that lingered in the air, making the room look as if a fog had settled.

Koa hesitated. She felt foolish for leaving her communication watch at the safe house. She didn't want Halston to track her. Now, Halston would never find her if something went wrong.

You can do this without him. For a second, she almost believed it. *Too late to run now.*

She nodded, sucked in a long breath to motivate herself, and stepped inside. The close of the door behind her sounded so final. Every inch of her was on alert. These vamps were unlike any she'd ever encountered. The Netherworld vamps were the purest of them all, and the males looked at her as if she was a piece of meat.

Koa's eyes scanned the room. There were four windows, barred and covered with black tarpaulin. A standard wooden bar stood in the corner of the large room. One vamp tended it, wiping it down, and pouring liquor into shot glasses. She immediately counted twelve other vamps and six dead human bodies being drained of their blood.

She was a little late for the party. The six women that were still alive looked as if they had been picked up from a sleazy club somewhere. All high-heeled pumps and miniskirts, sheath dresses and shiny costume jewelry. Koa wanted to help the women. She hated seeing them treated so carelessly.

Koa's jaw tightened when she saw a vamp snap the woman's neck he'd been feeding from. Koa's eye twitched. She resisted brandishing her sword. She was outnumbered. There was nothing she could do.

Koa felt herself become a little woozy at the scent. She should not be hungry right now, but the blood was everywhere. The sweet aroma was almost too much to handle. She closed her eyes and remembered the face of the young man she had accidentally killed when she was seventeen, and immediately regrouped. She would never forget the look of fear in the poor man's eyes.

In an alley, like an animal, she had feasted foolishly. Koa never killed a human again. The guilt would remain with her until the day she died. Koa ignored the scent of blood and eyed the other vampires in the room. They looked to be various ages ranging from early twenties, to early thirties. One could never tell how old a vampire was, especially one from the Netherworld. Because they were born vampires and not made, once they reached maturity, their bodies would remain captured in that state of youth for an eternity. These male vamps all looked young and strong.

And dirty and ugly. She raised an eyebrow at one who stood propped against a wall, staring at her. *Except that one. He's not too bad.* He almost looked attractive in his clean suit and tie.

Koa shook her head. *You're ridiculous,* she scolded herself.

The young looking vampire that had let her in settled onto the floor and rolled one of the girls over onto her belly. He slit her other wrist and held it over a bowl.

She stood there, feeling awkward, as she watched the blood trickle slowly into the bowl. *Perhaps he doesn't know who I am,* she thought.

"Oh, I know ya, Koa Ryeo-won. Every Netherworld creature knows the little half-blood."

Koa paled.

"Yeah, I read ya mind. No big deal." He drank a gulp of the blood. He glanced over his shoulder at the vamp who leaned against the wall. "Aye, Brice, our guest thinks you're right handsome." Everyone laughed. Brice revealed sharp, crooked teeth, as he laughed with the others.

Gross. Her eyes widened. She had to control what she thought about.

The young vamp grinned that he had heard her thoughts once again. He chuckled to himself. He wiped his mouth clean and came to his feet. "Hungry?" He offered her the bowl of blood.

Koa shook her head, but her chest heaved at the scent. She looked away.

"Ah, what's it? Too good for slut blood?"

The other vamps chuckled. He motioned for four of the vamps to end their game of poker and they all got up and went to sit on one of the leather sofas placed before a large projector screen. He slid a chair out from their poker table and nodded for her to sit.

"Why these are the best sluts in town. It's a delicacy, it is." He licked his thin lips. His grin sickened her.

Koa held her head up high. Her heart was beating so loudly that she could hear it. She was aware of all of the eyes on her. "Your leader. I will only speak to him… or her," she said.

He thought a minute and bit his lip. He gave her a look from under his thick dark brows. "You're lookin at 'em, lass."

Koa tensed. Everyone was staring at her in silence. *Is he joking?* Koa thought. *He looks to be about sixteen.*

"One thousand and sixty-two, but who's countin' anymore?" He sat in the chair and motioned for her to sit before him again.

Koa averted her gaze from the other vamps that looked at her with scrutinizing eyes and sat in the chair.

"You answer your own door?" Koa frowned at the concept. If she was the leader of a Netherworld clan, she'd have all kinds of goons doing her bidding.

He licked the blood from his teeth. "Aye."

Koa was uncomfortable. She didn't know why. He looked so young. Why should she fear him?

"A little short on help?"

He shook his head. "I like to check out visitors me self. That way, I can kill 'em and return to me business."

"Who are you?"

He sat back in his chair and played with the poker chips. "Should'a been ya first question, lass."

"My name is Koa, not 'lass.'"

He chuckled and the others joined in. "Didn't I already say we all know ya?" He leaned his face in close to hers and she nearly fell backward in her chair at his speed. He was no longer smiling. "But you gotta earn the *privilege* of learning me name…"

There was something about him. It was like Koa could tell that he was trying to be as unintimidating as possible. Why would he do that? Why would someone want to appear weaker than they were? The possibilities made her begin to fear him even more.

She cleared her throat. She put on a brave face. "Well, I just need a few answers."

"Depends on the questions." He swirled his finger in the bowl of blood as his dark blue eyes watched her.

Koa shifted in her seat. Her knee started to shake under the table. She hid it as best as she could. He wasn't so much as staring at her as he was leering at her. She hoped her voice would come out steady. "Tell me about this king from the Netherworld. You're all hiding from him, I know that much."

He snickered. "I hide from no one." He leaned in close as if he was going to tell her a secret. "Maybe some of them blokes fear this king, but not me."

Koa made a face. "Sure," she said sarcastically. She instantly wished she'd kept the sarcasm out of her voice.

He sat back and looked at her for a moment as his smile faded. His eyes darkened.

He licked his finger clean of the blood. "What ya want with Greggan?"

"I want to know why, you... I mean, those 'blokes' over there are afraid of him. Why does everyone know me?"

He nodded and kept his face serious. "Good questions. I can see why ya'd want to know those answers, lass." He tapped the table with a sharp, dirty nail. "But, me question is why do ya think I would tell ya anything? Why did ya walk in here, all alone, and think we'd just become quick friends and whatnot?"

Koa bit her bottom lip and tried not to look nervous. "Because," she cleared her throat again, "we have the same enemy."

His grin returned. He lifted an eyebrow. He shook his head and chuckled. "Silly girl. Silly girl." He came to his feet. "I sure thought ya'd figure it out. Thought you were all book learned an such."

Koa looked around. Everyone had stopped drinking. They looked like hounds, ready to pounce. Her palms started to sweat. She wiped them on her jeans.

She tried to turn the tables. "We are allies. We both want to stop Greggan. He wants to kill you for some reason, and he wants me for some other reason. I simply wanted to compare notes, you know?" She kept talking, hoping to buy herself some time to think. "I mean, if we work together, we can send him back to the Netherworld."

He walked around behind her, as if pacing, and mulling over her words. The room fell quiet. Everyone stopped feeding and looked up at their leader.

Koa prayed inside her head. There was something about him that just felt… evil. Something in his eyes made her feel worried. She should have told Halston where she was going.

"Well said, lass." He nodded his head as he thought. "But ya've still got one thing wrong, missy. Me and me crew are mercenaries and we ain't hiding from Greggan."

Something tugged at Koa… warning her. She gave him an odd look. Her eyes started to widen with realization. Her voice shook. "Who are you?"

He grabbed her by her hair and yanked her from the chair.

Koa panicked. *This was not a good idea,* she thought as she reached for his hands.

"You're right. It wasn't." He threw her across the room and straight through the wall. Koa cried out as she fell through the wall and into the pile of crumbed stone. She squeezed her eyes shut. She saw lights flashing under her lids. The pain was sharp and unwavering.

"Call me Bund," he said and Koa felt her face drain of color.

Bund. Her father's killer stood only a few feet away.

Koa started to count to herself. It was something she had done since she was a child. It sometimes calmed her when she was really afraid.

One.

She lay in a pile of rubble. Her heart raced too quickly for her to control her adrenaline.

Two.

Koa was outnumbered by Netherworld vampires that were ten times stronger than her.

Three.

She could barely move. Her head hurt from crashing into the stone wall.

Four.

Koa looked over at Bund who simply waited.

"Get up, you sneaky, *stupid* bitch. I've been waitin' for this."

Five.

Koa looked at that smirk on his white face and narrowed her eyes. "I won't kill ya. Naw, I'll slice ya up real nice, and present ya on a platter to King Greggan. How's that? And then, I'll roast that mother of yours right nicely."

Six.

A spark ignited in her head at the mention of her mother. Rage boiled within her. He had killed her father and now her mother was in his sights. She would harness that fear. She would fight like a madwoman. Rage filled every vein within her body, making her feel hot and sensitive to everything around her.

Seven.

Koa felt the power of her Lyrinian sword explode through her veins and let the rage loose.

CHAPTER 9

HER PULSE BEAT LOUDLY in her ears. Koa shot into the air. Her body moved too quickly for their eyes to follow. She grabbed her sword and flew straight for Bund. He seemed interested in what she was doing but not afraid.

Koa clenched her jaw. The hurt inside overwhelmed her. She missed her father.

Bund smiled at her. He knew what she was thinking.

Koa hated his hollow, pale face. She hated everything about him. She wanted to gouge his eyes out with her nails and smash the rest of his face in with her boot.

Read this, you asshole, she thought… just for him. She ran the blade along spilled blood and it burned red with hunger. The Lyrinian blade started to glow.

Bund smirked. He nodded. "Nice weapon. I'll give ya that."

The other vamps were up and ready for a fight. More than a dozen leisurely reached for weapons. Guns, crossbows, Netherworld weapons she'd never seen. Koa wouldn't wait until they grabbed them. She swept through the room like a cyclone of rage. Her sword glowed red hot and screamed for more blood. It was an extension of her. Her actions were no longer her own. The blade used her in order to quench its thirst.

Koa didn't mind. She needed the Lyrinian swords collection of skills to make it through this night. Her body ducked and dodged oncoming attacks. Her legs kicked through bodies, slamming organs to the floor. Her free arm grabbed loose hair and smashed heads to the tiled wall. The sword slashed with red hot, lightning speed.

Bund took a step back.

The lights in the room went out and Koa paused. She hovered in the air for just a moment, to get her bearings and let her eyes adjust. She couldn't see as well as them, but the Lyrinian sword worked like a heat missile. It would find its target no matter what.

She dove back in and closed her eyes. Like a blade dance, she swirled in and out of the crowd, listening to only cries of pain and angry shouts. She heard bullets. It didn't matter, the sword deflected it all. The bullets clinked against her blade and sizzled into dust at contact. Her movements were fluid.

Koa was as loose as a rag doll, and no one could touch her. Every time they tried to grab her, she would swirl out of their reach and dive to another vamp. Their hands tried to hold her, and it was as if she was as slippery as a marble; they hadn't a chance when Koa was in her trance.

There was so much blood that, in the end, Koa was drenched in it. When all was quiet she came to a stop and held her sword up. The red glow of the sword bathed the room in its dim light. There were bodies everywhere. Arms, legs and heads were sprawled about in a big mushy pile.

Koa nodded in satisfaction. She was surprised that she had killed them without suffering any serious wounds. Her arms were sore and she had a cut on her calf, but other than that, she felt fine. Her father had trained her in the ways of the sword. He had taught her well.

Koa felt her heart skip a beat when Bund reappeared before her. Her other hand slid a stake from a holster attached to her back. She threw it at him before he could even blink.

The stake lodged right into his heart and she grinned triumphantly. Koa would have cheered, but to her surprise, Bund grinned as well.

He looked down at the stake and his shoulders bounced lightly with his snickering. At first he laughed lightly, and then it became louder and louder until his laughter filled the room. "You stupid, stupid girl." He laughed even louder.

Koa gasped and covered her ears. His voice seemed to be everywhere. It filled her ears and made her shiver. His voice seemed to grate on her eardrums. There was something purely evil within it. Something she'd never encountered.

"What?" Koa breathed in disbelief as he pulled the stake from his chest.

Bund shook his head with a smile spread across his face. He tossed the stake to the floor and took a look around. "Nice job you've done here, lass." He clapped and took a step forward.

Koa sucked in a breath and held her sword out in front of her, hoping it would stop him. She was confused. A stake to the heart always worked. At least, she thought it did. Her only hope was that her sword would work.

Bund made a clicking sound with his tongue. "Sorry, Lyrinian blades only work on the dirty nephilim."

Koa knew he was reading her mind. All she could think was, *what are you then?*

Koa heard something. She stepped back and looked around with wide eyes as the carnage around her started to… move. She clutched her sword.

"Holy shit," she breathed as the pieces of bone started to reform. She looked at Bund with wide eyes. "What's happening?" She started backing away. She jumped when a hand reached for her shoe. She yelped and kicked the bloody thing away, sending it crashing into a wall.

She looked back at Bund. Her face was twisted in worry. This was not how she imagined this night going. This was not how she imagined she'd take out her revenge. Bund blocked the door. Koa hoped there was another exit.

Bund looked around and held his arms out. He lifted a brow. "Don't tell me this was ya first time killin' Netherworld vamps?"

Koa gulped. The bodies were reforming into grotesque creatures. The crunching sounds and squishing noises turned her stomach. She couldn't bring herself to speak. The fear clutched her even tighter than before.

When she looked back at Bund, his face had darkened. Red lines stretched across his face like pulsating red veins. His smile was gone. His face looked different, as if all the shadows in the room had absorbed into his flesh, turning it into an ash-like gray. His hair was already dark before, but it seemed to become even darker and shinier, like gloss had been applied.

"What are you?"

His shoulders jutted out and she could see his bones mutate.

Koa knew then that she was about to die.

Bund's voice deepened. He no longer sounded like a man, but a creature of darkness. The voice that she had heard in every nightmare she'd had as a child echoed through the room. His was the voice that one imagined a monster would have, like that of a…

Koa covered her mouth as a horrified squeal escaped her lips. She knew what he was, and she knew that she was not strong enough to kill him. Bund wasn't a New World vampire, he wasn't a Netherworld vamp.

Bund was a demon.

"Good girl," he sneered. His hands turned into bony claws and his legs bent like those of a beast from ancient myths.

Koa's brows furrowed. She felt like she might cry for her mother.

Bund tossed his head back and let out a feral laugh. "Go on, cry for ya mother for me. I love it when little girls cry." He pounced. His weight knocked Koa off her feet with such power that her scream was cut off. She fell backward into the blood. She banged her head against the cement floor and cried out. Lights flashed behind her eyelids as she squeezed her eyes shut to block out the pain.

Bund slashed her face and drew blood. She could smell the poison on his claws. She felt the blood leak from the wound. He licked her face, sopping up the blood with his rough, leathery tongue. Koa felt as if she was looking into the eyes of Satan himself.

She held up her sword and closed her eyes. "This is it then," she whispered to the sword as she prepared to fight with every ounce of life she had left, even though she knew the odds were against her. She opened her eyes and whispered a prayer. "It was a good run."

Bund cackled and held her face down with one strong claw. Koa stabbed him with her sword. Nothing. Not even a drip of blood.

He laughed louder and she held back a sob. His other claw jabbed her in her side and ripped upward until it reached her underarm, splitting her skin to the muscle. She felt hot tears soak her face. Her wounds stung as her salty tears pooled into them.

Koa was tired and weakened. She was completely exerted. She couldn't move. So, she lolled her head to the side and prepared for the end.

Bund leaned down to her ear. "Your blood will repair me men, and when they are whole once again... I will keep me promise, and roast that mother of yours."

Koa felt her face heat. Her eyes narrowed into slits of hate. She couldn't let him escape into the night and kill her mother. She would give anything for the strength to stop him. She wanted to scream out for Halston, but she knew that he would not hear her.

"But have no fear..." He licked her ear. His hot breath came out in a whisper. "I will not kill ya, love. No, you will be my prize and I will keep you as a *pet* for all eternity."

Koa felt her blood chill. Every inch of her flesh crawled with disgust and horror. The studio door crept open. Koa's eyes searched the doorway. No one was there. She looked out to darkness.

She screamed so loud that it made her ears ache. "No!"

Raven walked into the room and her green eyes started to glow. Koa frowned. It wasn't the normal glow that she was used to. There was something different about it.

Bund paused and looked over his jutted out shoulder.

"Run mother!" Koa shouted. She realized her mistake when she saw the look in Bund's eyes.

Bund looked stunned. "Mother?" He reached out a hand to Raven. "No. It can't be." There was real fear in his voice.

Raven sat. Everything stilled.

All sounds were sucked from the room and Koa started to shake. Koa didn't know what was happening. She thought that she was going mad. After all that Bund had said about roasting her mother and killing her, he sounded truly afraid.

Koa's vision started to fade. Her vision became blurry. "Raven... run!"

Halston stepped in behind her mother, and Koa nearly shouted for joy. He was like her guardian angel, always there when she needed him. She wasn't sure if she was dreaming but the room filled with the most radiant light she'd ever seen. Everything turned white in her eyes and she felt as if she was being lifted up to heaven. Her vision cleared.

Bund glared at her and howled. Then, he dropped her and flew from the room so quickly that he looked like nothing more than a black shadow.

Halston stepped into the empty space that Bund left behind and grabbed Koa into his arms.

Koa clutched his neck. "Oh, Halston, you came," she whispered and her eyes fluttered closed.

CHAPTER 10

HALSTON FELT his heart break when he saw Koa in such agony. She passed out in his arms and he held her there, close to him. He was furious. He was hurt. Koa had lied to him, and now she was injured. Bund's poisonous wounds would not be easy to heal.

Too many emotions filled Halston. More than he was used to feeling at the same time. Anger and grief. Fear and frustration. He no longer felt… in control.

Bund had escaped. Bund, a demon from his past, and a demon by nature, had escaped Halston yet again. Halston had spent centuries hunting him down. Once again, he had failed. He balled his hand into a fist and pounded the ground. The entire room shook.

Bund had seen Halston. Halston had taken his prize… Koa. Now, Halston feared that the demon's revenge would be more than they would be prepared for.

Raven ran over to him. "Halston! The vamps! They're taking their second form!"

Halston looked up from under his brows. His eyes were full of rage. He watched the pieces of bone reconnect in a new form. The Netherworld vamps had taken their second form. They had reanimated themselves.

Twelve reanimated men stood before him. They were deformed creatures. They looked like giant, feral wolves: all muscle and bone. No skin or fur, or anything but large fangs, yellow eyes, and sharp claws. Their legs were bent in, and even though they stood on all fours, they were nearly as tall as Halston.

Halston held Koa up with one arm and pulled out his infinity gun with the other. A metallic ring echoed throughout the room as the silver infinity gun was loosed from its holster.

The room felt smaller with the massive creatures crowding it. Things were about to get really messy. Halston glared at them all. He refused to let another creature escape that lair.

"Should I leave?" Raven asked in a whisper. Her green eyes had grown large as she watched the reanimated men prepare to try their luck with Halston.

Halston nodded once. "Go."

Raven ran, and with the sudden movement, the reanimated men charged. Growls were cut off when Halston held Koa's limp body close to his chest, lifted the barrel, cocked it once, and shot. A loud explosion drowned all sounds out. Time seemed to warp and slow as a single silver bullet shot out from the barrel and screamed with rage.

Halston narrowed his eyes in hatred. He watched the bullet collect speed, light, and energy as it raced through the room. None of the reanimated men had a chance to run. The single bullet ripped through them within seconds. The bullet cut through brains, hearts, lungs… and enjoyed every minute of it.

Like Koa's Lyrinian sword, it seemed to have a mind of its own. The infinity gun was more than a weapon.

It was judgment.

The bullet squealed like a train and returned to Halston's gun. It reentered its home and all was silent. Not even a full minute had passed. Reanimated bodies were sprawled on the floor.

There was a great deal of writhing. The bodies bubbled, popped, and melted into pools of thick black blood. There would be no third change. It was over for them.

Halston drew in a breath and let it out slowly. He looked at Koa's face and felt his brows draw in. He loved her. He couldn't deny it. The feeling frightened him. He wanted nothing more than to shelter and protect her.

Halston hugged her close and kissed her forehead. He closed his eyes and simply held her there, breathing her sweet scent, and listening to her soft heartbeat. He loved her, but he knew right then that he would have to do something that would hurt her. She might hate him for it—there was a lot that she might hate him for—but it was necessary.

Halston drew in another breath. Koa weakened him. His heart was tearing. "I love you," he whispered. He almost wished that she was awake to hear the words he'd been thinking for years now, but he was grateful that she didn't hear him.

He sighed. His jaw tensed. Halston knew what he had to do. "But you need to learn."

CHAPTER 11

KOA WOKE UP in the most comfortable bed she'd ever occupied. She sighed and sprawled out across the puffy white covers that felt as though they were stuffed with clouds. The smell of eucalyptus filled her nostrils. She breathed it in deep. The scent was familiar to her. She winced in pain and her eyes popped open. Sharp, searing pain stunned her into an agonizing squeal.

Koa held her breath, too afraid to make another move lest the pain get worse. She felt her heart speed. She wasn't used to this kind of pain. Sun spilled into the room through a wall made of glass. Koa looked around and the wrinkles in her forehead smoothed. She felt safe.

This was Halston's bedroom.

Koa covered herself with the blankets and looked around. He wasn't there. She looked down at her clothing and saw that she wore nothing but her bra and panties.

Koa had been in Halston's bed before. The first time she had seen Halston had been by chance. After her father's murder, Koa had been a ruthless girl. She had been lucky that Halston had found her. He had tamed her.

Five years ago, on a warm night in London, Koa had been drunk on bourbon and blood. She was sprawled across a park bench near a pub when Halston found her.

Koa remembered it well. She thought about it often. Like a guardian angel, there Halston had been, looking down at her with his bright golden hair and crystalline blue eyes. When Koa felt his hand touch her forehead, she had opened her eyes and had really thought that she was dreaming. He was perfect and she couldn't resist.

Koa had grabbed Halston by the back of his neck and kissed him. The kiss had been magical. Halston didn't stop her. Koa touched her lips at the memory. She could still taste Halston's tongue.

A smile came to her lips, despite the lingering pain. At seventeen, she had been a naïve girl, torn by feelings of revenge, guilt, and fear. Still, her vampire side made her impervious to fear.

Koa often suspected less than noble intentions from men, but the night she had met Halston, she knew she could trust him. She felt safe around him. So, drunk like a college freshman at her first frat party, Koa let him take her to his place.

When Koa had woken up the next morning, all those years ago, she found Halston sitting in a white leather chair by that glass wall overlooking the city, watching her.

Koa had been but a child back then… a child who had no idea what was in store for her future. She sighed and closed her eyes to keep the tears from falling. Once again, Halston had saved her from her own horrible choices. She hated to face him after all that she had done wrong.

She bit the inside of her lip and tried to remember what had happened. Another sharp pain in her side immediately reminded her. Bund.

Koa yelped as Raven leapt onto the pure white covers and tackled her. Raven licked her face. "Are you all right, darling?"

Koa held her tight and tried to keep from moving too much. She cautiously propped herself up on the soft pillows. Koa couldn't help but squeeze her mother tight. "I am. Where is Halston?"

Raven curled up next to Koa's head. "He is in the shower." Koa nodded and looked at the door to Halston's private bathroom suite. She almost smiled at the image of him in there without any clothes on. The pain made her grimace instead.

Koa sighed. "What happened… back at the lair?"

Raven licked her paw. "What do you mean? Halston rescued you."

Koa sat up on her elbows. "I mean, before Halston came in. You did something."

Raven tilted her head and gave Koa a blank look. She shook her head. "Nonsense. You are imagining things. Would you like some orange juice?"

Koa frowned. *Was I imagining things?* She shook her head. Koa knew what she saw. "Wait a minute!" Koa yelled.

The pain kept her from hopping onto her knees. She winced at the burning sensation in her side. Weakly, Koa pointed at Raven. "I saw you. What did you do? Don't lie to me!"

Koa pursed her lips when Halston opened the door to the bathroom and let waves of steam out. He peeked around the door to see what the commotion was about. His hair was wild and yet, he still looked perfect. Koa wanted to see more. Her cheeks flushed at her thoughts.

"Everything all right?"

Koa nodded and he came out of the bathroom and dried his hair with a towel. She looked away from his bare chest as her cheeks reddened even more. She had never seen a man naked before. Koa could only imagine what Halston was hiding beneath his towel. She squeezed her eyes shut.

You're ridiculous, Koa thought to herself. *This is not what you're supposed to be thinking about!*

"What's all the fuss?"

Koa looked at her mother, who licked her paws sheepishly. Koa knew something was up.

"How are you feeling? Do you need something for the pain?"

Koa shook her head. "It's okay. I can handle it." She searched his eyes, wondering when the scolding would begin, hoping he would let this incident slide.

Halston nodded and walked over to Koa. He sat on the edge of the bed and pulled the covers back. Raven moved out of the way and he took a look at Koa's bandaged side where Bund had split her skin.

Koa remembered just how deep he had cut her. She looked down expecting to see her side completely healed, instead, there was still blood on the bandage and she could still see some of her muscle. She was stunned. She'd always been able to heal almost instantly.

Halston sighed. It wasn't good.

"How long have I been here?" Her eyes were wide with fright. Halston sat on the edge of the bed and smoothed her hair. He was calm. She wished such calmness would rub off on her. She did enjoy the feel of his hand on her hair.

"Two days."

Koa covered her mouth. "Two days?" She looked at her wound in disbelief.

Halston put a hand on her shoulder and led her back down to the pillow. "It's all right. A demon wound will heal. It may take longer than you're used to, but your vampire side will fight the poison."

"Poison?" Koa felt her heart race. Halston pulled the covers to her neck.

"Relax, Koa. You need rest. Don't work yourself up or it'll take longer."

"Listen to him, Koa," Raven urged. "I hope you learned your lesson."

Koa shot a look at her, but her mother was right, she couldn't deny it. She had been stupid to think she could convince Netherworld vamps to side with her. The whole plan was foolish. She just didn't anticipate them knowing who she was.

"Bund recognized me." Koa sat up on her elbows and looked to Halston. "How did they know who I was?"

Halston stood and walked over to his wardrobe where he grabbed a shirt. He put it on and stepped inside his walk-in closet to change into black slacks. He sat on a seat inside his closet and carefully put on a pair of black socks and slipped into shoes. Halston seemed to be taking his time. Koa waited as he looked at himself in his full length mirror. He fixed his hair and she rolled her eyes.

"You just love looking at yourself," Koa couldn't resist saying. She hoped it would keep him calm, and make him forget that she had disobeyed him.

She smiled. Halston didn't.

He ignored her statement and sat back on the edge of the bed. "What exactly did he say to you?"

Koa cleared her throat. "Bund said that everyone in the Netherworld knows me. He said that he wasn't hiding, and that he wasn't afraid of Greggan."

Halston nodded. "It's true. Why would a demon fear a vampire? A demon is nothing more than an angel that has turned to darkness. When the fallen angels followed Satan from heaven their sexual desires led them to have intercourse with human women. Their dark spawn are what we know as vampires... and the other nephilim of the Netherworld."

Koa nodded. She knew all about the fall of some of the angels. She knew how their spawn were banished to the Netherworld centuries ago. Still, the Netherworld was only a place separated from the human world by a simple gate. "Yes, I know all of that, but why was he with those Netherworld vamps?"

"He was hired."

Koa slumped against the headboard. She blew her bangs out of her eyes. "That's right. He did say that they were mercenaries." She lifted a brow. "Hired for what?"

"To find you."

"Why? Why does Bund want to find me?" Koa needed to know.

Halston and Raven shared a glance. Koa noticed.

Koa slammed her fist on the bed. "Why are you two hiding things from me?"

"Don't get so worked up. I'll tell you everything, when you're healed."

"Tell me now!"

"Get some sleep, darling," Raven said and hopped from the bed. "Will you take me back home? I think my presence will only agitate Koa and prolong her recovery."

Koa reached out. She didn't realize how weak she felt. "No. Don't go." Koa wished she could hug her mother again. She would give anything to lie in her arms and cry like she did when she was a child.

Raven looked back. She ran over and leapt onto the bed. She licked Koa's face and snuggled her head into the crevice of her neck. "Rest up. I'll see you at home."

"Okay," Koa replied. She sighed and pulled the covers up. She did feel tired already.

Halston waited for Raven to leave the room. Koa watched him from a tiny space in the covers. He sat there in silence for a moment. The silence made Koa uncomfortable. She knew what was coming.

"I'm sorry," Koa blurted before Halston could put the words together to say what was on his mind.

Halston seemed surprised that she actually apologized. Koa thought that was a good sign. He hadn't expected that.

He nodded. His eyes were hopeful. "Thank you for that, Koa. It means a lot. But why did you go there without me? Why would you go against my orders and put yourself at risk?"

Koa groaned. She knew he would ask. She sat up and tried to scoot closer to him. Moving was a laborious task, but Koa needed him to forgive her. He still didn't say that he did.

"You fail to understand that we care about you, Koa. We only do these things to keep you safe. You're very important to all of us in the Netherworld Division."

Koa frowned. She didn't like how he kept saying 'we' and 'us' instead of, I care about you, or, you're important to me.

"I didn't want you to try to stop me. I wanted answers, and you just weren't giving them."

He turned his head to meet her eyes. She looked down. The look was too intense. She felt almost hypnotized by it. She drew circles in the covers with her finger, feeling sheepish, like a child who knew she had done something wrong and awaited her father's scolding.

"I told you already. I am here to protect you. You don't need to know everything. Some things are best left alone."

Koa didn't say anything. She heard Halston, but she was stubborn. She still wanted to know.

Halston sighed. "And now I see that I have to protect you from yourself."

Koa looked up. "What's that supposed to mean?"

Halston stood and wrapped his holster across his back and grabbed a vest from his wardrobe.

"It means you're out, Koa."

Koa fought through the pain and sat up. Her face paled. Her hands started to shake. He couldn't be saying what she thought he was. Koa stared at Halston with wide eyes. "What?"

He nodded. "I hate to do it, but it's for the best. You're a liability and it's better if you don't know what's happening out there. You're no longer part of the Netherworld Division. You revealed Raven's identity. It's best if you and Raven lay low and live a quiet life in your new home." He put his hands in his pockets and looked away. "You no longer have to let these things worry you. I will take care of it from here on out."

Koa stared at him. She wouldn't shy away from his eyes if he would just look at her. She could make him change his mind.

"Or you can move wherever you want."

Koa started to speak, but her voice was caught in her throat. He couldn't look her in the eye. That statement hurt her more than anything. She didn't want to be away from him. Couldn't he see that?

She felt as though Halston was breaking up with her. She was speechless. Her heart felt as though it was being twisted and crushed. The heartache hurt more than her side did.

Halston took a breath and started toward the door. He tried to make his voice sound light and calm. "I'll still protect you and make sure you're safe, you just won't live the life of a Netherworld agent anymore. Bund is still out there and I will do everything within my power to stop him."

Koa felt her body tense at the thought of Bund out there in the world, ready to strike at her once again. She thought of his promise to keep her as a pet for all eternity. Her stomach churned.

Halston gave her one last look. The look was too quick. "Now rest up." He left before she could protest.

The sleek black door to his otherwise all-white bedroom closed. She heard him head outside. He whispered to Raven and she felt her face heat with rage.

Koa balled up her fists. They were conspiring. She heard his footsteps walk down his long marble hallway and to the double curved stairs that led to the landing, and he was gone.

Tears dripped down her cheeks and onto the white blankets. Her heart sped. She didn't like this feeling. Halston was done with her. When would she see him again? How would she survive without the purpose the Netherworld Division gave her?

Koa screamed. She covered her face and yelled in anguish. "How dare you? How dare you?" She shouted and pounded her fists in the blankets with all of her might. She needed something more rewarding.

She wanted to hit something, to hurt something. She growled and came to her feet. Koa gasped as the pain made her double over. Her breath was knocked from her as her skin screamed in agony.

The pain was unnerving. The constant burning of her flesh only intensified her anger. Pain was rare for Koa. This was new, and she hated it.

Another feeling swept in and made her fall to her knees. Koa groaned. This pain was different. Still, Bund's pain couldn't compare to what overcame her. This was something that she was very familiar with. She had grown up with it. It had haunted her for years.

The hunger.

Koa looked up. She had an idea. Nothing would cure her faster than human blood. She crawled over to the chair and pulled herself up. She was so tired. All she could think of was how energized a little human blood would make her.

Koa thought of how disappointed Halston would be once he found out. He had worked hard to help her fight the hunger for blood. They had a strict feeding schedule, but once again, an intense battle had ruined it.

Koa shook her head and sucked in an agonizing breath as tears threatened to break free. She didn't care what Halston thought anymore. She didn't care about any of it.

Koa was out. She was free. She already hated it.

She knew Halston would be livid, and she welcomed it, he deserved to feel guilty for shoving her aside. She lifted herself into the air and flew toward that wall of glass and kicked it with all of her strength. It crashed into thousands of pieces of glass and Koa flew out, into the sun and as high as she could go.

She'd find a new home and a new family. Wryn Castle called out to her.

CHAPTER 12

IAN PRATT came when called. Koa smiled when he came to the door of her usual room in the Wryn Castle. His large, hazel puppy dog eyes lit up when he saw her.

He had a quiet, geeky quality. There was an undeniable intelligence that she could see in his eyes. That was what made Koa choose him out of all the others who had been presented to her three years ago at her membership meeting.

Ian was smart, *very* smart, and equally attractive. The thing that drew Koa to him though, was that he didn't know he was hot. That made her like him even more. His black hair was unruly, but it was soft and clean whenever she ran her fingers through it.

Koa watched him as he stood outside the doorway. He gripped the handles of his green, graphic-print backpack and smiled at her.

Koa did something she hadn't planned. She pulled him into the room, closed the door, and hugged him tightly. She almost sobbed into his chest but she bit the tears back. She breathed deeply.

Ian was so warm. He smelled so good. He smelled like youth. Real youth, not a young mask hiding a hundred-year-old creature. His scent was fresh, like freshly washed clothes. She held him close and nearly melted when he wrapped his arms around her back.

"What's this?" Ian asked when he felt the blood on her side. He looked genuinely alarmed. "Are you okay? What happened Koa?"

Koa didn't speak. She was grateful to have someone care about her. All she wanted was to feel cared for… to feel loved. She simply held him. She liked that he was thin. She liked that he was tall. Ian rested his chin on her head and sighed. He loved her. That fact didn't make Koa feel good.

His wasn't real love. There was no way that it could be... the glamour made him think he was in love. She wished it was real.

Halston's face haunted her. She squeezed her eyes shut and tried to block the disappointed look he had given her out of her mind.

"I'm fine, Ian, but you can make me all better." She gently grabbed the back of his neck and planted a soft kiss on his supple, human flesh. He nearly trembled with glee.

Koa gave him a gentle nudge, but it was enough to send him falling backward. She grabbed his collar, lifted him from the ground, and led him to the bed. The instant his head fell onto the plush black comforter, she was on his chest. She tied her hair back, getting it out of the way. Every vein and artery pulsed in her body. She needed him.

Koa moaned and plunged her teeth into his neck. She drank, greedily. She knew why she was so hungry, so out of control, and yet she didn't care. Halston could abandon her. Her mother could keep secrets from her. She would have a new family, one that wouldn't lie to her or hide things from her.

The blood gushed into her mouth and that familiar euphoria radiated throughout her entire body. She could feel his blood rushing and meeting with her own.

She felt powerful. She felt invincible. Koa could feel herself healing as she drained the blood from Ian's neck.

She nearly cried out from the intense pleasure. Her heart was breaking. Halston had hurt her, but Ian was sustaining her. He was rebuilding her. Koa sucked the blood until Ian was nearly dry.

Dry? Koa paled. *No!*

Ian let out a whimper and Koa froze. She realized what she had done and ripped her mouth away from his neck. Alarm overcame her when she looked down at his pale face. She grabbed him.

He was cold.

She screamed the most horrified scream she'd ever heard leave her lungs.

"Ian!" Koa tapped his shoulder. "Are you all right?" She shook him. He was limp and unresponsive. Koa's eyes widened. Terror overcame her.

Ian's eyes fluttered closed and she squealed.

"Ian!" She grabbed his face and shook his head from side to side. He groaned.

Koa slapped him. She couldn't let the young man die. She loved him, in her own way. He had been her pet for nearly three years. She was paying his way through the University. She couldn't lose him. He meant more to her than the blood.

There were nights when they would talk for hours after her feeding. She knew everything there was to know about him. She knew that his mother had died of cancer when he was in high school, and that his father had killed himself shortly afterward. He had been sent to live with an aunt until he was of legal age, and left the states as soon as he graduated.

Ian was smart. He studied chemistry and archeology, of all things. He'd always wanted to be like Indiana Jones. Koa nearly smiled at the memory of him telling her that. She couldn't let this good young man die.

An idea came to her. It hit her full force and wouldn't back down. Koa had no choice. She would set him free.

She leaned down to his ear. "Ian... do you want to live?"

Ian's head lolled to the side. He weakly opened an eye and stared at her drunkenly with it. Koa could feel her heart racing.

What have I done? I've become a monster. Koa swallowed. Halston was right to fire her. She had become the very creature they fought to stop.

His life was hanging from a thread. She could see the luster start to leave those hazel eyes.

She felt her heart skip a beat when he mouthed the word, *yes.*

Koa swallowed. She licked her lips of the blood and nodded. "Are you sure?" Koa whispered. "You know what I mean, don't you?"

Ian nodded and his eyes rolled into the back of his head.

Koa shot up and bit her wrist. She shoved her bleeding wrist into his mouth and squeezed her eyes shut the moment he started to drink from her. She'd never, ever turned someone before. She had no idea what it meant. She hadn't a clue what this would change. She was contributing to the vampire population, the very beings that she and Halston and his organization strove to decrease.

Koa almost forgot. She wasn't a part of the organization anymore. She could follow her own rules. Besides, Ian wasn't a bad person. Therefore, he would not be one of the bad vampires that she had once been sent out to kill.

She felt a pang of guilt the instant Ian withdrew his mouth and cried out in pain. She rolled off of him and onto the floor. Like a frightened child, Koa scrambled into a corner. She watched him with wide, horrified eyes and pulled her legs into her chest. She held her legs close with both arms wrapped around them and tearfully watched as Ian's human body died.

Ian writhed and cried as his body was thrown back and forth across the bed. He begged in agony for help. Koa couldn't control her sobs when he cried out for his mother. He was delirious with pain and it hurt her to hear him suffer.

Koa wished she could help him. She'd never seen this before. His cries cut into her very soul.

His cries continued for far too long, and then, there was silence. The silence was so thick that Koa realized that she was holding her breath. She looked at his body through a blurry film of tears.

Did I do it right? Timidly, Koa crawled onto all fours. She peeked over the side of the bed at his body. Ian lied there, sprawled across the bed, as if frozen… or lifeless.

His black hair was wild and covered his face. It was soaking wet from his sweat.

Koa sucked in a breath. Tears choked her. "No," she whispered. She climbed onto the bed. Something was wrong. "Ian. Please." She touched his face. It was cold as ice, even colder than before she fed him her blood. She buried her face in her hands. Her shoulders shook with her wracking sobs.

Koa was devastated. Ian had been more than a pet. Ian had been a friend. Koa felt her heart breaking. She'd never had many friends in her life, and she just killed one.

The bed creaked. Koa moved her hands from her face. She was almost too afraid to look… too afraid to hope.

Through tears, Koa looked at Ian's face. It was blurry, but she could see, with delight, that he was looking back at her.

Koa gasped and tackled him with glee. She littered his face with dozens of kisses. She laughed maniacally.

"Ian! You're all right."

He nodded and smiled. He hugged her tightly and Koa could feel that he was stronger. His arms no longer felt weak. His grip on her felt as hard as stone. She felt safe. She felt relieved and joyous.

"Yes, mistress. Thank you."

Koa pulled back. She held his face in both of her hands and gave him a serious look. "No more mistress. Understood? I am Koa to you from now on."

His smile widened. "Yes, mis—" He paused and laughed. Koa couldn't help but smile. "Yes, Koa." He ran a hand over her side again. He looked up in surprise. "You're all healed!"

Koa kissed his forehead. "Thanks to you." After all of the inner turmoil she experienced only seconds ago, she felt at peace.

A knock came at the door. Koa glanced at it. She knew who was there. She knew her scent. Cinnamon and sugar.

"Come on in, Lexi."

Lexi opened the door and peeked inside. She smacked on her cinnamon flavored gum and looked at the two of them. She sighed and shook her head. The door closed behind her.

"You two are getting a bit loud, don't you think?" Lexi looked at Koa who sat on Ian's lap in nothing but what she left Halston's loft in. Her panties and bra.

Koa came to her feet. She walked over to the nightstand where she kept a few of her belongings in case she actually wanted to stay longer than a night. Koa pulled out her credit card. She nodded to Ian. "Welcome Ian Pratt to the club. He's my sire."

Lexi looked at Koa in disbelief. "You sired someone?" She stared at Ian and smirked. "Not a bad choice."

Ian was on his feet and looking at himself in the mirror. Koa and Lexi watched as he checked himself out. He smiled as he fixed his hair which seemed to have a bit more luster. His eyes were a little brighter. Ian examined his neck, which was smooth and clear of fang marks. He looked over at them.

"Sweet!" He turned and looked at his profile and held his shirt up. "Call me crazy but is it just me, or did my abs become more defined?"

Koa shook her head with a smile glued to her face. It had worked. Lexi took her card.

"You know what this means, right? You sire him, you have to take care of him."

Koa looked at her and shrugged. "I have been taking care of him for the past three years."

Mischief danced in Lexi's eyes. "Oh no, Koa. That's not what I mean. He has to live with you now. He's like a baby, and you have to watch over him until he is prepared to go off into the world on his own." She mocked a curtsy and winked before leaving. "Have fun," she sang as she left the room.

Koa stood there after Lexi left and felt something new. She thought of what Lexi had said and it didn't bother her. She had purpose. This was just what she needed to take her mind off Halston.

She felt proud. After twenty-one years as a vampire, she had created something. She watched Ian, who turned to her with a sweet, childlike smile.

Then, she thought of her mother, Raven. She was still cross with her, but after all, Raven was still her mother. She had cared for her all alone for years, and it hadn't been easy. Koa felt a little guilty for being so vengeful all of the time. She had left Halston's loft with hopes of hurting him. She wanted him to feel the way she had felt.

Koa almost wondered if what Raven and Halston was keeping from her really was for her own good. She frowned at the thought. She wasn't prepared to let Halston be right about this too. Still, she had to go home or Raven would go insane with worry.

What will she think about Ian? Koa cringed. She could already imagine the scolding she'd receive.

Koa leaned against the door and closed it. She watched Ian. She felt a little motherly love for him now.

Her mind was set. She would bring him home, and she would have a real family again.

Her smile returned when she realized that she had just made herself an eternal companion. She didn't need Halston anymore. Koa sighed and fought tears. If only that were true.

CHAPTER 13

KOA WAS READY to move on from the disappointment of losing her place in Halston's crew. She waited in eagerness for Ian to shower and change and they checked out of Wryn Castle. Now, they would both need charges. Lexi set up a meeting for them to pick their new charges the next night.

Koa could wait at least a week to feed, but Ian was now a full vampire and would need to drink blood each night. Koa wasn't sure she liked the idea that they would have to be apart each night. She didn't really like the thought of him spending time away from her with a young beauty.

Shaking her head as she weaved down the dark roads in Ian's car, Koa realized that she was already being possessive. Ian wasn't her pet anymore. Now she knew how Halston felt about her spending just one night with a young attractive human.

The sun would soon rise, and so Koa drove as quickly as she could, but Ian had an old piece of junk that barely got over 50mph. She was excited to convert her cellar into Ian's living quarters.

She was surprised by how excited she was to bring him home. She was excited to be able to train and teach someone else for a change. Now, Koa would pass along everything her father, and Halston, had taught her over the years. She imagined Ian just soaking up the information like a sponge. She could tell that he would probably be a better vampire than she was.

Ian was full of energy just like a hyper child. She could only imagine just how much energy he'd have after his first full feeding. She wondered what special skill he'd acquire. Netherworld vamps were born with special skills, and sometimes even the New World vampires would inherit a small measure of such skills.

Koa grinned. Her imagination went wild. She was excited to find out if Ian would be so lucky as to have a skill. Koa and Halston sometimes talked about her ability to fly, and that perhaps she had inherited it from her father. Koa wondered if that was her skill, or if it was something else.

"Can we stop and grab some of my things from my flat?"

Koa gave him a sideling glance. "You have a flat now?"

He nodded. "Yeah, that money you put in my account let me leave the hostels and find a roommate. This kid named Robert. He's from the states, too, and we get along all right."

Koa shrugged. "Do you really need anything? I was going to buy you new stuff. New clothes and shoes. Whatever you'd like."

Ian laughed. "Um, okay. Is there something wrong with my clothes?"

Koa glanced at what he was wearing. Jeans that were torn at the bottom from dragging beneath his shoes and an old Super Mario T-shirt. She cleared her throat and looked away. "No, that's not what I meant."

"I think you want me to be your new toy."

Koa blushed.

Ian put a hand on hers. He gave her a sweet smile. "I don't mind. Honestly. I kind of like that you have an interest in me, even if you want to change me a bit." His smile widened. "It'll be like Beauty and the Geek and you can give me the whole makeover deal."

Koa laughed. "What's that?"

Ian shrugged. "Just some cheesy show that used to come on back home."

"I guess that does sound like fun." Koa's mind raced with ideas. Haircuts and a new wardrobe. Koa was afraid that she'd create a monster… a vampire that the women couldn't resist. It was an intriguing thought. She'd always wanted to do something like this.

Ian nodded. "It does." He looked out the window and became quiet for a while. Koa glanced over at him. She wished she knew what he was thinking.

"Are you all right?" Koa asked softly. She had known him long enough to genuinely care about him, and now, he was linked to her by blood.

He nodded, but kept looking out into the darkness of the countryside. They passed mountains and thick forests on either side. "I just forgot something is all."

Koa noticed the sadness in his voice. He looked at her with those large puppy dog eyes that made her want to just hug him. "What is it?"

"I won't ever see the sun again, will I?"

Koa took a deep breath. Her eyes went up to the sky. She felt ashamed that she was able to walk in the sun and she had just stolen that privilege from Ian. She gave a regretful look and shook her head.

Ian shrugged, but Koa could tell that it was still bothering him. He was being nice, to not make her self-conscious. "I guess that isn't too awful. I could be dead, right?"

Koa paled.

He made a face. "I'm sorry. That came out wrong. I don't blame you. I promise."

Koa put both hands on the steering wheel and focused on the road. Her brows furrowed. He should blame her. He was right. She'd nearly killed him. Halston had always warned her. She winced. "No. I'm the one who should be sorry. I've been reckless lately. I lost my self-control."

He tucked a hair behind her ear and Koa gave a half-smile. He was too sweet. He didn't know that he was only making her feel guiltier.

"I think I always wanted this. There's been enough death in my life already. Death scares me."

Koa nodded. She'd seen too much death in her short life as well. "Me too."

"I just realized that I took the sun for granted."

Koa realized just how much she had taken from him.

They drove the rest of the time in silence. Ian finally fell asleep and Koa hated to wake him when she pulled into the driveway of the cottage.

Koa watched him sleep for a moment and saw the sky start to brighten. She quickly got out of the car and ran around to his side. She opened the door and gave Ian a shove.

"Come on, let's get you inside."

He groggily nodded and took her hand. She pulled him along to the front door. Koa was surprised to find that Raven was waiting for her at the door.

Koa took a deep breath. Raven looked really confused when she saw Ian but she didn't question her when they came inside. She seemed to be happy just to have her daughter return.

Ian stepped inside and looked around in awe. He seemed to wait timidly beside the door, holding his backpack and looking around into the darkness of the cottage. Koa smiled and took Ian's hand in hers, much like Halston did when they were together. She knew the power such a gesture held.

Ian's hand was no longer warm like Halston's. It was cold.

She hid a frown and led him inside. She would have to get used to all of the changes Ian would undergo. She rubbed his back for encouragement.

Raven looked him up and down. "And who are you?"

Ian jumped when he noticed the black cat waiting in the shadows. He looked at Raven in surprise, and he gave Koa a wide-eyed look. "The cat talks?" He shook his head in bewilderment. A smile came to his lips. "Remarkable."

Koa laughed to herself. She smiled at her mother, hoping she'd see Ian's charm, his childlike innocence.

Raven didn't look amused. She merely stared at the young man, assessing him.

Koa cleared her throat. She whispered close to his ear, remembering how vehement Raven got when she mentioned their secret, even when they were alone at home. "Well, Raven is... special. Ian, meet Raven." She pointed down to the cat.

Ian was speechless.

"Well." Ian scratched his temple as he examined the black cat before him. "I always knew you were different, Koa. I always thought you were enchanted and so forth, but I can't say that I expected this." He gave a half-smile as if he still didn't believe it. "Wow." He knelt down and rubbed Raven on the head. "Nice to meet you... Raven."

Raven blinked at him. Koa could tell that she didn't approve.

Koa sighed. "She's not really a cat, Ian." She lowered her voice again. "She's my mother..."

Raven shook her head and licked her paw.

Ian's eyebrows furrowed in confusion. "What?"

Koa waved her arms. "There's a whole curse and everything, but

I don't really want to discuss the details right this instant. We have an eternity to go over such things."

She looked over her shoulder at Raven. "And, Raven, I'll explain everything to you in just a moment. Please don't be angry."

She led the way to the staircase that led to the cellar.

Koa heard Ian's footsteps stop, and she turned around. "What's wrong?"

She was a little disappointed that she couldn't give him one of the grand guestrooms of her father's manor and that she only had a cellar to offer him. She could see reluctance on his face. "What's wrong?"

Ian shrugged. "Nothing. I'm fine." He squinted as he looked down the staircase.

She could tell that he didn't like the idea but he didn't want to seem ungrateful. Koa sighed. "It's not what you think. I'm going to make it lovely for you. I will have a decorator in here tomorrow and she'll make it into the grandest one-bedroom apartment you've ever lived in."

Ian looked a little nervous. "I didn't mean anything. I'm really very appreciative. I just... don't really like cellars."

Koa lifted a brow.

"You see, in every horror movie I ever saw when I was a little boy, the cellar or the basement was always where the monsters lived." Ian's shoulders slumped. "I guess I'm the monster now."

Koa's lips parted. She didn't know how to respond to that. The comment was heartbreaking when she thought about it. She shook it out of her head. She couldn't bear to feel any guiltier than she already did.

She nodded. "I understand. Just take a look. It's not what you are imagining."

Ian grinned as he looked from the cellar to Koa. "This is a pretty old house. You sure there aren't any ghosts here?"

Koa shook her head and chuckled. "I can assure you, there aren't any ghosts." Koa was surprised to learn of Ian's fears. She felt drawn closer to him. She had her own fears. After everything she had been through, she was still afraid of the dark. Koa wanted to protect Ian from such fears.

"Just checking. With you, I can never be sure," Ian joked.

"Trust me."

Ian followed behind her. He kept talking and she could tell that he was trying to not think about how afraid he was. "I'm not really sleepy. I guess I'll get some homework done."

Koa paused on the stairs and looked back at him. Her face eyebrows furrowed. "You're going to try to go back to school?"

He gave her look. "What? I can't go back to school now?"

Koa thought a moment. She shook her head. Even though she could walk in the sun, Koa had never been to school. She'd been taught by her mother at home and later by a tutor her father had hired to come to the manor. "I don't know how you're going to do that. You cannot go out in the daytime. No vampire can."

Ian looked a little defeated. "Why can you go out in the daytime?"

"I really don't know why, Ian. No one knows for sure. I think it's because my mother was human."

Ian looked perplexed. "Your mother is a cat."

"Cursed. She was born a human."

"If you say so," Ian said, thinking. "I don't buy it."

Koa frowned. No one had ever questioned her mother's humanity, but something made her bite her tongue. She almost argued with Ian that her mother had been human, but then she paused.

How could she be sure? Koa was certain that her mother had done something to those vampires when she entered Bund's lair. Bund had been afraid when he saw her, even after all of his incessant taunting.

Bund had been afraid.

"I guess you're right." He put his hands in his pocket, "I didn't realize how much I would give up."

Koa stroked his cheek. She gave him an encouraging smile. "We will figure something out," she said with a smile. "Don't worry about it. Don't worry about anything ever again. I'm going to teach you everything. You don't even really need school anymore. You're a smart guy and now you're immortal."

Ian nodded. "You're right. Now, come on." He nodded for Koa to continue down the stairs. "Show me this grand cellar that I'll be spending the night in."

Koa walked down the stairs and entered a large room that covered pretty much the entire expanse of the cottage. The walls were made of stone and the floors were a dark concrete color. Koa could see what she could do with the room. She could only hope that Ian could see it too.

There were still boxes everywhere. She felt a little bad, but it was only temporary.

There was an antique sofa and a few tables strewn about. Koa hadn't quite set anything up yet. Her books were still lying on a desk, waiting to be put away on her bookcases.

She played with her hair. She was a little embarrassed. She prided herself on her cleanliness and preferred everything to be neat and in its place. She just hadn't the time with everything that had happened.

Ian didn't seem to mind. He sat on the sofa and set his laptop on a table. He leaned back and took a look around the cellar. "I admit, it's not as dark down here as I imagined. Still, a little creepy but I will survive. I don't think I am going to sleep well tonight— this morning, I mean."

"Do you want some company?" Koa didn't know if she could sleep either.

"I'm all right, thanks. You get some rest. From that wound you had earlier, it looks like you had quite the night. I am just going to do some research on vampires."

"Sure, you do that, but I think I could tell you a lot more about vampires than what you will find on the Internet."

"I'm sure you can, but I just want to do a little research myself, see what the humans know and we can compare notes later."

Koa nodded. "You big nerd," she teased.

Ian beamed. "Thank you. I take that as a compliment."

Koa rolled her eyes and laughed. She started up the stairs. "I'll come back for you at sunset."

"See you then."

She went upstairs and closed the door behind her. The sun was rising and the house was starting to brighten. She leaned against the door and Raven was waiting there for her.

Koa sighed and took a step toward her. She prepared herself for the scolding.

Raven surprised her. "He's a nice boy, Koa."

Koa was taken aback. She never expected that from her mother. She expected a major scolding.

Raven tilted her head. "I always knew you'd sire someone. I am surprised you didn't do it sooner."

"How did you always know that? I kill vampires."

"I can tell he's a good person. Therefore he'll make a good vampire."
Koa felt relieved.

"But now you have one more person to worry about. For instance, Bund will be seeking revenge. Who do you think he will target if he can't get one of us?"

Koa swallowed. She didn't know what to say. She looked at the cellar door.

It was her duty to protect her family. Raven walked into the darkness of the den. Koa looked up at the sky. She did something she rarely did anymore. She prayed.

CHAPTER 14

STRANGE THINGS HAPPENED at night. Koa was aware of most of them, but the Netherworld was new to her. She knew she'd been there once before with her father, yet she couldn't remember it. The Netherworld remained a mystery to her, and she was determined to unlock its secrets.

Koa knew she was dreaming. It was the same dream most nights, and so she let herself explore this world. She stood in a thick white mist and felt her hair flapping around her face. Drops of dew made her face slick, and her bare feet touched cool stones.

She looked up. Someone was playing a violin. She knew the tune and started to hum along. The song grew louder and yet Koa couldn't see who played the beautiful melody. She strained to see who played from somewhere in the clouds above, and then, she saw it.

The Gate, where the nephilim were escaping the Netherworld. Koa stared at it with wide eyes. She'd never gotten this far in the dream before. Now she looked at the stone gate and felt her skin crawl with anxiety. She knew she shouldn't be there, and yet, she felt as though it called to her.

Koa wanted to wake up. The violin was starting to play so loudly that she had to cover her ears. Koa felt weak. The Gate started to glide closer to her and she panicked. She couldn't move. Her feet were stuck to the ground. Koa gasped and tried to pull her feet free as the Gate continued its way toward her.

Something terrible waited inside that door, and she wanted to run from it. She knew it meant her harm and felt herself sweat with terror.

Shadows, like the ones Halston had managed to control, lunged at her. They grabbed her with their frigid hands and yet her flesh burned to the bone. Koa screamed. The hot, searing pain was unbearable and she fell to her knees. The Shadows held her steady, and she squeezed her eyes shut as they brought their faces closer to hers.

"Come back to us, Koa," they chanted. One of the Shadows leaned in close. The black face morphed into Bund's. Bund grinned at her. His tongue reached out to her and she screamed.

Someone shook her awake.

Koa grabbed Ian by the neck and he had to peel her fingers from around his throat.

"Koa," he gasped. He looked at her fearfully. "It's me!"

Realizing who he was, Koa quickly scrambled away. She was covered in sweat. "Ian! I'm sorry."

"You're strong!" Ian sat up and rubbed his neck.

Koa forced a smile. "Forgive me. I was dreaming."

"You were screaming."

Koa pulled her hair off her neck and grumbled at how heavy with sweat it was. She pushed herself up to her feet and sat on the edge of the bed. "What time is it?"

Ian put his hands in his pocket. He gave her a sheepish look. "I think it's time to eat."

Koa came to her feet. "Oh shit! Yes. Our appointment is tonight!"

Ian didn't budge. "Appointment?"

Koa quickly pulled her shirt over her head and tossed it to her hamper in the corner of the room. She darted into the bathroom to heat the shower. Ian avoided looking directly at her exposed body and turned away.

What a gentleman, she thought. She stood in the bathroom doorway. "We choose our pets tonight, at Wryn Castle."

Ian perked up then. "I get my own? Like I was to you? A pet?"

Koa nodded. "Exactly."

"Whomever I want?"

"Whomever you want."

Ian grinned and Koa smiled as she hopped into the shower. Once she closed the shower curtain, her smile faded. The fear from her dream still lingered. After all of those years of having the same dream of the mists and the violin, she'd never seen the Gate or the Shadows that waited for her inside of it.

Koa washed her hair and tried to forget the pain she felt when they touched her. The hot water ran down her body, and she closed her eyes. If only she could talk to Halston about things. She covered her face and sighed. She missed him so much that she felt physical pain.

She hurried and finished her shower to see that Ian had decided to wait outside. Koa didn't mind him seeing her nude. They'd have an eternity together, such things were trivial now.

She was surprised to see Raven waiting for her on her bed.

Her big green eyes looked up at Koa.

"This is a nice little house, Koa," Raven said.

"Perhaps." Koa sighed and continued getting ready. "It is a bit small."

"It is only the three of us now that you've increased our family," Raven pointed out and Koa couldn't help but smile. "We don't need a massive house with dozens of rooms. Never did."

"It reminds me too much of our old house in Korea."

Raven didn't say anything.

"I'm sorry. I didn't mean to bring it up."

Raven purred. "It's all right. I was just trying to remember it. It gets harder to remember things. Every day, I lose a memory."

Koa had many memories that she feared she'd forget as well. The sound of her mother playing the piano for her father still lingered in her mind. She'd give anything to hear her mother's music again. There was a time when Raven would cook for her every night. She let out a soft sigh. She missed those days. She grabbed her gloves.

"Going somewhere, darling?"

"Yes. I need to go and choose a new pet. Ian must do the same. Want to come?"

Raven blinked. "I don't think so. Why were you screaming anyway?"

Koa turned away and fumbled with her wardrobe. "You heard me?"

"Yes, the entire village heard you, Koa."

Koa shook her head. "It was just a bad dream."

"You've been having those bad dreams a lot more often lately."

"Well, consider all that I've been through in just the past month! Who wouldn't be a little traumatized?"

"Was it about the Netherworld again?"

Koa sighed and nodded. She lowered her eyes and stared at her feet. The last thing she wanted to do was worry her mother. Raven was intuitive though. Koa could never keep anything from her. Even when Koa was a child, Raven always knew when something was wrong.

"Don't drag the boy into this."

Koa's brows furrowed. "Into what?"

Raven was silent and Koa grew suspicious.

Koa huffed. "I was just trying to have a real talk with you. I'm sick of all of the secrets. I'm leaving."

"Wait."

Koa paused and glanced over her shoulder with a frown. "What?"

Raven sat up and looked at her for a moment. "There's something I need to tell you, Koa."

Koa's eyebrows lifted. She knew that, finally, her mother was going to reveal whatever secret she'd been keeping.

Raven nodded to the door that was open just a crack. Ian waited outside.

"Close the door."

Koa did so and sat down on the chaise lounge in the corner of the room. She folded her hands across her knee and sat up straight, like an apt pupil prepared for the lesson of a lifetime.

Raven took her time. Koa could tell that she was thinking of how to say what was on her mind.

"Koa, the first thing you should know… is that your father wasn't just another vampire. He was a Netherworld vamp. He was a king."

Koa slumped back in her seat and watched her mother with wide eyes. She felt her palms start to sweat and rubbed them on her knees. Her throat was dry. This was one thing she never expected to hear. Maybe she was suspicious that her father was a Netherworld vamp because of the Lyrinian sword he left her, but she could never have guessed that he was a king.

"He was king of the Northern Dominance, a major kingdom in the Netherworld, and was overthrown by King Greggan. He lost his kingdom and was banished to the mortal world."

"Wow," Koa said as she sat back up. She couldn't think of what else to say. All she knew of him was the difficult life without him and a privileged life with him. Still, although her time with him was short, she had grown to love and respect him. She remembered how much he loved her mother. That was a memory that stood at the forefront of her mind.

"That makes you not just half vampire, but half Netherworld vamp. You have one of the strongest strains of blood running through your veins."

Koa sat up. "Is that why I can fly, and other vampires cannot?"

Raven shook her head. "No, Koa. Not even Netherworld vamps can fly. That brings me to… your other half."

Koa tensed. She narrowed her eyes. "What do you mean?" Koa stared at Raven, and all she could see were those green eyes that had glowed so brightly in Bund's lair. Her skin started to crawl. The air in the room seemed to still with the anticipation she felt.

What are you, mother? What are you? Koa was almost too afraid to know, but she had to.

"Before I was cursed…" Raven took a deep breath. "I wasn't human."

Koa stood. She looked down at Raven in astonishment. She couldn't even speak the words she was thinking. Her throat tightened.

What are you? Koa shouted in her head. The suspense was maddening.

"I don't know what I was, Koa. But your father did, and so did Greggan, and that is why he wants us both. We are the only beings that can mate with a vampire and create day-walking spawn."

Koa's shoulders slumped. "What the hell are we?"

Raven's feline eyes closed and she sighed. "I wish I knew. I was an orphan. I was abandoned, Koa. I never had a mother or father. All I had was myself and my talents—" Her voice cracked. "And I lived a hard life before I met your father. It was even harder when you were born, with no one to turn to for help, but *you* gave me a reason to live."

Koa bit her lip. She had never heard her mother speak so bitterly about her past. She never knew her mother was an orphan.

"Who was Hayan then? I always called her grandmother."

Raven sighed. "All of the children did, Koa. She was a kind woman, and she helped me from time to time. She knew there was something special about me. I returned her generosity whenever I could."

Koa felt cheated. She never even had real grandparents.

"You see, I could do things that no one else could. I could… make people disappear. Bill collectors, enemies"—Raven cleared her throat—"abusive husbands..."

"Mother, why tell me all of this now? Why not sooner?"

Raven hissed. "How many times do I have to tell you? Do not call me that, ever again!"

Koa's eyes widened at her mother's tone. She looked down at the wooden floor.

"Not even in private." Raven settled and lowered her voice. She closed her eyes and breathed deeply. "You never know who is listening."

"I'm sorry." Koa reached for her. "What are you so afraid of?"

"Koa, you don't understand what I've done to protect you. There are so many creatures that want you dead, and then, there are those that wish to see you brought back for your birthright."

Koa folded her arms across her chest and walked to the window. Her mother could make people disappear. She thought of how Bund fled when he saw her mother. She wondered what that meant. She wondered if he was still out there somewhere, ready for revenge. Then she thought about what an amazing skill that was. She began to smile. *My mother is a nephilim…*

"There goes every shred of my humanity," Koa whispered, and her smile faded.

Koa pulled the heavy drapes open and looked out into the darkness. She glanced over at the neighbor's garden a few yards away. She could see lights and candles set up as they had a party of some sort. She could even hear the music playing and the people laughing and talking. She stared out at them and pressed her forehead to the cool glass. She sighed as she watched the happy people.

They looked so content. She wished she could feel even a fraction of that kind of happiness.

"What am I supposed to do?"

"Find Jax."

Koa swirled around. Something sparked inside her mind, but she couldn't decipher what it was. There was something familiar about the name, Jax. Something ignited both a longing and a fear within her. She felt uncomfortable. She shifted her weight onto her other leg and looked down at her mother.

She frowned. "Where have I heard that name?"

Raven stared at her. There was a long pause and Koa frowned. "What is it?"

Raven shook her head. "Nothing." She hopped off the bed and walked over on all fours to stand before Koa. "I don't know why you would have heard that name."

Koa looked at the ceiling and tapped her chin with her index finger. The name sounded so familiar, but she couldn't place it. She hated that.

"Who is he then?"

Raven hesitated. "He is Greggan's son."

Koa watched Raven. She could tell that there was more. She gave Raven a look and held her hands out, expecting her to elaborate.

Raven remained silent. She was still keeping secrets.

"Out with it!"

Raven glared up at her. "He is the one responsible for my curse."

CHAPTER 6

KOA DROVE all the way to Wryn Castle in silence. Ian tried to start a conversation but she could only give him short, one-worded answers.

Jax. The name repeated itself in her head a thousand times throughout that long ride. Her face was set with anger and her hands clutched the steering wheel so tightly that the leather grooves were engrained in her palms by the time they stopped. She looked down at her reddened hands and traced the grooves.

Ian stared at her.

"Koa?" He spoke in a timid voice, as if he was afraid that she might lash out at him.

Koa turned and gave him a blank expression. Ian looked afraid of her. She didn't care. He got out of the car and started to walk up the long stone pathway that led to the castle's entrance without her. He glanced back once and Koa was still staring off at nothing at all, with a scowl on her face.

Jax had cursed her mother. For years Koa had missed her mother's face. She had craved her mother's embrace for so long that she had forgotten what it felt like, what she used to smell like, and how she used to stroke her hair.

Koa slammed her fist on the steering wheel and screamed. Her breath came in quick gasps as she tried to control her rage. She wanted him dead. Koa wanted her Lyrinian sword to feast on his blood. She repeated Raven's words over and over again.

"Do not be hasty. Jax is Greggan's son. He is a Netherworld vamp and faster than anyone you've ever encountered," Raven had said. "Still, you must go to him."

Koa had asked many questions, and still, Raven only told her that she must go to him, and she must learn for herself the secrets of her past. Only Koa could find a way to break the curse and set things right with both the Netherworld and the mortal world. Koa leaned her head back against the headrest. Even Raven knew Koa had to go to the Netherworld. Raven tried to convince Halston that it was necessary. Halston would never let her go. He would never risk it.

Koa wasn't sure how dangerous the Netherworld was, but Halston's reluctance was an indicator. She didn't need his approval. Halston had abandoned her. She needed to start making her own decisions.

She hated to admit that was the reason he had left her in the first place—for making her own decisions.

She opened the door, stepped out, and slammed it closed. She lifted herself into the air and flew to the tall, black doorways that led into the castle.

Two guards with suits and slicked back hair opened the double doors for her without a second glance. Koa was a regular. She dared anyone to stand in her way on this night. Inside, she had no smiles for anyone.

Greta, one of Lexi's sires, and main girlfriend, started to greet her. She must have seen the scowl on Koa's face, because she decided to keep her mouth shut. Greta stepped back behind the mahogany podium and nodded to the side hallway.

Without a desire to acknowledge her, Koa walked through the black archway and into the dimly lit corridor. Black candles lined the paneled walls.

Koa walked along the red carpet that led to the end of the hall, and the parlor door. Koa smelled the heavy scent of perfume, cologne, and alcohol. There were fresh humans waiting. They were probably nervous to find vampire masters.

She took off her gloves and stretched her fingers. She was amped and ready to hurt someone. Only blood would calm her down. If she couldn't kill anyone tonight, she would stick to the plan, choose a new pet, and drink as much as she could without stealing a life.

There were guards at each door that led to a public room. They opened the door to the parlor and she stepped inside. Music thumped and vibrated the floor. She snatched a flute of champagne from a server and downed it. The server gave her an odd look as she put the empty glass back on the tray. She ignored him.

Koa shut her eyes and enjoyed the sensation of the music vibrating the floor. She wanted to feel anything but the hot, burning rage that pulsed throughout her entire body.

The DJ spun techno tracks and she let her head fall back as the music filled her. She smelled blood all around and found herself getting hungry and aroused. Her canines emerged and she licked them.

Koa waited until a particular scent caught her interest. She sniffed the air and her head lolled to the right. She opened her eyes and caught sight of the girl that emitted the delicious aroma. She was small, like Koa, and had a short blond bob. She wore a gold cocktail dress and ballet flats.

She smelled delicious.

Everything about her was petite, especially her waist and her small nose. Koa took two strides over to her and grabbed her by that tiny waist.

Koa kissed her. It was a passionate kiss that made Koa's ears grow hot and her heart thump. When she broke away, she felt dizzy. Koa didn't let the girl's tiny waist go. She held her steady as she swooned and looked up at her with bright blue eyes.

Koa always had a thing for blue eyes. She didn't smile at her. She couldn't even fake one. Koa gazed into the girl's eyes and in an instant, the girl was claimed. She would reveal everything Koa wanted without hesitation.

"What's your name?"

"Lindley," she breathed.

"How old are you?"

"Twenty-two." She had an accent, like one of those girls from the South in the states. Koa sure could pick them. She never knew she had such a taste for Americans.

"Why are you here tonight?" Koa had no idea what she was unleashing.

"My friends said it's the most exclusive place in Europe." Lindley lowered her voice as if she was going to tell Koa a secret. "Ann said that there were vampires here. Wait… are you a vampire? You kind of look like one… kind of pale. But pretty! You're so pretty. I could just lick your face, you're so cute! You know, I never even knew about vampires until I met Ann. I love you guys, though. Hey, I want to be a pet. I want a vampire to protect and support me, and buy me nice things. I hear some even let pets live with them, like mistresses. I don't mind being a mistress."

Koa stopped listening or caring. She had a feeling that the girl could go on... and on. She lowered her head to Lindley's throat and breathed her sweet scent in. It was nearly as good as Ian's and even a little dirtier. This girl wasn't as innocent as Ian.

Perhaps that was a good thing. She wanted something different. She'd never had a girl pet. Koa wanted to be daring.

Lindley was hers.

It was official, and Lexi smiled the moment she saw them together. She shook her head with a satisfied grin and logged the transaction in her little palm device.

Lindley was still staring into Koa's eyes with an empty headed, slack-jawed, look. Koa gave her one more soft kiss on her full pink lips and moved her hand from her waist to her small hand. She pulled Lindley along and started for the door. Ian stood near the bar with a stunning brunette, a glass of champagne, and a newfound confidence.

Ian watched Koa and gave a half-smile as if asking for her approval. He looked from the brunette and back to Koa. Koa gave him a slight nod and left the parlor. The second the guards closed the doors behind her and Lindley, it was silent in the corridor once more.

Jax. Jax. Jax.

Koa couldn't get his name out of her head. Lindley followed her without a word and all Koa could do was imagine this grotesque creature damning her mother into that feline body that she had been forced to live in. She hated all Netherworld vamps.

She would get her revenge.

They went up the elevator and to her usual room, and Koa closed the door behind them.

CHAPTER 16

HALSTON SAT on a wooden bench at a park. He watched the people walking by. There was soft music playing in the background as a young man played the guitar for a group of teenage girls.

It was a rare sunny day. He held something in his hand. A small gold bracelet.

Charms dangled from it. A train, a star, and a horse. Halston sighed as he looked down at the bracelet. There was a name etched into the inside.

Galena.

Sorrow filled his body every time he read the name. The bracelet had been given to Galena by her parents before they were killed by vampires. Halston took it from her dead body that very morning.

He'd never felt this way before. His heart beat rapidly. He could barely control his breaths. Halston was always in control. Now, everything was falling apart. A woman he was supposed to protect was dead, and another whom he had grown to love hadn't returned to her house in weeks.

How could I let this happen?

The guilt was too strong. He hadn't shaved or showered. He still had on what he'd worn on his mission the night before. He was glad that he hadn't had to shed any blood. He had found a newly emerged pack of vampires and convinced them to register with the Netherworld Division. They would now be monitored and set up with a clan of 'reformed' vampires.

Halston missed having Koa with him on such missions. She took more pleasure in reforming vampires than she did in killing them.

That was what he loved about her more than anything. She had a good heart.

Another pang of guilt filled his heart and he groaned. Everyday, he thought about the look on Koa's face when he fired her. Four weeks had passed, and he hadn't seen or heard from her.

Raven informed him that she had gone to Wryn Castle and he had followed straight there. He didn't venture in, but he had seen her step out onto her balcony one evening. He left then, assured that she was safe, but not before watching her stare out into the horizon as if yearning for something.

Halston imagined that she was calling for him. All he wanted was an apology—an indication that she knew that what she had done was wrong. He wanted her to mean it and finally learn from her mistakes. He wanted her to grow up and take responsibility for her actions.

Halston's hand shook as he put Galena's bracelet back in his pocket. Bund was loose, and he was on a vengeful killing spree. Halston investigated at least fifty murders of little girls within the last month.

The poor bodies had been nailed to the doors of their homes so that the parents would see them the moment they returned. The humans were in a hysterical frenzy.

"Serial Killer! On The Loose!" Those words were on every newspaper in London. The humans that knew of nephilim existence were looking to the Netherworld Division for answers. Halston and the others didn't know what to say. They couldn't stop Bund.

Halston winced. He knew who could.

Raven sat beside him, waiting for him to speak. Halston was grateful for her patience.

Halston held up a newspaper and folded one leg over the other so that his shoe rested on his other knee. He didn't look at the black cat. He looked at the paper and spoke. "It's time. Are you ready?"

Raven nodded. "I am. I've told you before that I've been ready. Do you finally think Koa is?"

Halston felt a pain in his stomach. He didn't like these new sensations. He missed Koa. He missed Galena. The thirst for revenge was too strong. He could not afford to allow himself to lose control.

"I can no longer wait for her to be ready. We've wasted enough time."

"And who is to blame for that?" Raven asked. "I know you want to protect Koa, but she is the key to everything. We have to let her know the truth at some point." She looked over at a little girl who came to pet her. "Before it's too late."

The little girl grinned at Raven, and looked up at Halston. "Is this your cat?"

Halston forced a smile. She was an adorable little brunette with a big blue bow in her hair. Maybe eight years old. Halston's face paled as he imagined her body being nailed to the door of her house. He tried to keep the smile. He didn't want to frighten the girl.

"It is," Halston said. He leaned forward and picked a fallen twig out of the girl's hair.

She smiled at him and adjusted her little black glasses. "What's her name?"

"Raven."

Meowing, Raven rubbed her head into the girl's palm. The little girl giggled.

"Nice to meet you, Raven," she said in a sweet little voice. "I'm Rebecca."

Halston looked around the park. There were so many people around. "Where are your parents, Rebecca?"

"Right there." She pointed over to a picnic blanket set out on the large green yard. There were dozens of other picnic blankets set all around. It was the first lovely day in a long time.

Halston nodded. "Good." He motioned her closer with his index finger. His eyes met hers. "Promise me something."

The girl's eyes widened as she looked into Halston's. She nodded as her smile faded.

Halston's voice lowered into a whisper. "Stay with your parents, Rebecca. Keep away from strangers. Even if they seem nice... *never* leave with a stranger. Can you do that for me?"

Rebecca didn't blink. She nodded slowly with her mouth agape.

"Good girl." Halston sat back and Rebecca stared at him. "Run along to your parents now."

Her lips trembled and she ran away toward her parents' picnic blanket.

Watching her run away, he hoped his chance encounter with Rebecca would keep her safe from Bund's treachery.

"I think you frightened the poor girl." Raven lowered her head to the wooden bench seat.

Halston remained silent. He hoped he'd frightened her. That was the point.

He frowned at the words he read in the paper. There were copycat killers out there already. Sloppy humans who wanted a piece of the fame Bund was receiving in secret. "It's my fault that we've wasted so much time. I've let enough people die."

Raven sighed. "I didn't mean to make you feel guilty. Bund is the killer here. Let's move past that and focus on the issue at hand. We need to stop him. *He* should be our main priority right now. We can go after Greggan later. Bund isn't only working for pay. This is personal to him."

Halston closed the paper and looked at the sky. There was something he hoped to hear, or see. A sign maybe.

Halston closed his eyes and sighed. There would be no more signs. Galena's body nailed to his door this morning was enough. He would never be able to erase the image of Galena nailed to his door by her wrists and feet. Her eyes had been pulled out of her head and replaced with silver buttons. Her mouth had been sewn shut. Worst of all, from the neck down, her skin had been ripped from her body.

Halston swallowed. His stomach still felt unsettled. He didn't think he'd be able to eat for a while. Halston had almost cried when he pulled Galena's body down. He would have, if the rage hadn't taken over. Halston had almost gone over the edge. He had almost lost himself.

"Will you go get her then?" Raven spoke quietly.

Halston looked at her. He pictured Koa's little face with her big, green eyes looking up at him. He missed cupping her face in his hands.

He missed her scent, humor, and bravery. He missed her smile. The way her eyes crinkled at the corners when she was genuinely happy made him almost smile. He believed that was her gift to him. Koa rarely smiled like that for anyone else.

Halston sat up straight. He watched Rebecca sitting in between her parents. She was staring at him. "No. She will come to me."

Raven made a face. "How are you so sure?"

Halston sat back and watched a couple standing near the fence surrounding a pond. They held hands and pointed to the geese.

"I just know."

CHAPTER 17

KOA WAS DRUNK on Lindley's blood. She stayed in the Wryn castle for a month and learned everything there was to know about her new pet. Lindley was asleep and holding onto Koa like a child holding onto a Teddy bear. Koa didn't mind. She enjoyed being held.

Lindley smelled like vanilla and sex.

She was one of the most alluring people Koa had shared a bed with, but she hadn't actually had sex with the girl. Lindley just had this seductive scent about her that Koa was sure drove the men mad. She only drank from her, though. Somehow, the thought of Halston's disapproval still bothered her.

She looked up at the ceiling and frowned. Koa shouldn't care anymore. She refused to. She played with Lindley's short hair. It was soft and silky, and fell between Koa's fingers with ease.

I don't want Lindley in that way anyway, Koa reasoned. There was only one man she wanted and she would save herself for him.

Koa sighed and glanced down at her. Lindley wore her panties and bra, and looked like a sleeping angel with her pale skin and blond hair on the cream comforter.

I made a good choice. She kissed her forehead and smiled. All of her pent up aggression had been somewhat relieved by her feeding.

Now she would just have to get back on a schedule. She'd had so much human blood lately that her energy was at an optimal level. She hadn't felt this strong in a long time. The thought of what damage she could do both frightened and intrigued her.

Koa's eyes widened. She gently moved Lindley's sleeping body aside and came to her feet. She stretched her arms and rolled her neck. She felt powerful.

"What better time than now to visit the Netherworld?" Koa spoke the word and her heart started to race. The adrenaline pulsed through her at an alarming rate.

I'm ready.

She wanted to go, and no one could stop her. She hurried and grabbed her things. She put on her gloves and grabbed her sword.

Something made Koa pause. She looked at the phone that sat on the sleek, black nightstand.

Koa knew what she had to do. Raven had known it, too. Koa picked up the phone and called Halston.

She held her breath as the phone started to ring. It rang twice. "Koa?" He yawned. "Is that you, Koa?"

Koa mustered her strength. "Yes. It's me."

"It's three in the morning." His voice perked up. "Are you all right?"

"I'm fine, Halston." Koa bit the corner of her lip. She felt her heart beating and her palms sweating. "I miss you."

Silence.

"Hello?" Koa panicked. *I knew this was a bad idea!*

"I miss you too, Koa. Where have you been?"

"Wryn."

"With Ian."

Koa walked over to the balcony and stepped out into the night. "Yes. I sired him."

"I knew that would happen."

Koa smiled. *Same old Halston.* "Of course you knew, Halston. You know everything."

"How does he like being a vampire?"

"He loves it. He gets along with my new pet," Koa hesitated. "Her name is Lindley."

"I see." He didn't sound thrilled.

"Halston," Koa said as she looked across the rolling hills toward the lake. "I need you."

"What is it, Koa? What happened?"

Koa held onto the stone balcony and closed her eyes. She had to be brave. "I am going to the Netherworld, and I need you to come with me." She stuttered. "I want you to come with me."

Halston surprised her. "Are you sure that you're ready?"

Koa felt her eyes water. "I am. I promise, I am ready." She closed the French doors to the balcony and sat on the cold stone floor. "I forgive you."

"Forgive *me*?" Halston asked. He sounded amused.

Koa sighed. "Yes. I was angry with you for firing me—so angry that I almost killed Ian." She squeezed her eyes closed. She'd never forget how horrible she'd felt when she thought that he was dead. She'd spent the month teaching him just as much as she spent feeding and learning about Lindley.

"Go on."

She growled in exasperation. "I get it, Halston! You taught me a lesson! There! Happy?"

Halston chuckled.

Koa pouted. Her brows drew in and she frowned. "It's not funny!"

He continued to chuckle. "I know. I can't help it. You just said exactly what I wanted to hear."

Koa's frowned deepened. "Well, this is not the appropriate time to be laughing."

Halston cleared his throat. "Right. Go on. You were talking about… learning lessons and so forth?"

Koa leaned against the French doors. She looked up at the moon. "Yes. I can be a little… headstrong sometimes."

"Headstrong, you say?"

Koa rolled her eyes. "Yes. You heard me."

"I see."

"I used to follow my own rules and look at where it got me. Nearly torn to bits by a demon, and I nearly killed a good friend." Koa played with the ends of her blue hair. She twirled a lock around her finger. "I just want a piece of my memory back. I want to break my mother's curse, and kill Bund. These are the things that make me lose myself. Whenever I want something, you know, I'll do anything to get it… and that's not always right. I realize that I cannot do this on my own." Koa closed her eyes. "I'm sorry."

"For?"

Koa shook her head. She had to bite her lip. Halston was dragging this apology out. She slowly let out a breath. "For not listening to you," she muttered.

Silence. Koa expected him to laugh.

"Koa, I believe you."

Koa's burned with tears.

"Together, we can do this."

Koa smiled and wiped a tear. "Thank you, Halston."

"But I must warn you, it's not going to be easy. There are so many who want you dead and I am not as strong as I used to be. But you have my vow that I will protect you with all the power that I have."

Koa nodded. "I know. Thank you, Halston." Koa opened the door and glanced at her sleeping pet. Lindley had given her more than she knew. She could feel herself radiating with newfound strength.

"Let's do this."

"Now?"

Koa grinned. She had her Halston back. She was more ready than ever. "Right now."

CHAPTER 18

THE GATE TO THE Netherworld started at the center of a craggy pit and reached up toward the heavens. It sat in the deepest part of the hidden forest, where humans would never venture. The Gate was invisible to humans. To them, there was nothing but a mountain with thick evergreen vines wrapped around its base.

Koa touched the cool vine. It trembled and coiled away from her. An outline of a door stretched along the stone and revealed itself to her. Koa took a long breath of the cool air.

This is it, Koa thought as she breathed in the scent of coal. *I am actually going to the Netherworld.* She almost felt giddy with excitement. She had butterflies in her stomach. She'd dreamed of this day.

Koa stepped through the wall and there stood Halston. She couldn't suppress her smile. She beamed at him and glanced back just in time to see the wall vanish behind her. She reached out and it reappeared. Koa pulled her hand back and it vanished again. She shivered and rubbed her arms as she turned back toward Halston.

He was dressed in black and wore a grim look on his pale face. No well-tailored suit or chic fedora and expensive shoes like she was used to: plain pants, shirt, and jacket. She knew that his long jacket only served to cover up his infinity shotgun.

Koa felt her excitement grow. She hadn't seen him fire that glorious weapon in ages. There was nothing sexier than when he was like this.

This morning, Halston was all business. His hair was so blond that it was nearly golden. Illuminated by the moonlight, Halston looked like a god.

"Ready?"

She gave a single nod. Her face was set. She would not turn away if she could help it.

"I understand you've always wanted to find out what happened to you when you were a child, but Koa, I am not sure you want to know. I've been protecting you all of these years. I just didn't want to see you hurt."

Koa's lips parted. She stepped before Halston and looked up at him. *Why would he avoid my eyes?* Koa could feel it— Halston cared about her.

The urge to squeal with joy overcame her, but she contained her excitement and the desire to reach up and kiss him. He might even love her. She looked at her feet.

"No matter how painful the truth is," she said, "I think it's time I know. I want my memories back. There is a black hole that I don't understand. From age twelve to seventeen— there is nothing, and I need it back."

Koa knew something horrible had happened, and whenever she tried to grasp those memories, an overwhelming nausea deterred her from further search. That same nausea overcame her now as she swallowed and tried to force it to go away.

"I want my mother back, and this Jax—" She paused when Halston winced at the name.

That's very strange.

"This Jax person is who can give me these things. I just want to help my mother and protect the mortal world."

There was a long pause and finally Halston's gaze met hers. She saw a hint of that smile she loved.

"Finally. I think you are actually ready." He started ahead.

A mixture of emotions flooded Koa. She thumbed the hilt of her sword for courage. She couldn't start doubting herself now, not after she had convinced Halston that she was ready for this. She took a deep breath and followed him.

Koa and Halston walked over the jagged rocks to the base of the gate. They were surrounded by a thick, white mist that swirled around their feet, hiding the ground. Blue strands of hair swept around Koa's face. She pulled her hair back and wrapped a band from her wrist around it, making a long ponytail that reached the small crevice at the base of her back.

The setting, and even how they moved toward the Gate, felt familiar to Koa. The sky was a mixture of gray and white. She walked along the black soil and gazed up at the imposing black structure that stood before her. The Gate itself was a metallic structure with bars and webs of fiery tendrils laced in intricate patterns along the door.

Black trees lined the path to the Gate. Koa marveled at the fiery totems that reached toward the heavens. There were paintings on them and symbols that Koa didn't recognize engraved in the smooth, dark wood.

Koa was captivated by the way the paintings seemed to come to life whenever she passed one of the totems. The figures followed her with their black eyes and pointed to her.

Koa's ears perked up. She heard whispering. She tilted her head and listened.

Someone played a violin. The soft melody was soothing. Whoever played it was a master violinist. The tune evoked emotions in Koa that left her in tears. She shuddered, confused by her wet cheeks. She realized immediately that the tune from her dreams was real. She'd dreamt of this very song for years. She hummed along to it.

As they walked closer, the song grew louder and vibrated against her very soul. Once Halston stopped, Koa was in tears, and could barely catch her breath. She couldn't explain why, but tears soaked her cold cheeks.

Stunned by her reaction, she tried to steady her breaths. Halston glanced over his shoulder at her. His icy blue stare seemed even more ethereal in the intensified light of the moon above them. He looked concerned.

"We are going on a journey to a place where most of the population would love to see you dead just because of your ability to come and go from the Netherworld as you please— because of your threat to the vampires that dwell here," Halston said. "Do not be fooled by the things you are about to see. This is not a place of beauty. This is not a place of love. You forget that, and you will be a prisoner here. Or worse, you will die. Now, stay close."

Koa nodded and he reached for her. She remembered when she was twelve. Her father had given her the same warning. She had no idea that this place that gave her nightmares had once been her father's home. He was a king and had been exiled. Her father had held his hand out to her as well.

Koa gratefully accepted Halston's hand and he curled his fingers in between hers. She instantly felt more at ease. She exhaled a breath of relief. That relief didn't last long.

A whistling sound swept through the valley. Out of the mists of the sky, a man landed with a soft thud. He stood tall— even taller than Halston who was considered abnormal by human standards. His long legs and long arms were thin, as was his entire body. His long black hair was straight and reached the middle of his back. His eyes were too big to be human. His mouth was wide, with thin rubbery lips.

Koa gasped. He held a violin. He brought it up under his chin and Koa was transfixed the moment he resumed his song. The tune was jarring on her mind, weakening her. She clutched Halston.

"Halston. What's happening?"

She was losing herself. Koa was afraid that she might pass out. Halston stopped walking and held her up.

"Make it stop!"

Cold wind slapped at her face as the mists swirled around her, dancing to the tune. The song made her feel as if her bones were cracking under a heavy weight. Her heart was breaking. Koa wanted to fall to her knees and weep with sorrow and pain.

Such a feeling frightened her. Gasping, Koa pressed her hands to her chest. Her heart beat too strongly. She could feel it beating against her rib cage. She gripped her shirt and winced.

The man's grin widened as he stepped closer to her. He wanted her, only her. Halston didn't seem to exist.

Koa felt as if her soul was being ripped from her body. She almost cried out in surrender when Halston brought up his other hand and grabbed the man by his neck. The man seemed stunned. He squealed and before her eyes, his body shrank. He shrank, smaller and smaller, until he was even smaller than Koa.

His skin hung loose from being stretched and his hair seeped into his head until he was bald. Grotesque scabs and patches of crust covered his scalp. His skin was a sickly green and dry like a lizard's in the desert.

Koa's eyes narrowed. She couldn't believe it. He had been an illusion. The man was no taller than a child.

"What... who's there?"

Koa looked at Halston in disbelief. The man couldn't see him. His eyes darted all around as he searched for whoever held him by his neck.

Halston's body started to glow. Koa gasped and stepped back as heat radiated from Halston's body. Discs of light as bright as the sun encircled Halston like crisscrossing planetary rings. Koa shielded her eyes and took another step away from him. The heat of his shield warmed her face. It was almost too much to behold.

Finally, the man saw Halston. The look of shock on the man's face was appalling. His eyes widened until they appeared to be too big for his face. He started to tremble and dropped his violin. He dribbled drool and started stuttering incoherent apologies.

"It can't be," he sputtered. "What are you doing here?"

Halston brought the man closer to his face. The man squealed as Halston's glow started to make his skin sizzle. "Tunes, open the Gate, or I break your neck."

Koa felt chills run up her spine at Halston's change of voice. He sounded dangerous. His voice lowered to a deep, grating tone that made her shudder. She was almost too afraid to stand by when Halston was in this state. Right now, he wasn't a friend, or a boss. Right now, he was much more. He was what he hid from the world. Halston was his true self.

"Master," Tunes said in disbelief. He nodded and Halston set him back on his feet. He bowed low and backed away from the oppressive heat.

Koa stared at Halston, her jaw hanging. Now she knew what it meant… to be an angel.

Tunes ran a hand across his burned and blackened face. When he rubbed it once, the skin smoothed and appeared much younger than it had before. He ran over to the Gate.

"Master, I wasn't expecting you back so soon. My apologies." He kept bowing as he made his way over to the Gate. His back was curved like that of a hunchback. He used his violin's bow as a key.

A loud lock clanked and the Gates pushed outward to open the path into the Netherworld. A swift wind blew by them and Koa shivered at the howling she heard it carry. Tunes bowed his head to Halston and peered at Koa. He blinked and his eyes changed. He looked at her with only sockets for eyes.

"Koa," Halston warned. "Stop looking at him. He's toying with you."

Koa grimaced as she noticed that he didn't have any eyeballs, just hollow holes that looked wet with a thick inky substance. He blinked again and his eyes returned, more bulbous this time. She winced.

"They've been waiting for you," Tunes whispered. He grinned at her. He had too many teeth to fit in his rancid mouth. His foul breath wafted to her nostrils. He smelled as though he had just feasted on raw fish and rotten eggs.

Koa looked away in disgust to the Gate at the narrow path. All that she could see was a world of darkness and she could already feel the bitter cold. Her heart thumped as she followed Halston into what appeared to be a cave.

She felt exposed when the cold air cut into her. There was a brief moment of doubt as to whether this was truly a good idea. There was no turning back.

Koa heard a low cackle as the Gate slammed behind them.

Koa's eyes widened in terror, as Shadows, black and wispy, appeared on both sides of the narrow corridor. She stiffened with a gasp as they reached out for her.

CHAPTER 19

SHRILL SOUNDS FILLED Koa's head. She covered her ears with her hands and turned to face an army of Shadows. The Shadows reached out for Koa with their thin, black hands that were all knuckles and knobs. She coiled back against the Gate and felt the cold steel press into her shoulder blades. The darkness of the cavern was only aided by Halston's angelic glow.

Koa's scream was trapped in her throat. She started to tremble as she stared into their faces in horror. This was the very moment from her nightmares.

They had no eyes. They looked to be draped in a black film, as if they'd been suffocated by a black plastic bag. They howled and their mouths opened in wide circles revealing red, lizard-like tongues. Koa gasped and reached for Halston.

He hissed. "Stay back, Koa!"

"Halston," she whispered, afraid to move. "What is happening?"

Halston motioned for her to stand behind him. "You're new to them. They want you." His glow intensified. "Step back, Koa." She was blinded and felt the heat of his shield on her face. The rings of light shot up and down his body and the Shadows backed away with a piercing shriek.

Halston glared at them. They hissed at him. His glare didn't falter until the Shadows made a path for them. They all lined up on either side of the path, and bowed.

Koa opened her eyes. She watched, wide-eyed, as the Shadows froze in their deep bows. Even though they were completely still, Koa could tell that they were still staring at her. Their heads were all turned to her. There was silence in the cavern. Koa could hear her own heartbeat.

She was in awe that they were all bowing to Halston. Sometimes, Koa forgot just how powerful he was. In the mortal world, he lived the life of a man. Yes, Halston was her leader, but even then she treated him as little more than her best friend.

She felt a wind. "Something touched me," Koa squeaked, and clutched Halston's waist. His light stung her. Koa shrieked and pulled her arms away. Her arms were burnt. The sting of her burns cut to her bones. She groaned and held them, trying to suppress the pain.

Halston shot her a look of concern and nodded for her to take a step back. Koa should have listened. She was stunned. She rubbed her burnt arm until it healed itself.

Her stomach bubbled with worry. She wanted to turn back.

There was so much doubt in her head that she began to forget why she had come. "Halston," Koa called.

Halston looked at her, forcing a smile. "You wanted this. I tried to warn you. But you never listen, do you?"

Koa swallowed hard. She didn't know what to say.

"But I won't let anything happen to you. I promise." He stepped beside her and motioned for her to go ahead. He cleared his throat. "All right, we can make it through the first cavern to the Wilds if I keep my shield up."

Koa looked uncertain. Her eyes scanned the hundreds of Shadows and darted back to Halston's face.

Koa frowned. "I am sorry." She looked down the narrow path toward the faint light at the end of the dark tunnel. "For making you come back here."

Halston shrugged. "It was bound to happen sometime. We've been preparing for years. We knew that one day you'd seek out the truth."

Koa looked at him. "We?"

Halston sighed. "There's a lot that you don't know." He looked down the path. "Honestly, I wish you never had to find out the truth, but that's just not an option. You're the key to many things. There are a few of us, powerful creatures, who have been protecting you, and watching over you in secret. We've made plans, and now, it's time to execute them."

Koa thumbed the hilt of her sword. It comforted her, knowing that it was only a flick of a wrist away. She wasn't comforted, however, to feel it pulsing in madness. There was evil all around. Her Lyrinian sword begged to be unsheathed.

Koa nodded. "So, you always knew you'd have to let me come here someday?"

"I did."

"And you made me beg you all of these years."

Halston ran a hand through his hair. He pursed his lips and his brows furrowed. "Well, I had to... to make sure that you were ready."

Koa forced a smile. "You sneaky bastard."

Halston returned the smile. He seemed relieved by her reaction. "So, are you ready then?"

Koa cracked her neck and rolled her shoulders. She took a deep breath and composed herself. There was a sudden surge of courage that she could only assume came from Halston's reveal.

Although Shadows waited on either side of her, she felt a little more in control. She gave a nod to Halston and he stepped back. She walked ahead and felt the breeze catch her hair. It blew fiercely and she felt the sting on her cheeks as her eyes adjusted to the darkness. She looked far down the path, toward the only exit. There waited another ring of terror. She said a silent prayer and looked back at Halston.

"I am." She took another step forward.

Koa felt an unseen force seize her body; with a guttural scream, she was catapulted ahead.

*   *   *

Koa was still screaming when she was dropped onto hard packed dirt. Halston was leaning over her. He let his shield down so that he could touch her.

Koa looked up, breathless, and in hysterics. "What was that?" Koa shouted. Her entire body felt cold. She was shaking.

Halston gave her a sheepish look. He helped her to her feet. "I apologize. I forgot to warn you about the Jem."

Koa gave him a perplexed look as she rubbed the gooseflesh from her arms. "What the hell is a Jem?"

Halston cleared his throat. He held her across the waist and turned her around.

Koa paled. They were in a mountainous valley where dim lights were scattered about the ground like tiny, circular electric disks planted in the dirt.

She assumed that it was female, only because of the bone structure of its face. But its glowing eyes stared at her from beneath the hood of its dark cloak. It held a rod with a jagged point at the top. It was red and dripped with blood. Koa gulped.

She spoke out of the side of her mouth, whispering, yet keeping her eyes locked on the creature before her. "What is that?"

Halston nodded to the creature. "A Jem. Guardians of the rings here in the Netherworld."

Koa was too afraid to move, least of all nod. "What does it want?" Her eyes were stuck on the Jem's eyes. They glowed from the inside outward, as if tiny light bulbs were placed in the sockets instead of eyeballs. Koa couldn't break her gaze.

Halston let her go and she clung to his arm. She wouldn't let go of his shirt, even when he tugged at it. "Let go," he told her gently. "It's okay."

Koa was hesitant, but she pulled her arm away and gripped her sword.

Halston turned his shield back on and the Jem took off its hood. The Jem had short yellow hair that matched the glow of her eyes. The wild tresses changed colors as it stood in the path of Halston's shield.

Koa was surprised to find this creature beautiful, even though it wasn't human, or like any type of creature she'd ever seen.

The Jem closed its eyes in bliss and Koa watched it grow younger and younger. The wrinkles smoothed out in her face and her hair grew longer and longer. When the Jem opened her eyes, she smiled. Her eyes still glowed, but now they glowed blue. Her hair was now blue as well.

Halston nodded to the Jem and she bowed. Koa blinked and the Jem vanished.

"Halston."

"What?"

"You're a terrible guide."

Halston chuckled.

"What just happened? Where are we now?"

"Well, like I said, Jems are guardians of the rings, they make sure unauthorized nephilim don't make it into the Netherworld, and that nothing leaves without permission. You are half Netherworld vamp, and heir to the Northern Dominance's throne. Not only that, but my presence with you cancels all doubt. I outrank everyone in the Netherworld because I am a pure angel."

Koa sat down. She was very tired. She didn't even know how long or how far that Jem had taken her. "I see." She looked up. "What happened with its face and hair?"

"I blessed her."

Koa shook her head. "I'm too tired to even try to make sense of what you just said." She rubbed her temples and groaned. She could barely see straight.

Halston let his shield dim. "Let's get off the road, so that no one sneaks up on us." He noted the look on her face. "Don't worry. I'll keep watch while you sleep, but we need to get to higher ground."

Koa grumbled and came to her feet. She didn't know why she was so tired, but she could barely keep her eyes open now.

"You still haven't told me where we are." She walked along the path, beside Halston.

"The Valley of the Jem. You'll probably see many of them, but don't worry. My presence will keep them away."

Koa sucked her teeth. "Of course it will."

He chuckled again. "Yes, you must be tired, we've been traveling for nearly thirty-four hours now."

"You're joking!"

He shook his head, with a smug grin. At least he had his humor back, but Koa's patience was growing thin. "Jems move fast. I move even faster."

"I don't remember a thing."

Halston shrugged and continued on. "Excellent. Now, let's go."

If she had known it was going to be so cold, she would have brought a jacket. She clutched her arms and scampered ahead. She followed Halston along the rocky path that led to a small opening in the mountain. The rocks and stones shimmered beneath the light of his shield. The gray stone went from dull to the brilliance of diamonds.

Sleep overtook her before she could fight it.

CHAPTER 20

KOA WOKE when a brisk wind blew her hair into her eyes. She rolled over and felt Halston's angelic shield warm her face. It was nice, like a warm fire. She yawned and sat up. She felt sore all over. She grimaced and rubbed her shoulder. She'd been sleeping with a rock underneath her.

Halston heard her and glanced over his shoulder. "Everything all right?"

Koa nodded and rubbed her eyes. She brushed her bangs from her lashes and scooted closer to him.

"Can you let your shield down for a second?"

Halston gave her a look. "Would you like to be snatched away again?"

Koa sighed. She shook her head and warmed her hands as close to his shield as she could. "No. Not really."

Halston gave her a side grin. "It's kind of nice to see you need me."

Koa couldn't help it. She returned the grin. She couldn't deny the power such a simple gesture had on her, even when she was angry, even when she was afraid.

"It doesn't happen very often," she teased.

He lifted a brow. "I protect you more than you know, Koa."

Koa met his gaze. "Do you now?"

Halston nodded, gave her an odd look that made his grin fade, and looked away. Koa didn't like that look. She was left with questions that she was too afraid to ask. She followed his gaze to the Valley of the Jem. She tensed. She didn't realize that she could actually see them gliding along the road, with their pikes, searching, patrolling.

Their feet didn't seem to touch the black pathway that was lit with those odd, circular bulbs. Koa leaned forward, nearly over the edge of the cliff as she watched them.

The Valley of the Jem actually had trees. They were black, and charred, but trees nonetheless. She could even catch a faint glimmer of a river. Koa squinted in the darkness. She'd never imagined that the Netherworld was such an odd depiction of the human world. It was a darker version, but it obviously mirrored the human world.

"So," Koa began as she continued watching the Jem. "How much longer do we have to walk before we reach the center?"

"About half a day."

Koa rubbed her arms. She wished that Halston would put his arms around her. She gave him a sidelong glance. "I missed you, Halston. More than I thought I ever could," Koa whispered. She didn't know where she had the courage, but she needed him to know how she felt.

Halston grinned and looked at her with longing. Koa held her breath. Everything inside of her waited.

"I think I missed you more," he said softly.

Koa smiled. She felt warm joy fill her heart. She felt like she could say anything.

"So, what was it like when you lived in the Netherworld?"

Halston's grin faded. Koa realized that she had chosen to say the wrong thing. She gripped the space between her eyes and winced. She shook her head then looked at him with one eye open. "Sorry. Bad timing, I guess."

Halston was silent for a long while. Koa was about to apologize again, thinking that he didn't hear her.

"It was bad."

Koa nodded, hoping that he would elaborate. "You don't like to talk about it?"

Halston looked down. "It's something that I am not proud of."

"We all make mistakes, Halston."

Halston shot her a glare that made her coil back. Her face flushed. "Don't compare petty mortal mistakes to what I did. You were born with sin. I was not. I was created to be perfect. I was supposed to be better."

Koa covered her mouth. His face went red with anger. Koa watched in terror as his shield went from gold to red as well, and his face was covered in black veins that moved like worms.

He almost looked like… Bund. Koa screamed. The scream echoed throughout the valley.

Halston's shield vanished and he caught her in his arms. She was shaking. She opened her eyes to see that his were closed.

His eyes were squeezed shut. He was focusing. The black veins slowly started to dissipate. He held her tightly, as if he needed her for strength. Koa was afraid, but she managed to stay still until he returned to normal.

She wrenched out of his embrace and came to her feet. She stumbled backward and caught herself with her hands. She slowly stood. Koa was afraid and worried for Halston.

After a moment, his shield returned to its prior intensity.

Halston's voice was as low as a whisper. "I'm sorry, Koa, for yelling." He put his face in his hands and rubbed his forehead. "It's just that I was a perfect angel when I was tricked into leaving heaven. I immediately saw my error when I arrived on Earth, and by then, it was too late to go back." Tears filled his ice-blue eyes. "I had already disobeyed. I wasn't allowed to return. I had lost God's favor."

She watched him with a deep sadness. Still, she was shaken up by what had just happened, Koa wanted nothing more than to take him in her arms and hold him close to her.

"Instead of trying to win back His favor, I took the darker path, and I am regretful of that."

Koa nodded as she bit the inside of her lip. She knew why he worked so hard. "That's why you do what you do, Halston. You do so much for the humans so that you can go home. I get it. I really do."

Halston sighed. Silence passed between them.

Pressing her luck, Koa pointed at his face. "What happened… when your shield turned red and your face got all weird?"

"Let's just say, you should never make an angel angry. Things don't go so well."

Koa shivered. She covered her arms with her hands and hugged herself. "I've never seen you that angry."

Halston looked up at her. He seemed embarrassed. He wouldn't make eye contact. "Only you can do that to me." He glanced at her. "For some reason, you do something to me that makes me forget my composure."

Koa frowned. She wasn't sure if that was a good thing or a bad thing. "Um. Okay. Thanks…"

Halston chuckled and shook his head while lowering his shield. To her delight, he pulled her close and held her to his chest.

He kissed her forehead and held her there for a moment. Koa closed her eyes and enjoyed that moment of closeness with him.

When he pulled from her he motioned to the smooth rock she had been sitting on before. "Sit down. You needn't fear me. I could never hurt you, Koa. I swear it."

Koa believed him, despite what she had just witnessed. The look in his eyes struck terror into her very soul. She took a deep breath and returned to her seat.

"So, why is it that I can make you that angry, Halston?" Koa spoke in a soft voice; it was almost timid, and she didn't recognize her own voice in that tone. There was something that she wanted to hear from him. She was excited, and yet fearful at the same time. Her stomach filled with anxiety.

"I don't know. I guess I care about you too much. Your opinion of me matters too much."

Koa sat up straighter. They locked eyes. "You care?"

Halston just nodded, then broke their gaze. He didn't look back at her. "Go on. Go back to sleep now. We will need to move quickly tomorrow."

Koa let out a long sigh, her hopes dashed. She nodded and snuggled into the little pocket of soft dirt where she had been sleeping. She lay there for a while. Tomorrow she would meet Jax. She would learn about her past.

Koa felt like she was waiting for Christmas morning—all giddy with excitement. She looked up at the dark sky of the Netherworld. No stars. No moon. Just faint streaks of light crisscrossed in every direction. She fell asleep trying to make sense of the pattern. The melody that Tunes played repeated over and over as she dreamed of Shadows and Bund's face over hers.

CHAPTER 21

HOURS ROLLED BY like days. Not being able to tell time made Koa feel anxious. She was tired of walking. The soles of her feet hurt and she almost took her boots off to give her bare feet a chance. There were actually bugs everywhere. Odd, giant, cockroach-looking bugs that made Koa decide to keep her boots on and deal with the pain.

Koa watched them skitter across the black path, busy with whatever it was insects did. Their red-striped bodies made Koa grimace. She kicked one off the path and shuddered when it took flight.

"Gross."

Koa heard a faint whistling sound. Her ears perked up to better hear. She narrowed her eyes as she saw a light approaching them. Halston stopped on the craggy path and held a hand out for Koa to do the same. "Wait."

A swoosh of air made Koa's hair blow furiously past her face. Whatever flew past them cast a dim light onto their surroundings. Koa drew her Lyrinian sword.

Halston stood his guard and they watched as a woman landed before them. She had blood-red hair, shaved on one side revealing a set of cryptic tattoos. The other side was long and wavy, reaching her elbow.

Koa stared at the woman and positioned her feet in a battle stance. Her Lyrinian sword was held ready. The power started to pulse within her veins. The feeling was intoxicating.

The woman smiled. It wasn't a friendly smile. Her eyes were large and a dark blue. Koa held her breath when the woman drew her own sword, massive and curved like a hook. The mists curled around it as she held it toward Koa's face.

"Don't draw that sword little girl. Unless… you plan on using it." Her lips curled into a grin that made Koa uneasy. The woman reached out toward Koa with her other hand.

Koa swung her sword up with lightning speed. It rested at the tip of the woman's throat.

"Oh, don't worry. I intend on using it."

The woman's smile widened, revealing perfect white teeth. She withdrew her hand. "Feisty. We might get along." Her eyes turned down to look at Koa's blade. She didn't move as Koa expected. Instead, she held her position before Koa's sword, and turned her gaze up to Halston's.

"What took you so long?"

Koa's eyes went from Halston to the woman. Her heart raced. She stared at the tip of her own sharp blade. Halston didn't draw his infinity gun as she expected. He stood completely still, and let his shield fade.

Koa felt her fury intensify. Why wasn't he protecting her? He just stood there.

Before Koa could react, the red-haired woman grabbed Koa's blade with her hands and yanked it from her. She held both swords and ignored Koa's frustrated gasp. She was quick… quicker than Koa.

No, the bitch just caught me off guard, she reassured herself.

"Stop playing around, Evina," Halston said as he glanced at Koa's angry face.

Evina stepped closer to Halston with a lascivious grin. "Oh, golden boy," she purred, pressing her large bosom into his chest. She played with a lock of his hair and he pulled his face away. "Who said that I was playing?"

Koa was furious. The woman had disarmed her as if she were a child with a plastic toy sword. Her cheeks reddened. She wanted to smack that smug look off Evina's face.

Koa noticed that Evina wore very little clothing. Her black and red corset pushed her bosom nearly up to her chin, and her tiny waist was wrapped with a belt loaded with weapons. She wore leather gaiters that reached to her thigh and a thin cloth that draped her front and back. She looked like something out of one of those fantasy books Koa had read as a child.

Koa didn't like how Evina was leering at Halston. Her brows furrowed and she balled up her fists. Koa's nails cut into her palms. She felt her ears grow hot.

"I didn't think you'd actually bring her back." Evina looked Koa up and down. She tilted her head with a curious look. "She still looks like a child."

Halston cleared his throat. He seemed uncomfortable. "Koa, meet Evina... princess of the Central Dominance of the Netherworld. Prince Jax's sister."

"Better known as Lyrinia," Evina said with a smile. She watched Koa expectantly.

Koa didn't return the smile, but she couldn't help catching the connection between Lyrinia and her Lyrinian sword.

Koa's perplexed look made Evina laugh. It was a seductive laugh that made Koa cringe. Evina tossed Koa's sword onto the rocky path as if it were rubbish. She stroked Halston's cheek, giving him a lingering look. She stepped out onto the path.

"A lot has changed since you left, Halston. I have changed. Jax has changed. But one thing remains the same. Father." Evina's eyes darkened when she mentioned King Greggan.

Halston nodded. "I knew Jax would be punished for what he did. We all did."

Evina watched Koa. Koa felt uncomfortable. She wondered what Jax had done to be punished. She frowned and looked at Halston instead, hoping Evina would stop staring at her. There was something about the vampire princess that Koa didn't like, and it wasn't just the fact that she was a pretty girl.

"When is the last time you saw your father?" Halston put his hands in his pockets and awaited an answer.

Evina looked past him, toward the Gate. She looked frightened for a second. "Not long." She looked back at them. "We'll talk more once we reach the city."

"Halston." Koa pulled Halston to the side. "What is happening right now? Why is she here?"

Halston glanced at Evina and whispered to Koa. "She's our guide to Jax."

Koa frowned up at him and put her hands on her hips. "Does she know that I intend to kill him?"

Halston made a face. He shook his head. "I don't think you understand why we're here, Koa. No one is killing Jax. We need him."

Koa dropped her hands to her sides. "What?" She'd been going over in her head just how she would kill the vampire prince. She would force him to change her mother back and then stake him. It was a simple plan. Why was Halston getting in the way?

Halston shushed her and she felt her rage simmer again. She narrowed her eyes at him. She hated being treated like a child.

"Don't you want him to break your mother's curse?"

Koa bit the inside of her lip and nodded. She tried to control her tone. "Of course. But, he's evil. Why can't I kill him after he breaks the curse?"

"Has she lost her mind," Evina asked as she glared at Koa. "You will not lay a finger on my brother."

Koa gave Evina a look, rolled her eyes, and looked back to Halston. "Can I hit her? Just once?" She held her hands up as in prayer. "Please…"

Halston sighed. "You'll understand why we simply cannot kill him soon enough. You'll know why once you meet him."

"Done whispering? How rude," Evina said. Koa could picture herself just flying over to Evina, grabbing her hair, and smacking her around—just a little bit—enough to make her shut up.

Halston turned to her. "Where is Jax kept prisoner?"

Evina picked up a black disc of some sort, and stepped onto it. She was lifted into the air. She hovered and waited. Evina folded her arm across her chest and tossed her hair out of her face. "Well, he was kept in the dungeons back at the palace, until he got free. Now, father keeps him in the Ivory Tower. Do you know how long it took to get him free from the palace?"

"What is the Ivory Tower?" Koa asked Halston in a whisper. She didn't want Evina to know how ignorant she was about this place.

Halston sighed. "It's a prison full of the Netherworld's most notorious, and dangerous, criminals."

"The most *notorious* and *dangerous* criminals," Koa repeated. She folded her arms and nodded. "Right… and we're supposed to trust this guy?"

"My, my. What a little, sarcastic bitch," Evina muttered.

Koa realized that she was just standing there, glaring at the woman, when Halston picked up her sword from the ground and handed the hilt to her.

"Come on, Koa. Take your sword."

Koa was too angry to speak. She accepted the sword wordlessly. She wanted to do something to that woman. The fact that she was the sister of one of her enemies didn't help.

Halston took her hand again. He gave it an affectionate squeeze. She looked up at him and let out a long breath, trying to push out all of her anger.

Koa shook her head. Why was she so bothered? She should not let Evina get to her in this way.

Halston brought his mouth close to her ear. "Calm yourself, Koa. You brought me here to protect you. I will do just that. But you must remain calm."

Koa nodded, her eyes locked on Evina's back. "Got it. But I don't know what I'll do if she touches my sword again."

Halston put up a finger. He had an intense look in his eyes. "Koa, listen to me." He held her by her forearms and brought her close to his face.

Koa sucked in a breath and looked into his blue eyes.

"You will do nothing. If you harm a hair on her head, an army will be on our heels within seconds. I cannot fend off an entire army. I brought you here because there is something you need to know. I agreed because you have to see it for yourself. The world is about to change, Koa. I will not let you run in there recklessly and get yourself killed. I've let you make too many bad decisions in order to teach you a lesson, but this time, you will listen to me. There is a plan, and we will stick to it."

Koa couldn't help but nod. There was no room for protests. His tone dared her to even utter a word against him. Halston searched her eyes to make sure that she really understood the severity of his words. When he was satisfied with what he saw, he let her go.

Koa gave Evina a sidelong glance and turned her back to her. "Well, what's this glorious plan you speak of?"

Halston straightened his jacket, covering his infinity gun properly. "Jax will tell you."

Koa glared ahead. "But!"

Halston raised a hand and she paused. Her shoulders slumped. He pointed to Evina. "What did I just say?"

Koa folded her arms and looked down at her feet. She nodded and bit the inside of her lip. She was a little angry for being scolded, but she hid a smile. Surprisingly, she was also a little turned on to have him exerting his power over her. She almost wanted him to grab her by the arms, and pull her close to him again. She hoped that he didn't see her grin.

Koa cleared her throat and glanced at Evina. She hovered in the air, watching them with her arms folded across her chest. Koa couldn't help but think that Evina looked like something you'd see in a comic book, perfectly mysterious and beautiful up there.

"Can we get on with it now?" Evina said. "I'm not a babysitter…"

Halston held his hand out toward the path. "Show us the way."

Evina grinned. "With pleasure. Jax is probably shaking with excitement in there."

Koa followed behind Halston and Evina and she looked in awe as the smothering, cavern-like path, opened into a large dome that buzzed with flying beings. There were so many lights that she was blinded. She shielded her eyes from the glowing palace in the center of the valley. She nearly tripped as the path became a narrow set of stairs.

Koa caught herself and she looked down to see the stairway plunge deeper into the dark depths below. She looked around to see that hundreds of other caverns opened up to similar stairways all around the dome. At the bottom of the stairs was a city.

There were skyscrapers and clustered buildings everywhere. This was the home of the nephilim, a safe haven for all that was inhuman. As they walked down the steep stairway, Koa examined the bright, gold-plated palace that stood in the center of the city. This was the place that haunted her dreams. Koa had been there before, she just couldn't remember why.

Golden towers stretched upwards, taller than the contrasting black skyscrapers. Like a sunflower in a field of rubble, the palace stood out. Hundreds of clustered buildings littered the city, and yet Koa was certain that from wherever you were in the city, that you could always see the palace. There were what appeared to be thousands of windows that reflected more light onto the city around it.

Hours seemed to pass until they reached the bottom of that staircase. By the time they reached the cobblestone platform, Koa had gone over her own plan in her head a million times. She wanted to see Jax's face as she lopped off his head.

Koa glanced at Halston. She was torn. She wanted to trust him and do as he said, but Jax had hurt her mother; how could let him live, even after he broke the curse? She would never be able to forgive him for what he did.

Cloaked beings walked past her. They almost knocked her off the platform at the bottom of the staircase and into the next level that waited underneath. She tensed when she realized what they were. They were Jems. Dozens of them. She could see the glow of their eyes.

Koa looked away. They ignored her as they hurried by with their pikes, ready to rip right through whoever dared try their luck at escaping the Netherworld. Koa related them to squads of police, patrolling the streets.

Halston whispered to her. "Just pretend like you belong here."

Koa frowned. "What did you think I would do, Halston? Fly around screaming, I'm the bloody half-blood you've all been waiting for?"

Halston gave her a look and straightened his shoulders. "Very well. I don't want to spend more time here than we have to, but there are preparations to be made. You'll go with Evina and I'll meet up with you two in a few hours."

Koa put her hand onto Halston's chest and grabbed the front of his shirt. "Wait a minute! You never said that I would have to be alone with that skank!"

Evina jumped off her disc and everyone within view gave a deep bow before hurrying off. She slid right up to Koa and bumped her with her chest. Evina was thin, tall, but solid muscle. She nearly knocked Koa backwards but caught her by wrapping an arm around her waist. She grinned down at Koa and locked arms with her.

Koa held her breath. She looked down at Evina's large bosom as it rose and fell with her breaths. She looked back up at her grinning face. Evina was so close, that Koa could smell her breath. She smelled like summer rain. It was sickening how alluring the woman was. How could anyone resist her?

Evina winked at Halston. "I'll take good care her." She locked eyes with Koa and pulled her closer into her body. "I promise I won't bite," she whispered to Koa.

Koa swallowed. She was frozen in a mixture of shock, rage, and arousal. Her first reaction had been to upper cut Evina in the jaw, but now… she stared at Evina in confusion.

Halston shook his head and muttered something under his breath. "We don't have time for games Evina, just take her to the docks and prep her for me. I'll come back with the materials we need to get her into the prison."

Koa's eyes widened, and so did Evina's grin.

CHAPTER 2

HALSTON STOOD in the center of the crowd as he watched Evina walk away with the only person for whom he had ever had real feelings. Yes, he fought for the humans and vowed to protect them for an eternity, but there was something more when it came to Koa. She stirred something in him that he should not feel as an angel. Love and compassion he had been created with, but whatever he felt for Koa went much deeper. He experienced physical pain whenever she was hurt or upset.

Halston couldn't explain it, not even after thousands of years of life on Earth. He watched the two women until they disappeared around a corner. His throat tightened as Koa glanced back one last time. Their eyes met, even though there was quite a distance between them. Like a bolt of electricity, her gaze burned into him. He was certain he saw a reflection of his own feelings within her eyes, but he could never be sure. He could never tell her. It would be the end of him if he did.

He sighed and his shoulders slumped as he stood there, alone, yet surrounded by the abominable spawn of his brothers and sisters. There was much to be done. Someone had to put the world back in order.

Everything rested on him. He waited. He kept checking his watch, as an hour passed; finally, he glanced over toward the direction that Koa and Evina walked and saw the signal.

It was done.

Halston cut through the masses and made his way to one of the staircases that led to the path toward the Gate. He paused at the bottom of those stone steps that had been built thousands of years ago. It was time to summon all those who had sworn secret allegiance to him and his cause.

He felt around in his jacket's inner pocket. He felt something cool and gripped it. Halston took out a pen. It was long and silver, and caught the light that came from the Disc Moon. It was a dim disc that stood at the very top of the dome, shedding light onto each level of the world and regulating time, so that everyone within its range aged much slower.

Halston hoped that one day Koa might forgive him, for keeping so much a secret. *It was all to protect her*, Halston thought. He took a deep breath and straightened his shoulders. It wasn't all for Koa. She was a big part of it, but he couldn't deny that it was supposed to be for the human race, and Koa had somehow taken precedence over even that. Still, he had done what was right by bringing her back—at least he hoped he had.

Koa was returned to the place where she belonged. Now, it was time to set other events in motion.

Halston pointed the thin tip of the silver pen before him and narrowed his eyes. A tiny blue light blinked, then glowed steadily. He swept the pen up gracefully, and wrote along the darkness before him. The air tightened, examining the light that sliced into it. Halston tried again, drawing with a delicate curve of his wrist as if he was painting a masterpiece. The darkness accepted the script, upholding tiny blue text.

The soft wind whistled as if curious about this oddity. Like an inquisitive child, it gathered around Halston and made his jacket flap open. His infinity shotgun was revealed. Annoyed, Halston covered it back up with his free hand and continued his message. The wind seemed to shiver with glee and floated each word along. It carried his message up the steps and down the tunnel, back to the human world. It was time to notify his Netherworld agents that it was time to recruit.

Raven knew her role in this. She would be waiting. She was never human, nor vampire. She was something... different. Something that would change both worlds. Now, it was her time to shine.

Halston finished his message and lowered the pen. He hoped that Raven was ready, that she would uphold her part of the bargain. So much depended upon Raven and her daughter. They were like two secret keys that the evil of the world fought to swallow.

Halston tightened his jaw. He hated to think of what was ahead for Koa. He could imagine that she was afraid, and yet hiding it very well. She was good at that. He almost smiled. She would be all right. He had taught her well.

Halston looked up toward the cavern. It was a cool night in the Netherworld. It was always a cool night. Daylight didn't exist here. Each level of this world led to more darkness and even more horrific creatures.

Vampires, demons, War-Breeders, ghouls, and fallen angels like himself buzzed by. They came and went up those stairs, returning to their homes in the maze-like city that was the Netherworld.

Halston shot a look at a flash of light. He let his guard down when Evina stopped before him.

"What do you think she'll do when she finds out the truth?" Evina hopped off her flying disk and stepped before him. She had a serious face. She had put her life at risk for Koa, but she could never resist a little challenge. He had almost thought that Evina would ruin everything with her little show in front of Koa.

The creatures around fled. Vampire mothers grabbed their children and ran into the safety of the many alleys.

Evina was daughter of King Greggan, a very powerful vamp, and they feared her even when she was nothing like her father.

Halston put his hands in his pocket. He took them out and folded his arms. He couldn't get Koa's face out of his head. That beautiful little face haunted him. There was no way that he could forget the first time he laid eyes on her. He felt his insides twist.

"Everything will work out according to plan. It has to." He raised a brow. "She's already asleep?"

Evina folded her arms across her large bosom and tossed her hair out of her face. "Of course. I'm not a novice, Halston."

"No. You're a temptress, and you cannot resist games."

"I don't have another century to wait. I wouldn't put the plan in jeopardy."

Halston raised a hand, shushing her. He listened to something.

She frowned. "As I was saying... games. I don't have time for them."

"But you love them more than anything."

She fought a grin. Instead, Evina sighed and turned her face. "You really think you know me. Just because I had a crush on you as a girl doesn't give you the upper hand. I'm not a child anymore. I've been a woman for quite a while now."

Halston smirked. "You had a crush on me?"

"You're horrible, Halston." She gave a soft laugh and looked at him with a warmness that she didn't reveal to many. "I cannot believe that I am actually entrusting my life to you—and my brother's."

"You are a smart woman for doing so. You need me. Therefore you will follow me to the end. Right?"

Evina didn't answer. She met his gaze and searched his eyes. She gave a slight nod and pulled her disc from her belt. Like a fan, she flicked it out and set it down. It buzzed and hovered.

With a quick hop onto the disc, she looked down at Halston. "I'm going back to check on things."

"No meddling. You can 'check,' but that is all. Don't use too much of your power on her. I don't want her remembering things just yet. It's best that we let Jax open Pandora's box."

Evina grinned. "Ah, don't worry, love. I won't harm her. I promise."

Shaking his head, he watched her fly away, above the masses. His mind went to Evina's brother. Jax was prince of the Lyrinia, the Central Dominance of the Netherworld and locked away for all eternity. He cringed. All of the things Jax would tell Koa could undo Halston.

Koa still believed that the night he found her drunk on a park bench had been the first time they'd met. Halston could never bring himself to tell her that he had known her since she was a child. Furthermore, he couldn't tell her that she had, in fact, been poisoned that night he found her and fed her the antidote while she slept.

At that time, telling her the truth had been out of the question. If she knew that he had been watching her for decades, secretly protecting her, she'd believe that he was some sort of stalker. It was ironic that their little joke, the nickname she had given him, was truer than she could have imagined. Somehow, Halston had become... her guardian angel.

"Halston," a familiar voice called.

Halston turned. His message had worked more quickly than he had anticipated. Halston turned and his gaze went up to a man who was a descendent of the giants. His eyes widened at the sight of a familiar, welcome face.

CHAPTER 23

"HOLY SHIT," the War-Breeder exclaimed. Seven feet tall and all muscle, the War-Breeder rubbed his eyes and stared at Halston in disbelief. "It is you! Is it time?"

Halston wasn't sure how to react when Tristan, his oldest friend, beamed at him. He had expected him to show up.

Tristan looked the same. No one down here really aged, unless they went up to the human world, where the sun had its effects. Tristan's bald head was tattooed, a common trend in the Netherworld, to display your social standing in its ancient hierarchy. His skin was a deep bronze, as if he had an eternal tan.

Scars covered almost every inch of his flesh. The scars didn't come from battle. Tristan never lost a fight, or a war for that matter. No, those scars were from a ritual from his childhood. His own mother was forced to do that to him, to teach him about pain, so that he'd never experience it again. The ritual lasted as long as the child could stand it. The instant they started to cry from the pain, the mother could stop.

Tristan never cried. The ritual had gone on and on. He had become a legend, and his mother had become the proudest woman in the village.

To Halston, it just made Tristan look like a runaway slave who had been whipped too many times, but to the War-Breeders, it served as a reminder that this was the strongest of their clan.

Halston sucked in a breath as he was swept off his feet by the big man. His bones nearly crunched in Tristan's abnormally strong arms. Once Tristan put him down, Halston couldn't help but return the smile. Tristan held him at arm's length. His thin brown eyes examined Halston with wonder.

"You look different," Tristan whispered with a perplexed look. Halston lowered his eyes. He was different now. He wished he could forget the past.

Tristan's look of wonder was quickly replaced with alarm. "Halston! What are you doing out here in the open? Someone will recognize you."

"Not likely," Halston said.

Tristan lifted a brow. "Right…" He folded his arms. "So, what's it been like up there with the humans?"

Halston stepped back. "You'll find out soon enough."

Tristan clapped his hands together. "Let's get on with it then! You've brought her back?"

Halston looked down at his feet. Koa. The child he had stolen.

Tristan let out a long breath. He shook his head with a side smirk. "Leave it to you, Halston, to get yourself in a mess like this, and to get me to join you. You started this war for Koa. What's so special about her? Why didn't we just leave things be?"

"I didn't start the war. I just put the inevitable in motion." Halston sighed at Tristan's expression. There was so much that even the War-Breeder couldn't know. The burden rested on Halston and his race of fallen angels. "You wouldn't understand."

"That half-blood is going to get us killed, isn't she?" Tristan shook his head. "She almost got us killed the first time we dealt with this foolhardy plan." He pointed to his chest. "I still have a nice scar to remind me."

Halston wore an eerie smile, hinging on bitterness. "I can't be killed. Remember?" If only he could, things just might be easier.

"Well, lucky you, Halston." Tristan's eyebrows bunched. He nodded. "I just love how you flaunt that when you know that I can be killed!"

Halston lifted his chin. "So what are you saying? You're no longer with me?"

Tristan rolled his eyes and shook his head. He hooked his thumb in his belt. "I'm just saying that this plan of yours had better work. Farrow got killed shortly after you escaped with the girl. She got swept up by Greggan's guard one night and decapitated in the citadel square."

Halston just stood there, feeling numb. He felt a lump in his throat.

Tristan cleared his throat. "I haven't kept touch with the others."

Halston could still picture Farrow's young face in his mind. She was one of the youngest in the crew, a Jem preparing for her final test to begin an eternity of patrolling the Netherworld. He had no idea that she was dead.

Tristan was silent for a moment. Halston straightened his shoulders when he noticed the War-Breeder staring at him. "At least it was a quick death."

Tristan nodded. "It was."

Silence. Halston felt a deep sadness for the Jem. Farrow was dead because of him. He couldn't take her with him when they took Koa. A Jem couldn't survive in the human world.

Halston shoved the guilt deeper inside the part of his heart where he kept his most valued emotions and locked it away. It would no longer bother him until he returned to unlock the vault.

Tristan tried to ease the tension. "Well, let's say we rebuild the old alliance then."

Halston looked up at the Disc Moon. It clicked and cast a darker green glow onto the kingdom. Each click, and subsequent color, was a Netherworlder's way of telling time here. It was getting later. "You're pretty eager for someone afraid of his own mortality."

Tristan took two steps over to Halston. His face brightened. "I never said all of that. You know me, I live for danger. I live to add another scar to my collection." He traced a long scar that went from his brow to the flesh beneath his right eye.

Halston found it odd how much Tristan valued his ghastly scars.

"King Greggan is trying to invade the human world, put up a fight against those soft, squishy creatures you call vamps up there. I want a piece of the action. I'm just not ready to die yet, is all."

Halston saw a flash of silver light and grabbed Tristan by his suspenders. "Shut up," he growled. "Someone will hear you." He pulled Tristan into a stone side street just as a royal guard stepped into the square. Halston caught a quick glimpse as they found cover in the darkness of an alley. The royal guard was comprised of Syths and Scayors. Halston's heart thumped when he saw the Scayor step into the square. They were tall, metallic creatures, combining Syth bodies and technology. Scayors were horrific creations. Those silver eyes were always searching, always ready to snatch someone off the streets.

Halston breathed. *That was close.* It was not yet time to blow his cover.

A group of ghouls lurked in the dank alley. They were thin, skeleton-like creatures with pasty gray skin and long, tortured faces. Hunched over and whispering, they looked up at Halston and Tristan with glowing green eyes.

Avoiding eye contact with them, Halston pulled Tristan further down the road. They stepped through black puddles of oil and slime and swatted fruit flies in silence. Tristan kept his mouth shut, but glanced at Halston as they traveled to the seedy part of the city, where the lower-ranked creatures tended to dwell. Tristan didn't question him.

Halston was, after all, the boss.

They ducked into a dark tavern. Two male vampires sat inside. Their faces were illuminated by the red overhanging lights as they looked up at the newcomers.

Halston looked up. A female vampire hung from an overhead light. Her black hair hung long as she tilted her head backward and swung as if she were on a swing. She opened her eyes and looked at them with disinterest. She closed her eyes again, fell lightly to the ground, and landed on her feet. She stood tall and walked over to them.

She lifted a brow. "Blood? Or booze?" Her voice and expression was indifferent. She had a sleepy look about her.

Tristan waited patiently, although he seemed to be on the verge of cheering. Finally, something exciting was about to happen.

Halston shook his head. "Nothing. Thank you."

She shrugged. "Suit yourself." She jumped back into the air, back to her light, and continued swinging.

Halston shook his head. "Has this place gotten weirder?"

"No, mate, you've gotten boring."

Halston slid into a booth and Tristan did the same.

Tristan grinned. "You know, I'm glad you finally came back, Halston. I was starting to get bored, anxious for a new adventure." He cracked his knuckles and Halston sighed. "I never thought you'd make me wait so long before I got to see some real action."

Halston's eyes scanned the room. "So you're still in? No turning back."

Tristan shook his head, still grinning. "Whatever gets me close to that Evina. She is still in on this, right?"

"She is."

Tristan chuckled. "Done. You have yourself a top-ranked War-Breeder. I'm in."

"How quickly can you gather vials?"

Tristan rubbed his chin. "The Alchemist works twenty-four hours. How soon do you need them?"

Halston thought a moment. He considered going to the Alchemist himself. "I need them, like, yesterday."

Tristan shook his head. "Well, you should have asked yesterday." He cracked his knuckles. "I guess I can have them by second light."

Halston nodded and thought about what Evina was doing with Koa at that moment. He shook his paranoia off and met Tristan's eyes. "That'll have to do."

"Who do you have on the outside? You'll need someone to track Greggan's thugs. You think Greggan is bad, wait until you meet his general, Bund."

Halston grimaced. "I have."

Tristan lifted a brow. "And?"

"He got away."

"Getting sloppy as well boring, I see."

Halston ignored the comment. "I don't expect this escapade with Greggan to last long."

"Look, Halston, you have an unlimited supply of blood up there. Human blood is expensive down here, and not many are even allowed out of the Gate these days. Greggan is setting up his empire to put the other levels of the Netherworld to shame."

Halston frowned. He was surprised. Tristan knew much more than he let on. He wondered how much the general Netherworld population knew.

"I plan on doing this quickly. I will hunt the renegade tyrant, kill him, and place Jax on the throne. Done. My plan is quick and efficient. I just want to be done with this all so that I can go back to my life, with Koa."

Tristan's smile faded. His hazel eyes darkened. "Oh. I get it. You fell for her?" He began to stand. "I can't do this if you make it personal. I'm not getting in between Jax and his girl. We're talking about Greggan's son here… not just any vamp. He's a damned prophet! You do know what he can do, right?"

Halston frowned. He grabbed Tristan by the arm. His eyes turned serious. "Sit down. I haven't fallen for her," he lied. He ground his teeth and Tristan stared down at him.

Tristan raised a brow. "What then? Why do this?"

Halston focused on the waitress that swung from the ceiling light. He kept his face straight, yet avoided eye contact with one of his oldest friends. "I just… care about her."

Tristan looked skeptical. "Yeah. Sure. I don't want to be around when Jax finds out you care. That little fact wasn't in the original plan." Tristan leaned across the table and spoke through clenched teeth. "You were supposed to watch and protect her, not fall in love with her."

"I know." Halston hated to admit it, but there was a lot resting on Jax's end. He wasn't sure if Jax could really be trusted.

Halston folded his arms and leaned into the leather of the booth. "Drop it, or go on, walk away. Pretend you never saw me."

Tristan shook his head but said no more.

Halston knew he would. The War-Breeder was not likely to run from a fight.

"So, who do you have on the outside? Spoons? Maybe Reddit? Or don't tell me… you found Glenda."

Halston shook his head. "No, mate." He met Tristan's eyes. "I found Al."

Tristan's eyes widened. He sat back with an amused smile. "Oh." He crossed his arms and let out a breath. He was impressed. "This is going to be *good*."

CHAPTER 24

RAVEN SAW THE MESSAGE carried along the wind and hopped to attention. She climbed out the window. She leapt across to a tree and dug her claws into the crusted bark. She glanced down into the darkness and her eyes reflected the light of the moon as she scurried down.

She had been a cat for far too long, and still, it felt odd to her. The black fur mimicked what used to be her beautiful, long black hair.

Raven always knew that she was… different. Still, she had never brought herself to reveal just how different she was. She only did what she had to do to survive. Now it seemed that she would have to do much more. She had to protect her child.

Her feline body *did* have its advantages. She could move around almost completely unseen. She bounded up and down hills and crawled across fallen logs to cross rivers and streams.

Raven had a mission. When Halston had come up with this plan years ago, she knew that he probably doubted her ability to follow through. She would not let Halston down.

Raven's only regret was that she had let Koa run off before she could fully explain things. Koa only had half of the story. She supposed that Jax would tell her the rest. That fact made her worry.

Halston and Raven had been working together for years on the plan. She prayed that Koa didn't ruin it. Halston had always watched over and protected her daughter. She hoped that he wouldn't let her down now.

Greggan was loose, and it would take an army, or a team of specially selected individuals, to track him down and kill him. She wished she had her body back, so that she could be of more help. Only Jax could give it back to her.

Raven narrowed her eyes. She needed to stay focused. She supposed she shouldn't blame herself too much. The nephilim had been trying for centuries to get back into the human world. Greggan would walk the earth, and all of humanity would suffer his wrath.

Raven paused and panted. She was tired. She had run for miles, for hours, and now, she had arrived. She needed to get things in order for Halston's return. She needed to get the rest of the crew together.

Nerves filled Raven, making her hypersensitive to the sounds of the night. Halston had intentionally kept her hidden from the other members of the crew.

Now, Raven would have her introduction to one of the most powerful of them all. There were rumors that this one had powers that rivalled even Halston's.

The wooden doors to the pub swung open with a creak. She heard loud laughing escape the swinging doors. She looked at the tall man. He had dark eyes, and wild black hair. He was big and intimidating, with a scowl plastered on his weathered face. He wore a black leather jacket and wrinkled slacks.

This can't be him.

For someone with such a notorious reputation, Raven expected someone a little more put together. Still, she could feel her senses drawing her to this place. It had to be him. It had to be the one they called Al.

Al pulled out a cigarette. He lit it and leaned against the wall outside the pub. His dark eyes looked around. Raven stood. She had to talk to him. She began to cross the street when a young woman came out of the pub. She was loud and clumsy. Her high heeled leather boots clinked along the slick asphalt with a deafeningly loud tapping noise that made Raven cringe.

Drunk, Raven thought with disapproval. *Great.* She willed the girl to go away. She had business to attend to.

The drunk girl stumbled onto the sidewalk and fell against the wall, trying to steady herself. Al gave her a sidelong glance. His gaze lingered on the young woman. She looked to be little more than a teenager. Her pale white skin was illuminated by the bright moonlight. It was a stark contrast to her short pink hair that ruffled in the faint breeze.

Raven frowned. *Of course, things can never be easy.* She urged the girl to move along. There wasn't much time. The girl laughed loudly, at nothing at all, and fell. Raven could see her panties underneath her short dress. She shook her head in dismay. She hated to think that once, Koa had been that drunk party girl.

Al grinned. He could see her panties too. He looked around, checking his surroundings. Satisfied that no one was looking, he strode over to the girl and reached out a hand. "Need some help, miss?"

The girl peered up at him and smiled. "Yes. Thank you." She was American. Her voice was thick and sultry, with a slight slur from the alcohol. She took his hand and yelped when he pulled her into his chest. He held her by her thin waist. She gave a nervous laugh and tried to pull away.

Raven narrowed her eyes. Al brought his hand to the back of her neck and turned her around. The girl tripped over her own feet. Growing impatient, Al picked her up as if she weighed no more than a child and disappeared into the darkness of the alley with her.

"Where are we going?"

Raven's eyes widened. She ran across the street. What was Al doing? She peeked around the corner to see him holding the girl by her neck and pulling up her skirt.

Raven was horrified. He was supposed to be good.

Why is he doing this? Her hopes were dashed and she sat back and sighed. The girl tried to get away, but she was too drunk.

Raven shook her head. If only she could help the poor girl. She turned away. There was nothing she could do. Al was supposed to be a Warrior. She was no match for a Warrior, an angel from the ancient times, created to keep the creatures of the Netherworld from spilling out into the human world. Raven felt her stomach churn at the girl's pleas. She begged for him to let her go, that she didn't want any trouble. She pleaded for him to stop.

Raven sighed and began to walk away when she heard a surprising crunch. It was quick and sent a frightening chill through her body. Raven tensed. It wasn't the *crunch* that surprised her… it was *Al's* cut-off scream.

Raven jumped and turned around. Her eyes widened. The girl was on Al's back. She had his head in her hands and twisted his neck. The girl held on as Al fell on his face. And then, she did something that made Raven catch her breath.

The girl *staked him*. A thin, wooden stake plunged into his back and scraped against the cold stone alleyway.

Al trembled and turned into dust.

Raven stared, stunned, as she watched that girl kneel in the remaining dust of a Warrior's body. She couldn't believe what she witnessed. It didn't make sense.

You can't stake an angel.

The girl paused. Her eyes rose to Raven's. She stared at her through chunks of pink hair. Raven stepped back, her heart thumping with horror.

Who is this girl, she wondered with panic.

The girl smiled. Raven couldn't help her curiosity. She leaned in for a closer look, prepared to take off running if necessary. She noticed for the first time that the girl had gray eyes. She finally released her grip on the stake and wiped Al's dust from her palms.

"What are you looking at, kitty?" Her voice was low, yet it felt as if it was tapping on Raven's mind like a fork tapping on glass. It was unsettling. It was unnatural.

She came to her feet.

Raven began to run away and felt herself held frozen. Raven yelped. She couldn't move. Something held her paralyzed. The girl laughed and Raven felt the fear wash over her like a cold bucket of water. She felt foolish, thinking she could be of help to Halston and his crew. She wasn't a Netherworld agent. How could she forget that she was only a cat now?

She had failed, again.

The girl leapt off Al's back and landed before Raven with such agility and speed that Raven flinched.

She stooped down and picked Raven off the ground. Raven began to raise a clawed paw when the girl gently smoothed her fur.

"Hey, now kitty, that's no way to greet a friend, is it?"

Raven perked up. She wasn't sure if she should reveal that she could speak to this anomaly of a girl. She had, after all, just killed Al once commander of the Warrior class of angels. Al wasn't a fallen angel, like

Halston, but one sent to set things right. And this girl had killed him.

The girl's smile widened. "Ah, don't be shy. I won't reveal your secret. I know who you are, and I've been expecting you. Eunju right? What took you so long?"

Raven tensed at the sound of her real name. She hadn't been called Eunju since before the transformation. She looked into the girl's eyes. Raven was perplexed.

Then it hit her. She tilted her head. "Al? You're Al?" she asked in disbelief.

The girl nodded with a grin. "Sure. Al works." She took her paw and gave it a shake. She laughed at how silly such an action looked. "I prefer friends to call me Alice."

Raven gasped. "You? You're a warrior?"

Alice nodded. "Why so surprised?" She carried Raven as she walked deeper into the darkness of the alley.

"You're so… so young!"

Alice giggled. "Oh, we both know that looks can be deceiving."

Raven was astounded. "How… how did you know I was looking for you? Halston didn't tell me much about you. He just said that I'd be led to you… when the time came. But, how?"

Alice peered into Raven's eyes. "What a good boy he is. I like it that no one really knows about me. I don't usually leave witnesses, but you can be an exception." She looked over her shoulder and paused. She listened and sighed, speeding up. "I'll tell you, since we're friends. We are friends, right?"

"I am friends with anyone that can protect my daughter."

"Splendid. Telekinesis is my secret weapon. Telekinesis sets me apart from the other warriors. This is why I was once commander. They used to call me Metal-Mind." Alice grinned at the memory. "I do miss those days. There was never a dull moment. I'd scoop up two, three, vamps at a time." She gave Raven a look. "I sure set fear into those pesky vamps, didn't I?"

Raven swallowed. She felt cold. She couldn't shake the feeling that something wasn't right.

Alice glanced down at her. "I know when someone is looking for me. I didn't become commander because of my looks." She gave a smug grin. "Although, I'm sure my looks did help."

Raven nodded. That explained how Alice made her freeze when she tried to run. Alice smiled. "Don't overthink it. I haven't been tampering with your thoughts or anything. It's just that in times like these, a girl has to be on her guard. Recruiting can be dangerous business. Especially with creeps like that guy I just killed lingering on these streets."

Raven looked up quickly. "He was a vampire, wasn't he?"

Alice nodded. She didn't speak. She looked around, scanning their narrow surroundings. She tilted her head, listening. Raven's ears perked up. There was a faint rustling sound at the back of the alley. Raven felt her heart pound at the sound of a low growl. It wasn't a dog.

Raven knew every predator now. Whatever waited in those shadows was no animal.

Before Raven could speak a word of warning, Alice bounded up the side of a stone wall, clutching Raven to her chest. Her feet seemed light and she ran along the wall of an office building like a spider, in and out of the darkness of the alley.

Raven was speechless. She tried to look back, to see if whatever had growled followed them. She coiled back, seeing eyes in the distance.

They were being chased. It was big, like a wolf, but Raven narrowed her eyes, it wasn't a wolf. The creature had no fur, just muscles wrapped tightly around bone. Claws scratched the wall as it ran behind, barely keeping up.

Alice moved quickly, like lightning. The swoosh of wind made Raven squeeze her eyes shut. She forced them open. She wanted to see where they were going. She wanted to make sure it didn't catch up with them. She could feel Alice breathing; it wasn't labored. Alice wasn't afraid.

"Hey, listen. I'm going to do something a little… crazy. You're used to crazy right, with that daughter of yours? You game?"

Raven swallowed. "S-sure." She craned her neck around. She saw the beast running through the fog, gaining on them. She remembered the night Halston had killed twelve creatures just like the one that chased them. She wished Halston was there.

Alice sucked her teeth. She frowned. "A damned reanimated man. I should have known that guy wasn't a normal vampire. Those Netherworld vamps are tricky. I don't think that big guy appreciates that stake I put in his heart." She reached a hand out and grabbed a pole above her head and catapulted them high into the air. She yelled. "Hold on!"

Raven shrieked as Alice tilted her head up to the heavens and outstretched her arms. Raven clutched to her with all of her strength, her claws firmly embedded into Alice's shirt. The beast lunged after them, and with a swirl of her arms, Alice turned herself in mid-air to face it.

Raven looked into Alice's eyes and shuddered. They had turned completely white, as if clouds moved within them. Alice turned out her hands, palms facing the beast and a sudden pop of air exploded from the small girl's body. It was like thunder, without sound, but Raven could feel her bones tremble and her teeth chatter.

There was a loud howl as the beast was torn limb from limb. Arms disconnected from shoulders, the fibers trailing along like streamers. Legs broke away from knees with a cringe-worthy popping sound. He split into a million pieces that flew out in all directions. Blood sprayed into the air and Alice's eyes returned to normal. Gray eyes glared at the carnage as she landed on her feet. Her boots made a splash in a puddle as they hit the ground.

Alice didn't stop. She wrapped her arms around Raven again and ran into the shadows. She breathed heavily then, glancing down at Raven.

"You all right, kitty?"

Raven nodded, staring at Alice's blood stained face. Pieces of bone and broken teeth were in her pink hair. Raven shivered—not from the cold, but from excitement. She was exhilarated. She looked at Alice in wonder. This was the one who could help them stop Greggan.

CHAPTER 25

KOA WOKE to find Evina staring down at her. She sat up in a panic. Her eyes darted around the room as she tried to catch her breath. The room was small, bare, and cold. A strange collection of candles hung from the ceiling. It was like a chandelier, but the candles were floating and encircling the apparatus that supported them.

"Where am I?" Koa's throat was dry. She swallowed. She felt hot. Her body was covered in sweat. "What did you do to me?"

Evina sat back in the only chair in the room, rested her elbow on the desk, and put her feet up on the bed, beside Koa. "You're at the docks. Why... don't you remember?"

Koa glanced at Evina's boots and back up to her face. The vampire's secret smile convinced her that something had indeed happened. Still, Koa could only remember being ushered away from the citadel. Now, she felt oddly at ease around the vampire princess, and she knew that she shouldn't.

Koa frowned. "What did you do to me?" Her body felt... strange. Her skin was cool and her blood seemed to rush. Her mind was a torrent of questions and memories that she couldn't make any sense of.

Evina shrugged, feigning ignorance. "I've no idea what you're talking about."

Wrong answer. Koa checked her sword and leapt off the bed. Evina was before her in a blink.

Koa glared at her. Her cheeks were hot with rage. "Move out of my way," she said through clenched teeth.

Evina held her arms out. The black tattoos seemed to move along her skin, like snakes.

Koa stepped away from her. "What are you doing?"

Evina wrapped her arms around Koa. Before Koa could react, she was asleep once more.

Koa was in a black room. The floor was red and Evina was standing in the far corner. Evina's eyes were closed. The air seemed to move around the vampire princess as she swirled her arms and sent waves of faint light toward Koa.

Koa ran at her and punched her in the face. Evina's eyes opened in shock. "What are you doing?" She was frantic. She hadn't expected that. "You're not supposed to see me in here! You're supposed to be asleep!"

Koa punched her again. She grabbed her by the hair and flung her across the room. Evina slammed into the black wall and vanished. Koa unclenched her fists. She was stunned. She was alone in the black room.

Her heart started to race.

What is going on! Koa was afraid. She had no idea where she was. She panicked. Her sword was gone.

This isn't real, Koa assured herself as she started to shake. She looked for an exit. Her hands beat the black walls and they pushed her back into the center each time. *This is not real!*

Evina reappeared and covered Koa's face with her hands. She tried to overpower her and push her to the ground, but Koa bit the flesh between her thumb and index finger and Evina pulled her hand back. Koa kicked her in the gut and Evina doubled over.

Evina flashed and appeared behind Koa. She gritted her teeth, pulled Koa's hair, and forced her to the ground.

"Stop fighting me! I'm trying to help you!"

Koa reached up and grabbed Evina by the throat. She swung a foot above her and kicked Evina in the chin. Evina bled from the lip but held her grip. Her eyes were wild with panic.

"Koa, please, stop fighting me!" Evina smothered Koa's face with her hands. "I'm trying to wake you up! You're not supposed to be lucid in this dream!"

Koa continued to fight and gasped. Something jolted into her. Evina's eyes were closed. Evina was screaming, but Koa could hear nothing but the sound of her own blood rushing to her ears.

Koa woke. She immediately drew her sword and placed the tip at Evina's throat. Evina was in tears. The vampire princess was breathless as she stared down at Koa's sword.

Koa was beyond enraged. She was past angry. Not because of what Evina had done to her, but because the Lyrinian sword refused to impale her.

Koa tried. She put force and strength behind it. The sword remained frozen. Koa growled and swirled away, sheathing the sword.

Evina was not evil. The sword would not kill an innocent being. Koa cursed under her breath. Her face was still hot from rage. She could still feel Evina's blows to her.

Evina rubbed her face, smearing blood. Koa frowned. She hadn't noticed that before.

Evina pulled her hand back and looked at the blood. Her jaw dropped. There was a look of fear in her eyes when she gazed at Koa.

"I'm sorry, Koa," Evina said, confusing Koa. "We all have our orders. Mine was to keep you safe, to keep you here, until Halston returns." Evina put her arms behind her.

Koa was silent, yet her glare was unwavering. It spoke multitudes. She was confused by Evina's sudden change in attitude. It was as if she dropped the whole, seductive, tough girl act. Maybe Koa was seeing her true self. Maybe this was the act.

Evina continued. "It just happens that I am a tempest. I cannot help what I was born to be."

Koa narrowed her eyes. "Tempest?"

Evina nodded and her blue eyes met Koa's. "I can get people to do what I want. I can make them dream what I want. Some call it persuasion down here in the Netherworld." She shrugged. "It's what I know. Never in a hundred years has anyone ever been lucid in one of my dreams. Never."

Koa thought to herself. That dream had felt pretty real.

"Koa, listen," Evina urged. "I never meant to hurt you. I swear it, on my brother's life."

Koa frowned. She didn't give a damn about her brother's life. She let out a long, slow, breath. She tried to force all of her rage out with it. It was difficult, but Koa managed to calm herself.

"When will Halston be back?" She couldn't shake the bitterness she felt. She hated being manipulated.

Evina turned the chair around and sat in it backwards, straddling it. "In an hour or so. We have to get you inside the prison before the third click of the Disc Moon." She wiped her face with a towel.

Koa cracked her knuckles and started pacing.

"Why don't you have a seat, Koa?"

Koa continued pacing. "You don't speak to me unless you have something valuable or important to say." She paused and gave Evina a look. "My Lyrinian sword may not work on you, but you better believe that my hands will go smoothly around your throat and squeeze the life out of you."

Evina frowned.

Koa had no regrets from her words.

Evina pursed her lips. She shook her head and murmured. "You always were a little hothead."

Koa spun around. Her eyes widened. "What did you say?

Evina played with her wavy, red, hair.

Koa stepped closer. "Tell me!" Koa felt her frustration start to overflow. She was tired of the secrets and lies.

Evina rolled her eyes. "I said that you were a hothead. What's the big deal?"

"You said that I was always a hothead!" Koa felt like she'd just discovered gold. She almost grinned, but her face remained serious. She had to know. "Have we met?"

There was a long stretch of silence, but Koa would not back down. Evina nodded.

Koa clapped her hands together. "I knew it!" She laughed. She wiped her face with her hands. She knew she had seen Evina before. There was a history between them. She couldn't remember it, but she knew that something was there.

Evina shot to her feet. "Please, Koa. I cannot say more than that. Don't ask me. Halston would be furious."

Koa's smile faded. She looked at the floor. Her boots were stacked against the wall. "Halston." She nodded. "Yes, I bet there're all kinds of things he's been keeping from me." She chewed her lip. She didn't know how to feel. She wished that Raven was there.

Evina put a hand on Koa's shoulder. Koa shrugged it off.

"Don't touch me."

Evina nodded. "All right. But trust me. He kept the worse from you. To protect you. Please tell me you can understand that."

Koa made a face. "No. I don't understand that." She looked away and pictured his face. "We were best friends. We don't keep secrets." Koa swallowed. She felt ashamed. She'd kept secrets from him before. Somehow she felt that this was different.

Evina gave Koa a look of disappointment. "You have no idea what he's done for you. What he's sacrificed, for you! You *ungrateful* little girl!"

Koa leaned her back against the door. She felt deflated. Her mind was torn. "I'll decide for myself. Once I learn the truth."

Evina gave her a bitter smile. "You'll regret those words when you get your wish."

CHAPTER 26

HALSTON FOLLOWED TRISTAN to the Alchemist. He lived in a hole in the west borough. They walked straight down into a dark pit where tendrils of vines with minds of their own reached down to them. For somewhere so dark, it was quite green. Vines and flowers grew here, when they grew nowhere else in the entire kingdom.

Discs lit the way, but just barely. These discs were the size of quarters and were spaced apart along the steep stairwell. They were all filled with oil and fire.

Halston held the rusty rail and kept an eye on those vines. Their little black eyes watched him curiously, from snakelike faces. He brushed one off his shoulder and it coiled back with a shriek that made the other vines vibrate.

"How many times do I have to remind you not to touch them?" Tristan scolded.

Halston shrugged. "It touched me." He watched the other vines huddle and share a steady glare at him.

Tristan shook his head and stopped at the bottom of the staircase. Halston recognized the long, narrow hallway. Vines and moss covered the stone walls. They became thicker and thicker and he had to squint to see the base of the Alchemist's tree with the wooden door.

Tristan sauntered over to it, ducking down as the ceiling became lower and lower. Halston had to do the same.

Halston let out an annoyed breath. "I do hate this part," he grumbled.

"Ah," Tristan said. "It's not so bad."

The further they walked. The lower the ceiling became, until they were on their elbows, pulling themselves through.

Halston felt squished. He was sure the big War-Breeder didn't enjoy it either, despite his comment. They grunted and forced their way through, all while the vines gripped at them and tugged at their legs.

"How much longer?"

"He must be busy. He has to open the gate for us."

Halston felt smothered. He didn't have time for this. "What is he doing, anyway? Taking a nap?"

"I told him that we were coming."

Halston grumbled to himself. The Alchemist had to open the gate in order for them to finally make it to his door. He was clever and not just anyone could approach his lair. This entire hallway was specially designed to keep out intruders and deter unsuspecting loiterers.

Before Halston could blink, he found the ceiling morph back to normal. He looked up as it ascended. He stood and dusted his pants. The Alchemist had accepted their visit and they now stood before the vine-covered door. The vines pulled back and the door swung open.

Music played inside. Drums. Halston had forgotten how… eccentric the Alchemist was.

"How appropriate," Halston said out of the corner of his mouth.

Tristan grinned. He started bobbing his head to the beat. "I kind of like it. It's odd, but it sets the mood, right?"

Halston made a face. The drums played fast and strong, in an almost hip hop rhythm. "If that's what you want to call it."

"Hey! Halston," the Alchemist called. "No one asked for your opinion."

Halston shrugged and the small boy, barely four feet tall, came from a back room and wiggled a finger at him. Halston wasn't surprised. The Alchemist still had the face of a ten year old. It was odd, being scolded by a child.

"And it's nice to see you again too, Roderick."

Roderick folded his arms. He wore black pants, and a white shirt with red suspenders. He was thin and pale, with short, wild, black hair.

"Payment first," the Alchemist held out his hand. "Then we can be friends again, even though you haven't visited me in far too long." He raised an eyebrow when Halston started to speak. "And messages on your little silver pen thingy don't count."

Halston gave Tristan a look and walked over to the boy. "I like to buy in bulk," Halston replied. "What can I say?" He searched his jacket's inner pocket. He felt around and grabbed an iPod.

Roderick's face lit up when he saw it.

Halston felt a little silly giving the Alchemist something that anyone could buy in the human world, but the boy was obsessed with human toys and technology. One could tell that just from looking around his front room. There were posters of boy bands, cars, actors and actresses all over the cement walls.

Roderick examined the sleek design of the iPod and a grin stretched across his youthful face. He giggled. The Alchemist, a grand wizard and immortal being, feared by all creatures... giggled.

Halston and Tristan stood back while Roderick put the ear buds into his ear and closed his eyes as the music played. He continued to grin and bounce his head to the music. 90's rap. That's what the Alchemist had requested.

Tristan chuckled and gave Halston a sidelong glance. "He'll never grow up, will he?"

Halston sighed and shook his head. "No. I'm afraid not."

They watched the boy start dancing. He jumped up and down and slid across the floor. Tristan was in hysterics by the time Roderick started trying to break dance.

"What is he doing?"

Halston was a little impatient. He had to get Koa in and out of the prison before third click. Halston checked his watch. "He's been observing human culture. He wants so bad to be human."

Tristan made a face. "Why? I'd rather be immortal than like the weaker race up there?" He nodded his chin up toward the ceiling.

Halston shrugged. "They have a few advantages, I suppose."

Roderick finally stopped dancing and swirled around to face them. "All right, let's get on with it." He swiped his lab coat off the back of a chair and put it on with grace. He was all business when that coat went on.

Halston nodded. He was ready. They followed the Alchemist into his laboratory. Wooden bookcases stretched all the way up to the ceiling that was at least a hundred feet high. There were cubbies along the walls that housed vials of ingredients. The equipment looked ancient, it was old and rusted, yet Halston thought that it was probably more efficient than what most humans used in their world. This lab was one that rivaled Halston's.

Halston wasn't a chemist or anything of that sort. He created weapons. He dealt with raw materials. Roderick dealt with magic and science. He practiced an ancient art that most creatures had never even heard of. Halston still didn't know where the boy even came from. He was an anomaly. He didn't really belong in either world.

"So, you need an advanced varnish of glamour, an orichalcum stone, and a fire stone, correct?" Roderick put on his goggles and looked to Halston with oversized eyes.

Halston nodded. "Yes, if you could make that for me, I'd certainly appreciate it."

Roderick nodded, his face serious. "Thank you for the music. I will make whatever you ask." He grabbed flasks of colored smoke and liquids and started mixing in two cauldrons. Then he pulled a black strand of light from the center of his small palm. It stretched and stretched and Roderick continued to swirl his hand so that the light coiled on the silver slab before him.

Halston watched in stunned curiosity. He had no clue where the boy had learned such things. How was it possible?

Roderick's face was completely focused. His big, brown eyes watched the light until it created a tall, spherical apparatus that he smashed down into the slab. He sprinkled white dust onto it and the light started to sizzle and pop. Roderick nodded and left it to sizzle and bubble. He was pleased with the results and returned to his smoking cauldrons. The first cauldron emitted a blue gas that illuminated Roderick's pale face.

"Why won't you let me see her?" Roderick asked.

Halston was taken aback by the question. "I didn't think you cared."

Roderick lifted a brow as he stirred in sand and salt. "What an odd assumption." He gave Halston a pointed look. Something in the boy's eyes displayed a wisdom that you wouldn't notice otherwise. "Of course I want to see her for myself. Stop being so stingy with her."

A child had put him in his place... again. He couldn't help but nod. "I suppose I can bring her by next time. Although, I hope we never have to return to this part of the Netherworld."

Roderick cracked a knowing grin. "You'll be back."

"If you say so," Halston said. He knew that Roderick was right. If they survived tonight, they would have to return eventually to finish what they'd started.

"Don't play coy with me." Roderick chuckled. "I get messages from the Oracle sometimes too."

Halston stood up straighter. "Since when?"

Roderick thought a moment. "Can't really remember. But yes, she speaks to me too."

"Who's the Oracle?" Tristan asked.

"I guess you'll meet her one day," Halston replied. He was more interested in what the Alchemist had to do with the Oracle. He wondered if they were from the same race. If so, then perhaps Halston had just solved one of the greatest mysteries.

"She will need to drink this one down in one gulp, while holding the enchanted orichalcum," Roderick ladled the mixture into a vial. He covered the two stones in a protective material and handed them to Halston. He looked up at him and their eyes met. "The fire stone is for in case she runs into trouble. Don't forget my instructions."

"I won't, " Halston said. The purple cloth felt warm in Halston's palm. He tucked it away into his inner pocket and nodded. He wanted to ruffle Roderick's wild hair, but he had to remind himself that, while he may look like a child, but he was not. He did look so innocent and Halston wouldn't dare say it out loud, but the Alchemist was quite adorable.

"Thank you."

Roderick nodded. He smiled. He looked tired now. Halston wondered how much these items — whatever he had just done to create them — had taken out of him. There were dark circles under his eyes that weren't there before.

"You're welcome, Halston." Roderick tucked his arms into the sleeves of his lab coat. "Do bring her to me next time. I hate being left out of these things. You'll make me feel like you don't trust me or something."

Halston sensed something off in his voice. He really did want to be included. He'd never thought about it. The Alchemist was lonely. Perhaps he wanted to be a part of the team. It was an interesting idea. He could always use someone like Roderick.

"I will," Halston said. "I promise."

Roderick smiled. "Good." He looked at Tristan. "This is for you." He handed the War-Breeder a small token. "You'll have a harder time leaving without this. Give it to the Jem."

Tristan lifted a brow. "Thank you."

Roderick nodded. "Don't mention it." He met Halston's eyes. "We are friends after all, right?"

Halston nearly did it again. He almost ruffled the boy's hair. "We are."

Roderick smiled again. There was a pain behind his eyes. "See you soon. Now leave before you run out of time."

As if on cue, the second click rung. The three of them looked up. Time was quickly running out.

Koa. Halston needed to get to her.

CHAPTER 27

THE DOOR OPENED and Koa beheld a massive man. He blocked the entire doorway and had to duck to enter the room. She and Evina had been drinking an odd blend of blood that Koa had never tried, yet she loved it. She didn't like it more than human blood, but it was almost as good. It was almost enough to make her forgive Evina for what she had done.

Koa came to her feet and tensed when the large man glanced at her. Koa looked him up and down and took a step back. He gave a nod and stepped out of the way. Koa's heart leapt.

"Halston!" She ran to him. She frowned, despite her happiness at seeing his face again. It hadn't really been that long, but she had been stewing over whatever secrets he was keeping.

"Koa."

She grabbed him by the collar and pulled him down to her level. "What is happening? I want to know what you are hiding, and what you are planning, right now!"

Halston nodded to Tristan. "Meet Tristan, our very own War-Breeder, he will help us defeat Greggan's army."

Koa looked at the large man. She almost asked if he expected to do it by himself and she stopped herself. His muscles were bigger than any she'd ever seen. Tristan smiled at her. He had a warm smile. That surprised Koa.

"You know Evina, she is a temptress, and you can't ask for a better skill than that when it comes to getting other vampires on your side. Al is recruiting others topside to infiltrate Greggan's organization. And Jax," Halston paused and Koa tensed at the name. "You are going to free him, because he is the key to killing Greggan and freeing your mother from her curse. Your mother, she is the only one who can stop Bund."

Koa didn't say anything. Halston had just revealed his plan, in simple terms. She didn't know what to say. She stepped back and let his collar slip out of her hands.

Halston searched her eyes. "Feel better?"

Koa let out a sigh. She was nervous but she nodded. "I just don't want to be left in the dark. I mean, it seems like I have to do the hard part and break this fool out of prison."

"Fool?" Evina made a face.

Tristan chuckled. "She's kind of funny."

Koa looked between both of them. "Well yes, I am not going to hide the fact that I don't think highly of him."

The War-Breeder and the temptress shared a look.

Halston pulled Koa back around to face him. "We don't have much time. Let's get going."

Koa thought about Raven. She knew that Jax could change her back and that he had valuable information for her.

"Whatever. Let's just get it over with." Koa shook her head and stared up at Halston. She felt like a puppet being controlled. She had her own motives, and she would get what she wanted.

Halston reached into his jacket and put something into her hand. Koa raised a brow. A vial. Koa touched the glass. The gravity of the situation was settling in. Things were about to get dangerous. Koa thought of Galena and how Halston had given her one of his vials weeks ago.

Koa eyes widened when he put two stones into her other hand.

"You went to the Alchemist?" She was awestruck. She felt a little cheated. She'd always wanted to meet that notorious being.

Halston nodded. "Yes. Drink this down in one gulp."

Koa swallowed. "You sure, it's safe?"

"Yes. He is the best at this. I promise."

Koa sighed and pulled the top of the vial open. A tiny spurt of air escaped and she smelled something foul. She gave Halston a look. "What will this do to me?" She licked the roof of her mouth as she imagined what the potion would taste like.

"I am not sure. It will transform you for a few hours so that you will be able to enter the prison without being questioned. If they saw you trying to go inside, they would immediately arrest you."

Koa thought of all of the possibilities. She could only imagine what she'd be transformed into. She didn't like the idea.

"Wait a minute," Evina cut in. She stepped closer to them and pointed to the Vial. "Won't it wear off the instant she enters Jax's portal?"

Halston ran a hand through his hair. "Yes. That's when she'll use the stones to escape."

Koa held them up. "How do they work?"

"She'll have to fight her way out," Tristan said.

Evina leaned against the wall. "Well, at least she'll have Jax by then."

A torrent of warnings flooded her mind. She felt strong, but she had a worrisome knot in her stomach.

Halston put a hand on Koa's shoulder. "Go on. Take it, Koa. We will be watching for you. We will all be outside and prepared when the time comes for you to escape with the prince."

Koa cleared her throat and eyed the contents of the vial. She felt queasy but the certainty in Halston's eyes gave her the courage to gulp it all down. It wasn't as disgusting as it smelled, but it was thick and she could feel it slowly creep down her throat and into her esophagus. It worked immediately. It burned her from the inside out.

She clutched her throat as it clogged her airway. Her eyes widened as she felt something enter her and take over. Her skin started to crawl and she felt her eyes roll into the back of her head.

Halston held her up. "You can take it Koa. It will all be over in a moment." Koa felt comforted by Halston's embrace, but the pain was almost too much. She cried out as a powerful force morphed her body into something that felt foreign. She fell to her knees with a crash of metal.

Koa opened her eyes. She heard Evina gasp. Koa gasped when she saw her hands. They were covered in metal. Her fingers were long and sharp. Koa felt fear enter her heart. She was afraid of herself.

"Halston," Koa called, but her voice was not her own. It had a robotic tone that made everyone cover their ears. Koa widened her eyes. Everyone looked odd. She saw them as colors now.

Evina was red. Tristan was green and Halston was yellow. They still had their forms, yet she could see their inner aura, the difference between their races.

Koa stood. She sucked in a breath when her head hit the ceiling. She bent over and towered over them all. She saw that her legs were covered in black metal as well and her metallic boots were sealed to her gaiters. She wore a metallic breastplate and she touched her face to feel it covered in metal as well. As far as she could tell, she was completely covered in smooth, black, metal. She felt heavy, yet strong.

She looked at the others as their auras pulsated. "What am I?"

Halston was staring up at her with wide eyes. "A Scayor."

Tristan stroked his chin. "No one would dare question her like that."

Evina nodded. Her blue eyes twinkled with wonder as she looked Koa up and down. She clapped. "It's brilliant."

"Damn, you look awesome." Tristan grinned. "It even adapted to her female features. It's rare to see a female Scayor." He knocked on her belly, which was nearly as tall as his face. Koa had to be nine feet tall.

She felt awkward. She had never been taller than anyone. She was so used to standing in the shadows and getting lost in the crowd. Now, everyone would see her, and run.

Halston swallowed hard and shook his head. He looked at her with wide, surprised, eyes. "Roderick is a genius."

Koa clasped her hands. It felt odd, hearing the metal clink against each other. "What now?" she asked.

Everyone looked at Halston.

"It's time."

CHAPTER 28

KOA APPROACHED the Ivory Tower. The prison was the one structure that passed through all of the levels. All of the worst criminals were housed in those ivory stone walls. She'd never seen a building so tall. The Ivory Tower stretched upwards and went through a circular hole that led to the upper level of the Netherworld. Made of stone and bone, the building looked like an ancient castle. It was clean and bright, and yet one could feel the evil radiating from it.

The evil was palpable.

Even as a metal creature, Koa could feel the eerie, oppressing, tension in the air. She could hear the cries coming from inside the tower: cries of pain and cries of anger.

Koa felt her heart thumping in her new, foreign body. This is where Jax awaited her. She swallowed and realized that her throat was dry. She licked the roof of her mouth, trying to moisten it, and trying to distract herself.

Halston, an angel and her best friend, had led her here. She could trust him. She had no choice. He never led her astray before. She was in a place where everyone was a stranger.

She checked the pouch that was secured around her waist and made sure that her sword was secure. It pulsated against her belly inside the armor. She felt the subtle vibrations running up and down the armor.

There was so much evil surrounding her that she didn't even need the sword to warn her. Evil was thick in the air. She said a silent prayer for strength and joined the ranks of the other Scayors that lined up to enter the prison.

Koa blended in with seven other Scayors. They all walked in unison, very precisely, like robots. The loud clink of metallic shoes on the black path made her cringe with each step. Still, she couldn't help looking around at the tower in wonder.

Syths were stationed everywhere. Some walked in different directions with their weapons in hand. Others patrolled and shuffled visitors into and out of the tower.

Koa raised a brow. A vampire woman dressed in all black with a teenaged boy was ushered from a side entrance. The woman screamed at the top of her lungs. She slapped the Syth and hissed at him. The Syth roughly shoved her aside and walked away.

The boy covered his ears and fell to his knees. Koa almost stopped, but remembered that she had to keep up the façade. Curiosity almost ruined everything. Still, she couldn't pull her gaze away from the two. The boy put his face in the black dirt that covered the land around the Tower. His bony shoulders shook as he sobbed.

Koa swallowed and turned her attention back to the path to the front entrance to the Ivory Tower. Chills ran up her body as she heard what the woman was screaming.

"You killed him! You didn't have to kill him!"

Koa tried to shake the feeling of dread as she kept up with the other Scayor's quick steps and felt her breath start to quicken. She was grateful that no one questioned her when she entered the Ivory Tower.

No one even dared glance at her. Even the other Syths that stood guard, kept their distance. Besides, who would dare try to sneak into the prison?

Koa smirked as she passed by. Then she wondered if they'd be able to smell her differences. It made her worry.

The Alchemist is the best, Halston had said. She held the stones in her pouch as well. This had to work.

The harsh reality that she might die settled onto her. She felt nauseous. Koa turned to the one memory that made her smile every time: the day she met Halston and kissed him. She had been drunk, and he simply laughed and picked her up like a rag doll and took her back to his car. Koa hadn't been afraid. Even then, she had known that he was someone special.

When she woke up, there he was. "Good morning," Halston said, as if they had been close friends for years. It was that simple, and for the next twenty years, they had become just that, but more than close friends. They became best friends, and it was their secret, inside joke… that Halston was Koa's guardian angel.

Koa felt better. She breathed deep. She had to keep her cool. There were too many narrow hallways that she began to feel dizzy. Creatures she'd never seen before stalked the hallways, carrying electronic devices and taking notes. Koa was amazed by how much technology the Netherworld utilized. They seemed to enjoy a balance between technology and Medieval and Gothic architecture.

Koa checked exits and noted the number of Syth guards posted. Her brows furrowed at how many children walked the corridor. There she was, in the dimly lit prison and there were children swarming the halls. They all wore the same uniform, gray slacks and blouses, with their hair pulled back into ponytails. Their eyes all had the same hollow look in them.

Koa studied their aura's. It was more similar to the vampire race. They were not human children. Her gaze followed a procession of two straight lines as they walked from one door and across the corridor to another. Two more groups like that did the same, except they came from the opposite side and disappeared into a door on the right. Koa noticed that each child carried a tiny dagger. They ignored her. She felt as if they had an arrogant air about them, as if even as a Scayor, that she was beneath them.

Once the children disappeared through those massive steel doors, Koa's mind went back to Halston's face. His image kept her calm. Even though he wasn't there, he kept her from focusing on the skeletons that lined the walls like gruesome art. The other Scayors were horrific enough; just being near them made her anxious.

Koa went over Evina's directions in her head over and over. It was simple, the temptress had said, Jax's cell was directly down the main entrance corridor. She would know it when she saw it. Evina was right.

Turning a corner at the end of the main corridor, she could feel that she was close. Her eyes widened in awe. With a gasp, she pulled her face back as black liquid hands reached for her. She stopped before a portal.

She took a breath. It was similar to the portal that stood in their safe house back in the human world. The royal seal of Lyrinia was posted on the four silver brackets: snakes and golden swords. Between the brackets stood a black pool, stretched like the faces of those Shadows, except this was a liquid. The outer edges were illuminated by an alien light.

It reminded her of the inkwell portal in the safe house. Koa wondered if it worked the same way. She knew that the portal would let anyone in… but it wouldn't let anything back out. She didn't want to go. She had no choice. Koa held her breath.

This was what she came for. She never expected it to be easy.

Koa braced herself and before she could talk herself out of it she jumped inside the black pool. She felt the disguise start to melt away. Her scream was cut off as the liquid filled every orifice of her face. The thick liquid seeped into her mouth filling her lungs, coursing into her veins. It tasted like black licorice and bitter herbs.

Koa was frozen in terror. There was no fooling the black mass of the portal. She felt smothered and found herself searching in panic, hoping that the end was somewhere near.

It seemed to take an eternity. Her lungs burned for air. She clutched her throat, falling to her knees. She crawled along the floor, the sticky substance gripping her like glue. She couldn't move. Like a spider web, it held her there, immobile.

Koa began to panic. She choked. Her lungs burned as if hot acid had been poured down her throat. A hand reached out to her and she recoiled backwards. Black tears trailed down Koa's cheeks. The hand grabbed her by the top of her head and yanked her through. The instant her face emerged she gasped for breath.

Terror struck her when she looked into those blue eyes. He frowned at the look of shock on her face.

"My darling Koa," he said in a tender voice. Tears filled his eyes. He came to his knees and put his hands on either side of her face. Koa stared in frozen bewilderment as he caressed her face. He littered her face with kisses, holding her as if he was afraid to let her go. He fought sobbing aloud. "You've come back to me. After all of these years, you've returned. I always had faith that you would, even when Halston took you from me."

Koa felt her terror replaced by loathing. "Jax."

Jax nodded and pulled his face back. He held her at arm's length and smiled at her. He examined her face with his eyes, then stared at her hair. "Your hair is blue now. I like it."

Koa frowned. Something wasn't right. He wasn't what she had been expecting. He appeared to be a gorgeous young man, but she knew that it was just a mask. Still, there was such innocence in his eyes.

Koa shook her head. She couldn't afford to let herself be swayed. *What am I thinking? He needs to die!* Koa thought to herself, but then… there were the tears. Genuine tears. She felt an anxiety building in her stomach. He laughed. He looked embarrassed and wiped his eyes with the back of his hands.

"Forgive me. I should have contained myself better." Jax let her go and came to his feet. He was tall, like his sister Evina.

Jax wore a suit. His dark red hair was perfect and polished. His skin was milky white, like porcelain. His blue eyes stared at her in longing.

Koa looked away. Her frown deepened. She pushed herself up to her feet and stepped away from him. Koa stole confused glances at his face. She felt out of place. She opened the pouch and drew her sword.

"What is this?" Koa looked around the large bedroom, searching out hidden spies or guards. It appeared that they were alone. "Is this some kind of trick?"

Jax's brows furrowed. "A trick?" he asked. "What kind of trick?" He stepped toward her and she gasped, bringing up her sword. To her dismay, the sword felt heavy in her hand. Perplexed, she lowered it. Why would it not work?

"Stay back, Jax," Koa warned.

Jax made a face. He looked hurt. "You're… *afraid*… of me?" He took another step and Koa clawed at his cheek. All of what little color was in Jax's face drained. He stood there with his mouth agape, staring at her in disbelief. He didn't even move to touch his wound. The small trickle of blood trailed down his face.

Why do I feel like I just struck a child? Koa thought with dread. Her hands shook as she looked down at her lowered sword.

The sword didn't glow. Like his sister, he was not evil.

Jax pursed his lips. He looked away from her in pain. He straightened his suit and walked over to a table. He picked up a cloth napkin and dabbed the blood from his cheek.

"You drew blood," he said staring at the white clothed stained with his blood. He glanced over at her. His shoulders slumped, as if all of his hopes and dreams had been crushed. "What has happened to you?"

Koa was without words. She felt odd. She looked around, expecting someone to jump out of a corner somewhere and reveal the meaning of this strange encounter. She swallowed, and unsure of herself, spoke. "You're trying to confuse me. Stop it." Jax's eyes widened. "What's wrong with you?"

Koa lowered her sword, defeated. She narrowed her eyes as she looked at Jax. "What is going on here?"

Jax shook his head. "You mean to tell me, you really don't know? You don't remember *anything*?"

Koa shrugged. "What is it that I am to remember? All I know is that you hurt my mother and yet I am supposed to release you in order to kill Greggan. I am not so sure I trust someone who harmed my family." Thinking of breaking her mother's curse gave her courage. She had to be brave for Raven. "But I trust Halston. I will only let you live because of him."

"So Halston is the one who did this to you?" He nodded with a bitter smile. "He's the one who erased me from your memory." Jax fell backwards into a chair. He lowered his head in silence. The silence stretched for an eternity.

Koa wanted to be patient. It wasn't one of her strongest qualities. She cleared her throat. Jax looked up, tears of blood falling from his eyes. "Why would I harm your mother, Koa? All I've ever wanted to do was protect you. I've loved you from the day your father brought you into the palace."

"You cursed my mother!" Koa countered. She wanted to know more about when her father brought her to the palace, but she needed to stay focused.

Jax shook his head. "Cursed!" He shot to his feet. "Who has spread these... vicious lies about me?" He frowned. His voice lowered. "Was it Halston?"

"My mother told me what you did."

Jax looked stunned. He walked to her with his eyes on her sword. He lowered his voice. "I loved your father and mother. Without them, I wouldn't have you. I would never have dreamed of hurting any of you. I would destroy that world you live in up there… and *everything* in it to protect you." His face turned serious. Jax spoke with passion. "I had your mother changed because she would have been killed otherwise. I did it for you. I pledged an eternity of love to you, Koa."

Koa saw his hands balling into fists and felt her resolve waver. He was sincere. She was baffled and unnerved.

"Lies," Koa whispered. She wanted to hold on to that hate. All of those moments spent plotting her revenge on whoever cursed her mother.

"I could never lie to you Koa. You mean more to me than anything."

"What are you talking about?"

Jax sighed and covered his face. He shook his head and ran his hands through his red hair. Koa watched him as he sat back and folded his hands on his lap. He looked up at her. "From the beginning then?"

Koa nodded. She was eager to hear what he had to say. "Everything. Every bit of it."

CHAPTER 29

"WELL, WE DON'T HAVE much time. So, I will try to be brief," Jax began. "I suppose this all begins with Halston and the rebel angels. You see, Halston was just one of thousands who left heaven to follow one whom you might know as Satan. They were all tricked into leaving their perfect existence and abandoned here on Earth. Halston was the first to try to make it back. He and another angel known as Al tried to find a way back. They have been trying for centuries. But on the other end, there were the angels who didn't want to go back. They fell in love with human women." Jax met her eyes.

Koa felt uncomfortable whenever he looked at her. She tightened her grip on her sword. Koa refused to turn her back on him, or anyone else. She would keep her guard. Her eyes briefly scanned the cell. She was surprised that it appeared to be more of a luxury suite than a damp, old prison cell like she'd imagined. Jax had everything he needed. A big comfortable bed sectioned off by a sheer divider, a tall wardrobe, tons of bookcases, a lounge area with a mini bar, and even a golden telescope that pointed out a small hole in the wall.

Koa frowned. *This is weird*, she thought, but nodded for him to continue.

"Their spawn were the first nephilim. Vampires, giants, and War-Breeders were considered the more stable of the creations. Ghouls were considered failures."

"Giants? War-Breeders? Like Tristan?" Koa took a step back at hearing her own voice echo across the large room. She looked around, still paranoid that somehow this was all a trap and that at any moment Jax would make a move toward her.

Jax perked up, excited that she was showing some interest. "Yes, the giants were wiped out in the great flood. They didn't follow the others to the Netherworld." He frowned. "I'm not really sure why." He shook his head. "Anyway, War-Breeders are big, muscular creatures. They were created to fight against whatever the Royal Army sent down to stop them."

"Royal Army?"

Jax tilted his head. "You really know nothing. You know, the Kingdom of Heaven? Well, they have the Royal Army. There's a war going on, my love. It's been going on since humanity came into existence."

Koa swallowed. This was bigger than she could have imagined. She felt so small and insignificant. Koa nodded and licked her lips. "And what about demons?"

"They're different. They're what angels become when they cross over to the dark side." His eyes darkened. He pointed at her and spoke in the tone that made the hairs on the back of her neck stand. "You don't *ever* want to make an angel angry enough to turn." He slid his finger across his throat.

Halston had never told her that before. Then she remembered how he had changed right before her eyes in the Valley of the Jems. "Noted. Now, where do I fit into all of this? What is the story of… us?"

Jax smiled then. "Why that's the best part of the story." He began to stand. Koa whipped her sword up and he sat back down. He looked down at the blade and sighed. "Calm down. I'm not going to touch you."

Jax sighed and ran a finger along the now-healed wound that Koa had given him. He looked up at the vaulted ceiling, mock stars hung like thin, glittering lights. He was thinking.

Koa huffed.

Jax frowned. He gave her a knowing look. "You're still impatient, I see. You were always a little… anxious."

Koa's eye twitched.

Surprisingly, Jax chuckled. Koa felt a shiver run up her spine. Something about that laugh made her feel a little wary. Jax stood, quicker than she expected. He was before her so quickly that she gasped and nearly tripped backwards. He caught her with one arm behind her back. His arm was strong, like solid stone.

She froze. Jax looked down into her eyes, as if hypnotizing her. She felt her heart quicken and her knees grow weak. Koa gulped and swirled out of his embrace. She fled behind him and pointed her sword at his back.

Jax stood there completely still, his arms still held as if she were still leaned against them. Like a statue, he remained that way. "You know, it probably was unwise to believe that you would still love me." He straightened his back and turned to face her. His face was emotionless.

"I guess I always hoped that true love would stand the test of time. But, it seems as if Halston has blocked your memories. It seems he has taken it upon himself to shield you from everything that happened here so long ago." His shoulders slumped. "He shielded you from me."

Koa watched him approach again.

He took a step toward her. "Koa, put the sword down sweetheart."

Koa shuddered, but didn't move her sword. She watched him come another step closer. "Stop right there, Jax." She was afraid. He scared her more than she had thought possible. It was his quiet, calculating, way.

Jax moved closer. "You will not use that sword on me again, Koa. Are we clear?"

Koa's eye twitched again. There was something about the way he spoke to her that signaled something within her.

Jax raised a hand and gently moved the blade to the side. "Let me show you, Koa. Let me remind you of what we had." He took her hand and with a yelp he pulled her into his chest again.

Koa's lips trembled. He was so close that their faces nearly touched. She felt as if she might scream. Jax... was in complete control. "Get away—"

"Stay still," he warned and Koa's voice was caught in her throat. He traced her lips with his finger and closed his eyes. When he opened his eyes again, they had gone completely black.

Koa's eyes widened in panic. He grabbed the back of her head and yanked it back. His eyes bore into hers again and before she could scream... something happened. A flash of light, and then darkness overcame her. Her scream rang in her head, but nothing audible came out. Jax had her. For that second, she was his. For that second, she saw everything that he had meant to tell her.

Entering the palace years ago with her father. Greggan, sitting on the throne with his long red hair pulled back into a ponytail at his nape. His intense blue eyes landing on Koa as he examined her.

Koa's father had left her there. There was some sort of treaty. She still didn't know why her father agreed to it. But then, Koa saw Jax, standing in a hallway, watching her and her heart thumped in her chest.

She remembered the first night she and Jax snuck away to be with each other. His kiss was unlike anything she'd ever experienced. His kiss made her feel as if she was weightless. Every nerve in her body cried out for more. She could even remember the taste of his tongue and craved to taste it again. Koa's nether regions grew hot with yearning. She gushed with wetness at the memory.

Then, she remembered the pain. Greggan had found out she and Jax had been sneaking to be with each other. Koa gasped. Greggan had found out that Koa… had given her virginity to Jax. Greggan had wanted her for himself. He was furious. He punished them both. Koa was in tears. In that second… she remembered it all. When Jax let her go, she returned to the present and her fear evaporated.

Koa opened her eyes. Jax stepped away from her. Tears soaked her cheeks. He looked expectantly at her. She could see it all over his face: he was hopeful that she was his again.

"I agreed to help Halston take you away from the palace, so that you wouldn't have to suffer the way I have," Jax said in a soft voice.

Koa opened her mouth to speak but gasped instead, when Evina buzzed by. She hopped off her flying disc and grabbed Koa's sword. Koa fumed.

"Put the sword away, Koa. I'm tired of you walking around like you fear us."

Koa fumed. "Give me my sword!"

Evina looked to Jax, ignoring Koa. "Brother, have you told her everything yet?"

Jax shook his head. "Not everything"

Evina looked confused. "Why? I'm tired of waiting for her to know the truth."

"I had it under control."

Koa looked from one to the other. She balled up her fist and glared at Evina.

Evina spoke a little softer. "I just wanted to make sure you didn't hurt Jax before he could remind you of the truth. We all took a great risk to smuggle you out of the Netherworld. My father still doesn't know that I had a part in it. He still thinks I'm his obedient daughter." Evina's eyes searched Koa's. "I couldn't sit back and watch him hurt you the way he did. You and I were like sisters back then, before everything fell apart and we had to help you escape."

So much information overwhelmed Koa. Looking into Evina's eyes, she saw something strange, and new. It was love…for Koa.

Jax sighed. "There's still so much to tell."

Koa stepped forward. "Tell me then." Her eyes didn't leave Evina's. Memories flooded her mind. It was true.

Koa and Evina had been like sisters during her time in the Lyrinian palace. Koa had revealed her secrets to the vampire princess. They had shared so much. Koa could no longer keep a glare on her face as she approached her. She understood it all.

Evina massaged her temples and sighed. "Look, Koa. Jax is the only prophet in the Netherworld, he saw what our father had in store for you when he forced your father to bring you here. We all helped you escape because we believe in an alternate future for both worlds—"

Evina gasped when Koa wrapped her arms around her, embracing her.

Evina sighed, she rested her head on Koa's. "I did miss you," she whispered.

Koa was overwhelmed with emotion. There was something unnatural about remembering so much at one time. Her body was filled with both sorrow and joy. When she pulled away from Evina, Koa was smiling. She felt whole somehow.

Evina wiped a tear and took a deep breath. She threw her hand out, pointing at her brother. "Jax *loves* you. But we all know that you are the key to changing the Netherworld. You are the key to our ability to coexist with the human world. Father locked Jax up in here so that he couldn't change the future that he predicted. Now, Koa, you're the only one that can release us from this prison, because you wield the ancient Lyrinian sword. Its power is the only thing that can cut through that portal's power." Evina looked back at Jax. "Oh yes, I almost forgot, the Lyrinian Royal Guard marches on the corridor as we speak."

"They're here? So soon?" Jax rushed over to a telescope and peered into the glass lens. He stood. "They're here."

"Yes!" Evina clapped her hands together. "Now, can we get moving?"

Jax gave a single nod. He rushed over to a cabinet near the fireplace. He pulled out a couple of tightly wound scrolls and stuffed them in his suit's inner pocket.

Koa's breaths quickened. She could hear them coming. Lyrinian Royal guard? She could only mention what monstrosities were coming for her. She rushed over and grabbed her sword from the ground. She hid a grin as she remembered the way she and Evina used to play and compete.

She gave Evina a look that was full of mischief. "I'll slice your hands off if you do that again."

Evina grinned, catching on to their old game. "You're not quick enough little girl."

Koa took Evina's sword, and sliced a chunk of her hair off before Evina could blink.

"See? I can do it too."

Evina looked appalled. Koa grinned triumphantly as Jax grabbed her hand and pulled her toward the portal. Her grin faded as she watched Evina's hair immediately grow back.

Evina winked. "Bet you wish you could do that, don't you? You forgot just how spectacular I am." She laughed.

"Enough Evina!" Jax's voice boomed, making them both freeze. He quickly composed himself. "Let's go."

CHAPTER 30

JAX RAN for the portal. He waited for Koa to catch up.

"You must lead the way."

Koa thought of how that black mass had almost suffocated her, and took a deep breath. Evina tapped her feet. Horns blew in the distance.

"Get on with it!" Evina shook her head. "We have to get out of here quickly!"

Koa took another deep breath and plunged in. Koa nearly panicked when she was lost in the black, oppressive, darkness again. Jax took her hand and she felt a slight comfort. She glanced down at her sword. She hadn't noticed it before, but it started to glow. The light it emitted was dim but it lit the way.

"Keep going, Koa." Jax had his hands on her waist. She felt safe. "Don't stop."

The black mass tried to grip Jax as she pressed on, but somehow Koa's presence was distracted it. It soon forgot about him and focused all of its attention on her.

Evina was completely fine. If she was uncomfortable, she hid it well.

Koa wondered why their father trusted Evina over Jax. Her lungs started to itch, and burn.

Koa's lungs ached and when she saw the light at the end of the portal she felt as if she'd never been happier. Time seemed to stand still. How long was the portal? How long did it violate her with its smothering hands?

Jax gave her the final push that she needed to emerge from the darkness. She fell to the ground and the black mass evaporated from her skin as she coughed and cleared her throat and lungs of its presence.

There wasn't time to recuperate.

Footsteps thundered down the corridor. Koa looked over her shoulder.

"God, I hate them," Koa said under her breath. Dozens of Syths charged toward them.

The Lyrinian Royal Guard.

"Are you all right?" Jax whispered into her ear as he helped her to her feet.

"I'm fine. It's not the first time I've dealt with Syths." She'd never seen that many in one place before, and her hand shook as she gripped her sword.

"Stop them!" One of the bigger Syths with a golden spear on his helmet gave out the orders. They wore armor: thin, black and metallic.

Jax straightened his suit jacket. He checked his watch. "Excellent timing. Thank you for this, Koa. You won't regret it." He casually sauntered into the center of the hallway.

"What are you doing? There are too many!" Koa held her sword in one hand. She snatched a dagger from her boot and held it ready as well, in case there was some close combat.

Jax grinned. "Really? You'd have to be pretty quick to take all of those things down…" He shrugged. "I suppose I can show you a thing or two." Jax reached into his pocket. He pulled out a fan much like Evina's. It flicked open and turned into a hovering disc. He stepped onto it and outstretched his arms. Two blades slid out of his sleeves. They were blood red, with crystal hilts. "Just watch me, my love."

There was a blast of wind, knocking Koa backwards. She gasped. Jax moved too quickly for her eyes.

Screams.

Gulps of pain.

Crunches of bone, and spurts of blood.

Koa blinked and all of the Syths were dead. Blood still sprayed in the air and Jax darted past her. He caught her by the arm and yanked her up into the air. Koa's voice was caught in her throat.

Dumbfounded, Koa looked at him with such respect that she rarely felt for anyone but Halston. No one was that quick. To behold the skills of Netherworld vamps was sobering. She thought the special skills she'd witnessed from New World vampires was something amazing, she had no idea what pure blood vampires could do.

Koa looked over her shoulder at the carnage. In a trance, she shook when she looked up at Jax's face. Not a trace of blood tainted his white skin.

"What was that? How?" Koa looked down at his daggers. They dripped with blood.

"What?" Jax gave her a sidelong glance, and then looked at his daggers. "Oh, nothing really." An eerie grin crept onto his lips. "I've been locked away for a long time. I think it's only fair that I get to stretch a bit." He gave her a quick kiss on the cheek.

Koa smiled.

"Fly!" He shouted and let her go.

Halston warned her against revealing her secret power. The time for secrets had passed. All Koa needed was the permission to soar. Koa's ducked and flew away as Jax grabbed two Syths by the necks and crushed their windpipes. Jax dropped them to the maroon carpeted floors without a second look.

Koa should have been frightened by his power. Now that she remembered the love they'd shared and the passionate night when she lost her virginity to him, she couldn't help but feel a tingle of affection flood her body as he displayed his power.

Koa's eyebrows furrowed when the same two trails of children came out into the corridor. She paused in the air. "Jax," she called.

He sped up.

"Jax! What are those things!"

"You better use that sword of yours, Koa! Those are not children!" He jumped from the disc and barely missed a step. He ran into their ranks without a second thought.

This is crazy, Koa thought.

"Wait—" Her voice sucked into her throat as the corridor turned into chaos. The scene before her went mad.

Koa frowned in confusion. Even in her Scayor suit, she couldn't tell what their aura was. Their eyes went black and their mouths turned into snarling openings filled with sharp fangs. Those little monster were definitely not children.

They swarmed Jax. They threw silver darts at him, yelling and growling like animals. Jax dodged the darts and killed two with one swirling arm.

The blood, it made Koa feel queasy. She cursed at herself, letting her morals get in the way. She should have known that it would be ridiculous to have children here.

An abnormally large Syth came crashing down the corridor. Koa's mouth opened in awe as he slammed through the double doors, sending shards of wood and brass into the air.

That wasn't a Syth. It was a giant.

Giants don't exist anymore!

Apparently, Koa was wrong. The floor trembled with each stomping step the giant took. He picked up Jax by his hair with a massive hand covered in rings on each finger. Jax clenched his jaw and he stabbed the giant in its gray-haired chest, slicing him as he slid back down to his feet. Intestines spilled onto the carpet and the giant crashed to the floor with a deafening thump.

Koa flew as fast as she could when the childlike creatures jumped onto Jax. They tried to bite him and stab him with their tiny daggers.

"Don't let the prisoner escape!" A woman called from the other end of the corridor. She was tall, with a shaved head revealing tattoos. She wore red armor and pointed at Jax with the muzzle of a long red gun.

The exit was so close. Koa was just thinking of how frightening that woman looked, when Evina came up behind the woman and lopped her head off. Her curved sword sliced through with expert ease, spraying red blood into the air. The body crashed after the head and Evina smashed the face of that severed head into the ground.

Evina stood and tossed her hair out of her face. "Jax! Hurry it up! We don't need to kill everything we see. Let's just fly away!" She yelled at them before running back the other way.

Koa tightened her hand around the hilt of her sword and clenched her jaw. She didn't know what those children really were, but she no longer felt any sympathy for them. One bit her leg and she cried out. The bite stung like hell.

Koa kicked that abomination into the wall. She took a deep breath and ran into the chaos. Evina and Jax were skilled, and Koa had to keep up. She wanted to show off, just a little, to not appear weak in comparison. She couldn't help feeling inadequate in the midst of the royal Netherworld vampires.

The sounds of squeals and yells were overwhelming. More and more of those little creatures poured into the corridor from every direction.

Koa dove into the masses. Her sword screamed with yearning. Koa swirled in the air and caught the throats of four of those creatures. She sent their decapitated heads flying in different directions. Koa took a breath and embraced the pain of the Lyrinian sword.

Too much evil.

The Lyrinian sword begged her to quench its thirst. Koa would not let it down. She closed her eyes and the sword took over. Koa's mouth was open as she focused on the feeling of the sword. Its power soared through her veins as she slashed through bodies and listened to the satisfying sizzle. No one could touch her when she was lost in the trance.

A loud bell broke her from the trance, leaving her feeling empty. Not enough blood had been spilled.

She stood and opened her eyes. She'd killed at least seven more of those creatures. She took a look around. One of them stabbed her in her thigh.

"Little bastard," Koa cried out and covered the wound with one hand and ran her sword through her assailant's face with the other. Four toppled onto her with sharp daggers and Koa could barely catch her breath.

Koa growled as she fought her way out of their huddle. She reached out her sword and sliced them all across their middle in a circular motion that resembled a dance. When she emerged from the huddle, she was covered in blood. Cuts covered her arms. They would heal.

A loud bell went off again. It was an alarm.

Koa looked up. Down the corridor ran Scayors. Koa paled. Robotic yells filled her ears. Five of the giant, metallic monsters stopped at the beginning of the corridor. A long, metal finger pointed at Koa. She started to panic.

Evina stepped forward. The Scayors all turned in unison and looked at her. Koa narrowed her eyes, curious to see what the vampire princess would do.

Evina tossed her sword in the air. Her tattoos moved just as they had before. She closed her eyes and waved her arms around slowly. The sword hovered in the air. With the movement of her arms, it started to turn in a circle. Purple haze surrounded Evina as her tattoos danced. Her eyes were closed and she seemed to be in deep focus. The Scayors fell to their knees and bowed with their heads low.

"What is she doing?" Koa shouted over the alarm.

Jax caught his breath and nodded to his sister. "A blade dance," he replied. He smirked. "She'll have them fighting for us before the dance is done."

Koa now saw what purpose Evina served in their new 'crew.' She watched Evina and couldn't help but feel impressed. That woman could bend anyone to her will.

Evina didn't stop. Her eyes remained closed. She spoke softly, calmly. "I will run out of energy in about two minutes. Do something now, to clear a path. The Scayors are programmed to resist my dance, but they are not completely immune. They will be free from their trance the moment I stop."

Halston's voice whispered in her head. *Focus. Focus. There's always a way out, Koa.*

The Scayors blocked the exit. The gate was shut and Koa could see more Scayors lining up outside. They had half a minute to think of a way out.

Koa felt around in her pocket. She felt something smooth, and warm. Koa's eyes widened. "Jax, Evina, get down!" She grabbed the fire stone from her pouch and tossed it. She held her breath and rolled onto her stomach. The explosion made the Ivory Tower tremble. It destroyed the tapestries, walls, carpets, and everything in its path.

Jax grabbed Evina and spun her out of her trance. She cried out, grabbed her sword from the air, and they both ducked into the outer hall that led to the exit.

The ringing in Koa's ears was deafening, but she didn't have time to recover. She was on her feet within half a second. Her face was set. The creatures doubled over on the floor.

Koa ran a finger along the blade of her Lyrinian sword, spilling blood onto its blade. It absorbed the blood and screeched with pleasure. The blade turned red and Koa was lost in a trance. The lights flashed and the wails filled the hollow corridor. The night air of the Netherworld bit at her and she didn't care.

No one was safe. Scayors filed in, stomping and pointing their fingers at her. Koa gasped. Blue light shot out of their fingers. Koa watched as the light seared what was left of the Ivory Tower floor. She held her sword up and blocked the light. It bounced back and the Scayor was eviscerated. Koa breathed with relief.

She kissed the blade of her sword. "Thank you," she whispered to it. She shook her head with a smile and ran out with newfound confidence. Through the remaining fire from the fire stone, Koa jumped and ran her sword through the middle of a Scayor.

The sound of metal meeting metal made her ears hurt. She gritted her teeth as she sawed through and left the Scayor in two pieces. He crawled away on his arms and met his legs again. Koa cursed as the body fused back together. Sparks flew as the pieces became one. The Scayor stood and towered above her.

"Shit," she whispered.

Koa grunted as Jax grabbed her from behind. He held her with both hands. "No use trying with those things," he said to her as he looked up at the Scayor's face. "Your sword can't kill them."

Koa nodded. She shivered. Jax cupped her chin and brought her face up to his. Koa closed her eyes to his touch. She remembered the softness of his palm on her cheek and moaned. She had no idea how much she had missed him, and now, she remembered.

"Don't worry, my love," he said softly, even as the Scayors filed into the tower in perfect battle formation. "We haven't come this far to lose." Koa couldn't believe how optimistic he was, even when death seemed imminent.

The ground shook.

Jax pulled her close. Evina covered her mouth.

"Oh no. They let the Wraith out!"

Koa looked up at Jax's face in alarm. "What's a Wraith?"

Jax gulped. "Fly Koa! Fly away now!"

Koa shook her head. "I'm not leaving you here." She couldn't believe she had just said that. She was frightened. Still, she could no longer picture life without Jax.

Jax looked down at her and his eyes sparkled with mist. He smiled. "My Koa. You're back."

CHAPTER 31

HALSTON AND TRISTAN gathered all of the supplies that they could carry from Tristan's home. They tucked away knives and guns, filling their bags with stakes and various vials from the Alchemist. There was much to do, and so little time. Koa should almost be done in the Ivory Tower. They needed to get back in case Evina's assistance wasn't enough.

Tristan lived alone. He had taken a wife, and she had been executed. Halston couldn't get Tristan to tell him why. He had an idea, but kept his mouth shut. Halston also didn't ask why Tristan had chosen to live in an abandoned storage building with creaky staircases and boarded up windows. The furniture was sparse and there was an old, musky, smell of rot.

"How long has Greggan been gone? Has anyone in Lyrinia noticed his disappearance?"

Tristan nodded. "I've noticed. I'm sure others have noticed something strange happening as well. Of course he took some of his best men and women up to the human world. I'd say Greggan has been back and forth for the past six months. But Greggan was never a very social king. He doesn't exactly walk the streets of his kingdom shaking hands with his subjects."

Halston sighed. Greggan would have assembled his own army up there by now. The humans would be defenseless. Tristan was close. For the past year Halston had been keeping track of the disappearances and the murders. Greggan was taking innocent people and farming them. Greggan was merciless.

To Greggan, humans were like cattle, mindless meals that he could do what he pleased with. Not only did he feast on humans, but he was also creating more vampires and turning them into eternal slaves. He was trying to single handedly repopulate the world of vampires after Halston and Alice's centuries of ridding the world of them.

This was unacceptable. If there was anything Halston valued most, it was the fate of the humans. He had sworn to protect them. It was his last chance to return home to the Kingdom of Heaven. It was all he'd ever wanted. Well, it used to be all he ever wanted.

"Evina, where will she meet us?" Tristan slipped metal gauntlets on each wrist, and a jagged dagger at his hip. Halston knew what those gauntlets could do, and hoped they'd never have to make use of them in the human world.

"At the south gate. Hopefully Jax has convinced Koa that he is not our enemy and that she can get him out of his cell."

Tristan nodded. "Right, it takes Lyrinian metal to cut through that black matter."

Halston nodded. "That's right."

"Why is that?"

Halston sighed. "Really? Do I have to go over this now?" He shoved a watch into Tristan's hand. "Put it on now. We need to get out of here."

Tristan pursed his lips. He held the black watch up into the dim light that spilled through his boarded up windows. "What's this?"

"Communication device," Halston answered. "I'll be able to reach you whenever I need to, and vice versa."

Tristan grinned. "Excellent. I do miss working with you, Halston. You certainly have the best gadgets." He put the watch on. "I'll let you stall on the whole Lyrinian thing if you give me a decent gun."

Halston scoffed. "You don't need a gun, Tristan. You're a War-Breeder, remember?"

Tristan laughed and followed Halston outside. They walked out into the cool air of the lower tenements of Lyrinia. It was quiet. It was the dim hours of second light. The Netherworld's night. Everyone was sleeping.

Halston lowered his voice. "Don't worry, I already have something nifty in mind for you."

Tristan smiled. "Good man." He patted Halston on the back. "I knew you'd come through for me."

They walked quickly through the shallow alleyways. The city was a labyrinth, but Tristan knew his way around. The only time they were slowed down was when they had to step over sleeping packs of ghouls. There weren't many of those creatures left in this world, but it seemed as though they had figured out that there was safety in numbers.

Within an hour Halston and Tristan were at the central plaza. The staircases all led to that plaza and they quickly ran up the stairs two at a time. They screeched to a halt when they heard a loud explosion in the distance.

Halston looked back; there was a loud commotion coming from the palace. He stood tall and grabbed his infinity gun's handle. His jaw tightened with worry.

"Koa."

Tristan stumbled back as Halston bent his knees and took off into the air. Tristan shielded his eyes from the breeze that swept around his friend. It was a sight to behold, Halston in his golden, angelic, glory. He nodded to himself. "I guess I'll wait at the gate then."

Tristan gasped when Halston buzzed in on the new watch that he gave him. He didn't like technology. He frowned at the gadget.

"Yes, wait at the gate, I'll send them to you."

Tristan nodded. "Sure thing, boss."

CHAPTER 32

THE GOLD in the sky caught Koa's attention. She looked up and felt her heart soar. It swelled with joy. Halston flew across the black sky in all of his angelic glory. Embers and tiny sparks still fell from the damage her vial had caused to the front of the palace, and yet Halston glided along the air with expert agility and grace.

Koa couldn't help but smile. He had come back for her. She forgave him of everything. The secrets, the lies, everything... was forgiven.

Jax didn't let his grip on her lessen. He glared at Halston.

Koa turned away, toward Halston. He landed and she ran to him.

Halston grabbed her with one arm and hugged her tight to his chest. "I'm sorry."

Those words were simple, and yet they made Koa hold him even tighter. She didn't care anymore. She buried her face in his chest and breathed in his scent. She smiled. His scent was always the same: eucalyptus and flowers, as if he'd been born in a garden. She looked over her shoulder, remembering Jax. He watched them with furrowed eyebrows. His glare went back up to Halston.

Halston turned her to face him and Koa felt a little embarrassed. Jax watched, and she wondered if he could see how she felt for Halston. Could Halston sense how she now felt for Jax?

A blank mask covered her shame. All of this time, she'd thought that she was saving herself for Halston. She hadn't known that she'd already given herself to Jax.

A loud, bestial cry came from the dungeons of the Ivory Tower.

"It's coming," Koa whispered.

Halston held her at arm's length. He bent to her level and met her eyes with an intensity that made Koa hold her breath. She didn't want him to let her go.

"Listen. We have to separate. I will draw the beast away from you all while you make a mad dash for the Gate. Do not stop for anything. Do not look back. You run for your life, Koa, and I will do my best to return to you. Understand?"

Koa couldn't speak. She stared at him and nodded. Her skin tingled. Her hands began to sweat. She couldn't let him go again. Another cry shook the floor and what remained of the walls and Koa knew the seriousness of Halston's request. Whatever a Wraith was, she was certain that she didn't want to face it. She'd seen countless monstrosities this very night. She was weary and didn't feel ready to face another.

Halston stared at her for a moment, as if taking her all in for what might be the last time. He kissed her forehead and pushed her away. "Go!" He took off down the hall at lightning speed and all Koa felt was the whoosh of air as he flew away.

She hadn't a chance to call out to him as Jax pulled her out of the wreckage. She came to her senses and turned around. Evina jumped on her disc, and still holding her, Jax did the same and they went higher into the air.

Koa looked down at all of the lights and sighed. The Central Dominance sparkled like an enchanted city. That Disc Moon above turned and their sky began to brighten. It was a slight change, but Koa could tell that it signified that morning was coming.

She was worried. She hadn't felt such worry in ages. Halston and Koa had been separated only once before. It had been during a mission two years ago. She had tracked down a hellish clan of vampires that were rampaging through Eastern Europe. The memories of blood still lingered in her mind. The bodies of Romanian villagers had been piled up like small hills across the countryside.

It took five months for them to make it back to one another. She couldn't imagine being apart from him for so long again.

Koa swallowed her anxiety. She hoped Halston would make it out of there. Deep down inside, she knew he would. He had to. He was her teacher and protector; he had to know what he was doing.

Jax held her firm against his chest.

Her heart thumped as she thought of Halston.

The Ivory Tower began to fade into the distance until it became a tiny spot against the backdrop of that city of darkness.

Resting her head on Jax's shoulder, Koa realized just how tired she was. The potion that changed her into a Scayor and the fight in the tower exhausted her. The hunger would start to creep on her soon.

Koa's eyes brightened when she saw the staircase that she and Halston had taken hours ago. She knew what that staircase signified.

Freedom was so close.

Jax and Evina sped up and Koa wanted nothing more than to make a dash for the Gate. She knew that would be unwise. The Netherworld discs were faster than she was on her own. Those discs covered what would have taken another two days to travel in what felt like minutes.

Now, they would just have to get past the Shadows that waited for her within the tunnel. She swallowed and squeezed her eyes shut. She kept them closed as they entered the tunnel. Halston's voice spoke to her as they entered the darkness.

Do not be afraid, Koa, Koa imagined him saying. Wind swept her hair around her face, blowing tears from her cheeks. *We will be together again.*

THE END

Thanks for reading! If you enjoyed this book, please consider leaving a review.

Dark Prophet: The Chronicles of Koa Book Two is now available <u>on</u> Amazon.

* * *

Don't Forget to Subscribe to K.N. Lee's Newsletter to Receive Freebies, Exclusive Content, Cover Reveals, Giveaways, Sales, and More!

www.knlee.com

AN EXCLUSIVE LOOK AT

DARK PROPHET

The Chronicles of Koa Book Two

CHAPTER 1

KOA FROWNED DOWN at her body. A red dress. Koa hated red, but she did not have a choice. Like the blood that Koa had spilled the night before when she had been cut with a glowing dagger, the dress was dark and rich.

Ceremonies such as this were normal in the Netherworld. The wound on her white wrist healed before her eyes. Within minutes, the ceremony was complete, the tests were run, and it was confirmed that she was indeed the daughter of Alsand Vangelis, the vampire king of Elyan.

Only hours ago, Koa was awakened by a team of violet-eyed women tugging at her limbs. They washed her in scalding hot water, scrubbed her raw with oils, and slathered creams onto her snow-white skin. They straightened her thick black hair and painted her face with colors that Koa only thought older women were allowed to wear. Then, she had been dressed.

In a gaudy red wedding gown… at the age of twelve.

Koa wanted to run from the black temple that she and her father had slept in. On the side of a mountain, the temple faced the back of the dark kingdom that was meant to be her prison for an eternity. She wanted to break free from the parade of attendants sent to accompany her and fly home.

The human world seemed so far away.

No one understood just how much she did not want to do this. This wasn't to be a human wedding, but a Netherworld wedding... a vampire wedding.

Koa scrunched up her nose as she looked down at the billowing gown, littered with sparkling crystals and black taffeta. She looked like a gothic spin on a Disney princess.

Vampire Barbie, she thought to herself.

Even at such a young age, Koa knew she did not fit the role of such a character. She was not a doll or a character from the books she read. She closed her eyes and tried to calm her nerves.

Like boiling acid, anxious feelings churned within her stomach, making her feel like she might faint, or worse... vomit at any moment.

How embarrassing that would be, Koa thought as she chewed her lip. She grimaced. Her lips tasted horrible, like tar. She'd almost forgotten that she was covered in makeup like a clown. Her small hands shook and she wanted to cry. It took all of her strength to keep the tears from escaping and causing an even bigger scene. With hot cheeks she held her breath, and prayed for an escape.

Koa was afraid of this dark place, where neither the sun nor moon existed. The entire population was composed of millions of creatures that would have given normal girls nightmares. "Nephilim" is what her father called them. The spawn of fallen angels. King Alsand was a nephilim.

Koa was as well.

She was glad that her father was by her side. He never let go of her hand. With her free hand, Koa tugged at the high collar of her gown. She groaned. The black lace made the skin on her throat itch.

Koa looked up at her father. She was small, and her father always looked like such a giant to her. King Alsand walked regally by her side. He commanded such attention. With his head held high, his face depicted an air of authority. Together, they walked at the head of the procession through the wide streets of Lyrinia, while the citizens watched in uneasy silence.

Netherworld vamps, War-Breeders, Jems, Syths, and even ghouls came out of their hiding spots to catch a glimpse of the mysterious half-blood princess.

Koa tried not to stare back at the horrific creatures all around. The sound of metal and robotic buzzing noises caught her attention as a quad of Scayors entered the crowd. Everyone stepped aside to let them through to the front. Like metallic giants, slim, and sleek, the Scayors patrolled the event like silent police.

Their eyes cast a dim green glow over what they scanned.

She shuddered when their gaze lingered on her. She feared that they were reading her thoughts and knew that she was afraid of them. That was one thing that Koa hated, the admission of fear. Even the monk-like Syths scared her. They were big, pale, creatures with bald heads and faces covered in tattoos.

Lightning broke out and everyone looked up to the sky. Koa clutched her father's arm and paused.

He smiled down at her. "Don't worry, Koa. It's not a real sky, my love. That is simply the ground of another Netherworld level. I believe they are having a battle up there."

Koa's eyes narrowed as she looked at the dismal black sky. Lightning struck again, but it wasn't the kind of lighting that she was used to. It was green and took the shape of various symbols as it faded into the dark. To think that they were only on one of the many levels of the Netherworld, and that entire civilizations and kingdoms were going about their business with little to no care about what an important day this was for Lyrinia was too much for young Koa to grasp.

When she looked back down, she saw that everyone had returned their attention to her. Vampire women and men stared at her. They were the only creatures that she wasn't fearful of. Father had various vampires over at the manor from time to time, but none of them looked as picturesque as these Netherworld vamps.

Painted faces stared at her. The vampire women were the most beautiful women that Koa had ever seen, and yet none compared to her mother's simple and natural beauty. These women were like painted dolls whom she imagined tipping over and watching crack into pieces of porcelain.

Koa noticed how they seemed to be separated into groups. The red lipsticks on the left and the black lipsticks on the right. Koa didn't know if it was simply a fashion trend or something more, but all of the women wore the most elaborate gowns and jeweled arrangements on their perfectly sculptured hairdos.

They watched her, unblinking, unsmiling. She could see the judgment in their eyes.

"Father," Koa breathed. She looked away from their violet eyes and clutched her father's arm.

King Alsand looked down at her. His green eyes were serious today. "What is it, darling?"

Koa looked ahead at the sparkling golden palace before them. The golden plates along the palace's walls shimmered and reflected all of the light from the Disc Moon, the artificial moon of the Netherworld. Her voice was caught in her throat. Something felt odd and yet she felt drawn to the palace. It stood out like a candle in the dark and pulled her in, as if by magic, like a moth to a porch light.

Koa's face paled. This was the place that would be her new home. King Greggan's teenage son, Prince Jax, would be her new husband.

Koa stopped. The guards that were leading them looked back and seemed ready to seize her and force her forward.

King Alsand leaned down to her ear. "What's wrong?"

"I want to go home."

Her father patted her hand and when one of the Syth guards stepped forward, he whipped out the Lyrinian sword with lightning speed. Everyone drew in a breath and stepped back as they beheld its power. The ring of steel rang throughout the air. It pulsed, audibly, and visibly as the red glow made the air heat and crackle.

Even Koa held her breath as her eyes shot to the Lyrinian blade.

King Alsand's raptor-like glare burned into the guards, warning them to keep their distance. He didn't have to say a word. The red glow of the black blade was enough to make the large brutish creatures rethink their actions.

King Alsand waited a moment longer, making sure that they knew how serious he was. Koa had only trained with that sword once. The power was too great for her now, but one day it would be hers.

She flinched when her father's glare landed on her. "Koa, this is your home."

Koa shook her head, but avoided his eyes. She looked around. The air was stale, not like the fresh, fragrant air of France. The sky was dark, lit only by the Disc Moon that cast different colors across the land whenever the hour changed.

She missed the moon of Earth. She missed the sun, the trees, and the flowers. The Netherworld felt like a nightmare from which she would never awaken. No matter what color the day was in the Netherworld, it was always too dark for her. Koa's father didn't understand her love for daylight, for he had never seen real daylight.

The sun's rays would kill him just as surely as it would kill any vampire, Netherworld or New World. Koa was the only exception and she wished that he would at least try to understand.

"You are half Netherworld vamp, Koa," her father gave her hand a squeeze. "This is where you belong, amongst your people."

"I am also half human."

King Alsand looked down at her and pursed his lips. His eyes hid something from her.

Koa tried to soften her voice and sound as sweet as possible. "Bring mother here, and maybe I won't feel so homesick," Koa reasoned, her green eyes hopeful.

King Alsand shook his head, but his features softened for her. "My darling girl. You will see that this is the place for you. You belong here with your people. The treaty has already been signed." He leaned closer to her ear and whispered. "Your mother cannot come here Koa. She is safe in the mortal world. If we do not fulfill our side of the treaty, she will be in danger. Now, is that what you want?"

Her lips trembled. She shook her head quickly. Just the thought of someone harming her mother made her feel sick. She didn't know what she would do if she lost that sweet, loving, woman.

She looked into her father's eyes.

"Do you understand what I am telling you?"

Koa nodded. She understood, but she still didn't agree with what was happening.

Alsand smiled and stroked her pale white cheek.

"But I don't want to do this," Koa whispered.

Alsand's smile faded, but his eyes didn't turn cold on her as she expected. He knelt down to her level and cupped her cheek.

"I know, my dear girl, but sometimes we have to do things that we don't want to... to protect those that we love."

"May I?" Faun asked of Alsand.

Alsand nodded and Faun gathered her white skirts in one hand and scampered over to fix Koa's long black hair. Koa didn't take her eyes from her father's. She hoped that he would see how miserable she was.

Koa ignored Faun as she examined her face with violet eyes. She was adamant about making sure that Koa's part was perfectly straight and that her hair fell in long ringlets.

"Smile," she said.

Koa twisted her mouth. "I don't want to."

Faun put her hands on her bony hips. She scrunched up the space between her thin brows as she narrowed her eyes at Koa. "Just do it. It's only for a second."

Koa rolled her eyes and faked a quick smile.

"That wasn't so hard, now was it?" Snickering, she gathered her skirts in her hand. "You have red lipstick on your teeth," she said and returned to her place in the procession behind Koa and her father.

Frustrated, Koa rubbed her teeth with her finger. She knew just how ridiculous she looked. Black liner, red lips, and rosy cheeks.

Alsand locked arms with Koa. He leaned close and gave her a kiss on the cheek. He lowered his voice into a whisper. "Remember, never mention that you can walk in the sun. Never."

Koa swallowed and squeezed her eyes shut. "I know, father. You don't have to keep reminding me."

"Good," he stood back to his full height. His eyes widened and he leaned down again. "Or that you can fly."

Koa nodded, her head down. "Yes, I know."

He pinched her cheek. "Good. Shall we continue, darling?"

"I don't know, father." Koa couldn't bring herself to look at her father again. "Is there anything else that you want to remind me not to say or do?" Her eyes were burning from the tears that threatened to gush forth.

Alsand noticed and simply shook his head. He patted her hand.

She hung her head. Once again, they were walking down the black stone walkway that led to the gate and stone doors of the Lyrinian palace.

Koa's heart pattered against her ribcage. She felt like she might have an anxiety attack. So many eyes staring. So much anticipation in the air.

Those golden gates that she'd been staring at for the past hour, as they walked through the entire kingdom, were held open for them and heavily guarded.

When Koa stepped through the gates and entered a massive courtyard of stone. Their path was lit for them. On either side of the carpet were artificial trees of stone and black clay. They weren't real, but they were beautiful. Art.

Even Koa could appreciate the mastery. She examined the sculptures as she followed her escort through the courtyard and to the stone doors that led into the palace. Once inside, light seemed to fill every dark space. Chandeliers, torches, candles, mirrors reflecting the light, and light discs were positioned all over the wide corridor.

It was then that Koa contemplated flying away. She'd thought of it often. It would be her last chance. She took a peek over her shoulder. She could still see the door. She'd just promised her father that she would keep her abilities a secret. She wasn't sure why such things were so important.

She could simply lift herself into the air, and head for the Gate, but visions of her mother being harmed kept her firmly planted to the purple carpeted floor.

Koa felt numb, like she was walking to her prison cell.

Each corridor led to another corridor of a different theme. From one of light and mirrors they stepped through grand arches to a corridor of dim candles and artificial flowers in vases painted with paint that seemed to have a light of its own. There was a corridor with walls filled with paintings and soft music played by a small creature that resembled the one at the Gate. Tunes was what her father called him, but all Koa remembered was how creepy he was. She shuddered as she recalled Tunes' bulbous eyes.

Koa watched it buzz around with short black wings as it blew eerie melodies out of its flute. She tapped her chin and furrowed her brows as she tried to remember what kind of creature it was.

With bat-like wings and rubbery, yellowish skin, she was sure she'd seen that creature in a book from her father's study. Koa spent hours in there, reading anything that she could get her hand on. The Netherworld tomes always intrigued her. Now she was faced with the creatures she'd studied.

"An imp!" Koa shouted triumphantly. She covered her mouth with her hand and looked around in horror. She hadn't meant to say that aloud. Everyone glanced at her with disapproval, but the imp continued playing its flute until they went into the next corridor.

Koa was relieved to find that the maze of corridors had finally ended, and that they were finally in the main ballroom where the prince and the royal family awaited them.

She stepped into the room, from carpet to shiny granite floors and a flood of light and decorations overwhelmed her senses. She didn't want to admit how beautiful it was, but her eyes widened at the spectacle. Hundreds of chairs draped with gold silk lined either side of the alleyway that led to the dais where the thrones stood.

Her heart thumped. She felt something she hadn't expected. Koa's face flooded with blood as her eyes met those of the prince.

No one else mattered. Nothing else existed as Koa's eyes cut through the crowd and down to the set of five thrones as Koa and her father stopped before the platform.

"Princess Evina, 1st Queen Katya, 2nd Queen Lera, your highness, King Greggan, and Prince Jax, behold King Alsand of Elyan and Princess Koa."

Koa heard the introductions but something odd was happening. She stared at Prince Jax with her mouth agape.

He was the most attractive person she had ever seen in her life: piercing dark blue eyes, dark blood-red hair, and a perfectly sculpted chin and nose. Koa felt her face flush as he looked her up and down. Then, he did something that made her grin, despite her previous fears and doubts.

Prince Jax winked at her.

DARK PROPHET
(The Chronicles of Koa #2)
Available now on Amazon **&**
www.knlee.com

BONUS MATERIAL

Someone has stolen classified documents from the Netherworld Division's secret vaults.

The following interviews were leaked to the press.

Read at your own risk...

TOP SECRET

Netherworld Division #265

Potential candidate for agency

Rank: #2 out of 44

Name: Koa Ryeo-won

Age: 17

Sex: Female

Hair Color: Black

Eye Color: Green

Ethnicity: Asian/Caucasian descent

Height: 5'6

Weight: 122lbs

Interviewer: Captain Patrik Kramer

Cpt. Kramer: Good evening, state your name. Please speak clearly so that Marlina can hear you. She'll be typing everything you say tonight.

Koa: Sure. I am Koa Ryeo-won. And good evening to you too.

Cpt. Kramer: Thank you Miss Ryeo-won. Where were you born?

Koa: Daegu, South Korea

Cpt. Kramer: And your parent's name?

Koa: Eunju Ryeo-won and Alsand Vangelis

Cpt. Kramer: And your parent's race?

Koa: My mom is Korean and my father is…well, I guess he's just white. Like you.

Cpt. Kramer: No, I mean, what race are they: human, vampire, War-Breeder, Syth, etc…

Koa: Oh. My mom is human and my father is a vampire

Cpt. Kramer: Interesting. I looked over your profile and I was quite impressed. You ranked fairly well against the other candidates. Skilled in the sword, dagger, and martial arts. Where did you get your training?

Koa: My father taught me everything I know.

Cpt. Kramer: And you speak, French, Korean, English, and Russian?

Koa: Yes, and Spanish. And a little German

Cpt. Kramer: Impressive for a seventeen year old.

Koa: I guess. I grew up isolated from others. My early life was spent in a one room cottage in Korea with my mother. When my father came to claim us, he moved us into his massive manor in France, but still, I wasn't allowed to go to school. I didn't have friends. What else could I do but read and study?

Cpt. Kramer: But I see here, that you can walk in the sun. No other vampire can do that.

Koa: I'm not full vampire. I only have to drink blood once a week. Of course I prefer human blood, but it can be blood from any living creature. But, Wryn Castle has changed that. I will find myself a pet and I won't have to hunt anymore. But don't let that influence your decision. I assure you, I can do this job. I can do many things that even full vampires cannot.

Cpt. Kramer: You can fly.

Koa: Yes. I can fly. How many of your agents can do that?

Cpt. Kramer: Quite a few actually. We are mainly comprised of angels, but I see what you're getting at. None of the other candidates can fly. But, why should we accept you into the Netherworld Division when our main goal is to reform or exterminate the vampire race?

Koa: Because it needs to be done. Someone has to keep order in this world. I may be half vampire, but I am more human. I've seen what some vampires can do. I want to protect the humans.

Cpt. Kramer: But you killed a human.

Silence

Cpt. Kramer: Do you wish to stop the interview now?

Koa: No. I'm fine. I just don't like to think about that.

Cpt. Kramer: You cannot have any secrets here. We know everything.

Koa: I see that.

Cpt. Kramer: Tell me about Bartov Gorski, the Polish student you killed.

Koa: It was an accident. I didn't mean to kill him. I was just started to date him and I got a little carried away when I was feeding. Trust me, I've punished myself enough for that. I will never let that happen again.

Cpt. Kramer: You come highly recommended by Agent Halston.

Koa: Yes. He saved my life. He found me at my lowest point and helped me get my life back together. I'll never be able to repay him. I want to do this job, and do it well, to prove to him that I was worth saving.

Cpt. Kramer: And yet, we still have that human murder on your record. What would you suggest we do about that?

Silence

Cpt. Kramer: Koa?

Koa: How the hell should I know? Lock me up. Kill me. That won't bring Bartov back. But let me be an agent and redeem myself. Let me use my skills, skills that you need, to bring vampires to justice. There are many out there that need to be shown that there is another way. I want to be a part of that more than anything.

Cpt. Kramer: More than finding the demon that killed your father?

Koa: How did you know about that?

Cpt. Kramer: I told you, Koa. We know everything.

Koa: I will find him. And I will kill him. Until then, I will do what it takes to keep the humans safe. Even if you don't make me an agent, I will be out there. I'll do it alone if I have to, but trust me, you cannot keep me or my Lyrinian sword from seeking out and destroying the evil of this world.

Cpt. Kramer: I see. That's all the time we have. You can see yourself out. Call in the next candidate, a Miss Galena Volkova, and we'll contact you if you've made the team. Otherwise, you will never hear from us again, unless, you kill another human. Then, you will be punished. Have a good night, Miss Ryeo-won.

Koa: There's nothing good about the night Captain Kramer. The night is filled with demons, vampires, and creatures from my worst nightmares. I'll be out there, hunting those monsters...one by one.

Cpt. Kramer: You're a determined young lady, aren't you?

Koa: I am.

Cpt. Kramer: Take this to the receptionist. Tell her to show you to Agent Halston's office.

Koa: What is it?

Cpt. Kramer: You'll see when you get there.

Koa: Sure. Bye, and thank you for considering me.

Cpt. Kramer: Goodbye, Koa.

RESULTS

Status: Accepted

Team: Agent Halston

Trainers: Agent Halston and Agent Alice

Location: United Kingdom

Restrictions: None

Special Notes: **Signed by Viktor Smead, Head of the
   Netherworld Division**

The half-blood, Koa Ryeo-won will be accepted on a probationary
   agent visa. Until more information is acquired on the
   "human" mother, Eunju Park-Vangelis, she will be
   allowed to live. Keep a close watch on them both. The
   mother is considered extremely dangerous.

TOP SECRET

Netherworld Division #265

Agent: Halston

Sex: Male

Height: 6'3"

Hair Color: Blonde

Eye Color: Blue

Weight: 220lbs

Race: Angel

Rank: General

Territory: United Kingdom & Central Dominance, formerly known as Lyrinia, of the Netherworld

Interviewer: Cpt. Patrik Kramer

Reason for Interview: Request to recruit Netherworld creatures for mission.

Mission: Execute the demon named Bund and the vampire king named Greggan.

Cpt Kramer: Good evening General Halston. Thank you for taking the time out of your busy schedule to speak with me. Please speak clearly, so Marlina can document everything that's said in this hearing.

Halston: Good evening to you as well. Let's keep it short if at all possible.

Cpt. Kramer: Very well. Let's get started, shall we? How long have you been here on Earth?

Halston: Since the ancient times. Before the Great Flood.

Cpt. Kramer: And why did you leave Heaven to come to Earth.

Halston: Do we really have to go over this? I came to request a specialized team. Why do I feel as though I'm being interrogated?

Cpt. Kramer: Forgive me, General Halston, but my questions were written out by Viktor himself. I'm afraid he outranks all of us angels on Earth, and I must follow orders.

Halston: I followed the traitor Satan from Heaven and I've been stuck here ever since.

Cpt. Kramer: But you never swore allegiance to the great traitor, did you?

Halston: No. I was tricked. It's no secret that I've been trying to redeem myself for centuries. No angel has done greater work on Earth to protect the humans and right the wrongs of my mislead brothers and sisters.

Cpt. Kramer: Can you elaborate on those wrongs?

Halston: Honestly, Patrik. As if you do not know.

Cpt. Kramer: Once again, I apologize. Please, for this interview, could we keep it formal? Please answer the question.

Halston: Many of the fallen angels produced dangerous spawn. The creatures we see today, vampires, Syths, ghouls, etc, are the abominations of angels. It is my duty to clean up the mess my… I mean *our* brothers and sisters have made.

Cpt. Kramer: Thank you, General Halston. And you've never created a Netherworld creature, have you?

Silence

Cpt. Kramer: General Halston?

Halston: No.

Cpt. Kramer: Why the hesitation?

Halston: Move on to the next question, *Cpt.* Kramer.

Silence.

Cpt. Kramer: Very well. Let's just get to the matter at hand. What creatures did you have in mind for this mission?

Halston: Of course I'm bringing my second in command, Al. A Metal-Mind is absolutely necessary. I also need a War-Breeder. I have one in mind. An old friend, Tristan, I would like to bring him to this world.

Cpt. Kramer: You'd actually let a War-Breeder loose?

Halston: Why not? It's not like they are true Netherworld creatures. They are the only natural predator of vampires, created to fight them in the Great War. Tristan is one that I trust.

Cpt. Kramer: And the prophet, a Prince Jax?

Halston: He is a necessary evil. I need his power and knowledge.

Cpt. Kramer: He is King Greggan's son and rightfully imprisoned in the Ivory Tower. He is too dangerous for this world. So is the daughter, a Princess Evina. She's a legitimate Temptress. Can you imagine the damage a vampire with her powers could do if she was around humans? You actually intend on bringing them here?

Halston: Whatever it takes to rid the human world of Greggan and Bund. If we don't stop them, the human world could be thrown into absolute chaos. The Vampire Registration System would be obsolete, humans would be farmed for blood, and I don't even want to think about what Bund would do if he was free to roam Earth without consequence. I have a plan to prevent all of this. I have it under control.

Cpt. Kramer: How exactly do you intend to destroy the demon, Bund? As angels, we have no power against our own kind, even if they turned to the dark side.

Halston: I have my ways. I know of someone that can take care of him for us.

Cpt. Kramer: Oh yes, you believe the half-blood's mother has such a gift?

Halston: I do.

Cpt. Kramer: You show great trust in such Netherworld creatures. You are aware that the half-blood, Koa Ryeo-won, and her mother are under surveillance. You know that we cannot actually let them live.

Silence.

Cpt. Kramer: Did I say something wrong?

Halston: This interview is over. Send my request to Viktor or I will go to him myself.

Cpt. Kramer: General Halston? General Halston, come back here. We're not done! Halston!

Silence.

Cpt. Kramer: I guess that's it for this interview, Marlina. He's not coming back. Go ahead and shut it down.

ABOUT THE AUTHOR

K.N. Lee is an award-winning author who resides in Charlotte, North Carolina. When she is not writing twisted tales, fantasy novels, and dark poetry, she does a great deal of traveling and promotes other authors. Wannabe rockstar, foreign language enthusiast, and anime geek, K.N. Lee also enjoys helping others reach their writing and publishing goals. She is a winner of the Elevate Lifestyle Top 30 Under 30 "Future Leaders of Charlotte" award for her success as a writer, business owner, and for community service.

Author, K.N. Lee loves hearing from fans and readers. Connect with her!

knlee.com
  Street team: facebook.com/groups/1439982526289524/
Newsletter: eepurl.com/3L1gn
Blog: WriteLikeAWizard.com
  Fan page: Facebook.com/knycolelee
  Twitter: twitter.com/knycole_lee
  The Chronicles of Koa Series Page: facebook.com/thechroniclesofkoa

TITLES BY K.N. LEE

THE CHRONICLES OF KOA SERIES:
Netherworld
Dark Prophet
Lyrinian Blade

THE EURA CHRONICLES:
Rise of the Flame
Night of the Storm
Dawn of the Forgotten (Coming Soon)
The Darkest Day (Coming Soon)

THE GRAND ELITE CASTER TRILOGY:
Silenced
Summoned (Coming Soon)
Awakened (Coming Soon)

THE FALLEN GODS TRILOGY:
Goddess of War
God of Peace (Coming Soon)
Love & Law (Coming Soon)

STANDALONE NOVELLAS:
The Scarlett Legacy
Liquid Lust
Spell Slinger

MORE GREAT READS FROM K.N. LEE

Rise of the Flame (Young Adult Epic Fantasy) *Six races. Four realms. One human girl who can bring them together in peace... or war.*
Lilae has been hunted since the night of her birth, for she is heir to a god's throne. But everything that her surrogate family has done to protect her may have been for nothing. After Lilae is stripped of her powers and enslaved by the emperor of the Mithrani, she finds herself desperate to survive in a strange new world.

The Scarlett Legacy (Young Adult Fantasy) *Wizards. Shifters. Sexy mobsters with magic.*

Evie Scarlett is a young wizard who yearns from an escape from her family's bitter rivalry with another crime family. But this time she may be the only one who can save them.

Goddess of War (Young Adult Fantasy) *Unsuspecting humans. Fallen gods in disguise. A battle for the entire universe.*

After escaping the Vault, a prison for gods, twin siblings Preeti and Vineet make a desperate journey to the human world where they must impersonate the race they are meant to rule and protect.

Silenced (New Adult – Paranormal Romance) **Silence kept her alive. Magic will set her free.**

Willa Avery created the serum that changed the world as humans, witches, and vampires knew it.

Liquid Lust (New Adult Romance) **Sohana needed a fresh start. Arthur--a British billionaire has an enticing offer. Neither expected their arrangement to spark something more.**

Discover more books and learn more about K.N. Lee on knlee.com.

76675144R00120

Made in the USA
Columbia, SC
12 September 2017